A Summer Sanctuary

Scottish Island Escapes
Book 3

MARGARET AMATT

Cover designed by Margaret Amatt
Map drawn by Margaret Amatt
ISBN: 978-1-914575-96-9
eBook available: 978-1-914575-97-6

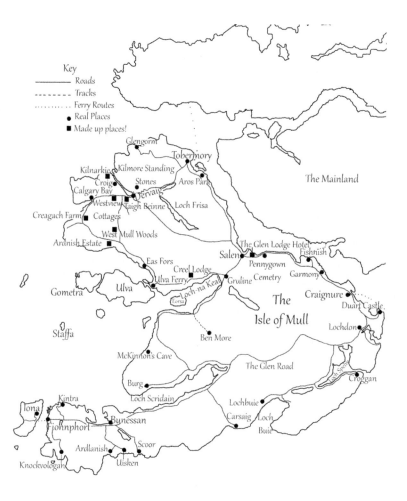

Key
Roads
Tracks
Ferry Routes
Real Places
Made up places!

Glengorm
Tobermory
The Mainland
Kilmore Standing
Kilnarkie
Stones
Aros Park
Croig
Calgary Bay
Dervaig
Westview
Taigh Beinne
Loch Frisa
Creagach Farm
Cottages
West Mull Woods
Ardnish Estate
Eas Fors
The Glen Lodge Hotel
Salen
Fishnish
Creel Lodge
Pennygown
Ulva Ferry
Gruline
Cemetry
Garmony
Loch-na Keal
Gometra
Ulva
Eorsa
The
Craignure
Isle of Mull
Duart Castle
Staffa
Lochdon
Ben More
McKinnon's Cave
The Glen Road
Burg
Croggan
Loch Scridain
Lochbuie
Kintra
Carsaig
Loch
Iona
Bunessan
Buie
Fionnphort
Ardlanish
Scoor
Knockvologan
Uisken

For Ian and Ossian

FIVE YEARS AGO

Chapter One

Kirsten

If seeing the end of a rainbow positioned over the Hidden Mull tour vehicle wasn't enough for Kirsten McGregor, finding a shiny pound coin by the front tyre convinced her this was her lucky day. She smiled as she stooped to pick it up, her long dark hair tumbling over her shoulders. The rainbow faded, but it left a neat reminder that life could be good. Things were getting better.

As Kirsten opened the car door, she heard Roddy Hunter's voice like the monotonous hum of a dentist's drill. It burst the bubble of happy thoughts from moments before. She dropped the coin in her pocket and rubbed her eyebrow as she turned to see him hurrying across the driveway, waving a pamphlet, and flipping his grey combover into place, neatly concealing a growing bald patch.

'Before you go, don't forget to warn the guests not to swim at Eas Fors. I heard some silly teenagers were scaling the waterfall and jumping off. Our insurance doesn't cover that, so don't let anyone get any funny ideas,' he said.

'Ok.' Kirsten straightened her large glasses, fixing her gaze on a fluffy grey cat stalking out the door of Roddy's bungalow. Her eyes blurred, and the cat slipped out of focus. Before her dad had died two years ago, she and her sister, Beth, had loved spending days at Eas Fors, fooling around in the water. She bowed her head, feeling Roddy's disapproval even though he couldn't possibly know what she was thinking.

'And take this.' He thrust the leaflet into her hand. 'It has a money off deal for the curry house in Tobermory. The guests might use it. I won't, I'm not fond of spice. Now, off you go. We don't want you late for the pickup. And don't forget to tell them about the latest sightings of the fledgling sea eagles. Also, remember to let them know the history of Ulva, and make sure you do it justice.'

'I will.' *Or I'll try.* With a brief smile, Kirsten shut the car door before he said anything else. If he decided to spout the rule book at her, she'd be late, and Roddy liked nothing more than waxing lyrical on rules, regulations, policies and procedures, but he also didn't tolerate lateness. The Alhambra's engine choked into action. Kirsten gave the steering wheel an affectionate squeeze. As the car was ten years old, its days were surely numbered and with the mileage they put on it doing the tours, it couldn't hold out much longer. As she headed south from Roddy's house in the coastal village of Lochdon onto the Glen Road, bright blue sky twinkled above the calm seas, and only a few fluffy clouds surrounded the mountainous peaks.

Snaking her way through the heart of the island, Kirsten hummed to herself, hoping she'd make good time on the twisty single-track roads. What was Roddy like? How much time did he need to spend on admin? Maybe his real reason for taking Kirsten on was so he could spend all day making up complicated company policies and playing with the new online booking system. Although he and his wife Linda claimed employing Kirsten was to help them wind down, neither of them seemed in any rush to let up. Linda wanted to invest in a new minibus so they could take twelve tourists all together rather than split them between the two people carriers. *I hope she doesn't get one.* Kirsten let down the window. The idea of driving a minibus was terrifying. Plus, who'd lead the tours? They'd be limited to one a day, she'd end up redundant. This way, she could visit one place and Linda another. *We don't need a minibus.* But as someone they'd only employed for the summer, Kirsten didn't really have a say.

After almost an hour, Kirsten reached the sleepy fishing village of Bunessan. A small group had assembled outside the Argyll Hotel. Kirsten pulled up next to them and adjusted the laminated sign in the window. Roddy had spent hours perfecting it with the company name, the logo of a sea eagle making a dramatic catch, and his contact details prominently displayed. Despite hardly ever doing a tour himself these days, all correspondence had to go through him.

As Kirsten got out to greet the passengers, a familiar sickening sensation rose in her stomach and her limbs felt heavy and achy. She fiddled with the hem of her baggy shirt, pulling it low over her walking shorts. Meeting strangers wasn't easy. *Just breathe normally, in and out.* What if she made a mistake and said the wrong thing? Roddy's fury might simmer quietly, but she'd feel the burn. She couldn't afford mistakes if she wanted him to keep her on. Her career options weren't exactly all-singing, all-dancing.

'Good morning.' She pulled out a smile, glancing around, but not looking too closely. Sticking to Roddy's number one rule, *the clients are not your friends,* gave her prickles of panic. Was it possible to make a warm connection without being too friendly? She hadn't mastered the skill Linda had for being warm and professional at the same time. Making too bold a connection might seem overly familiar, so Kirsten let her eyes flutter from guest to guest, not resting too long on any of them. 'Are you waiting for the Hidden Mull tour?' The silly high-pitched chirrup in her voice betrayed her pesky nerves.

'Yes.' The robust young man, whose shoulder she'd been staring at, took hold of a woman's hand as he spoke, 'Shall we get in?'

'Just a second, I need to check my list. I should have a Mrs Baxter and one other guest.'

'That's us.' An older woman with dark curly hair put up her hand. Kirsten nodded at her and the man beside her.

'And a Craig Hamilton with two other guests.'

'Me,' said the robust young man. 'And this is Shelley, my fiancée, and somewhere we have Fraser… where's he got to? He was right here.'

Shelley, still holding his hand, pointed. 'Over there, looking at the view.'

'Fraser!' Craig bellowed. Kirsten tottered back as the sound rang in her ears. 'We're going.'

Following Craig's gaze, Kirsten swallowed as she caught sight of the man they were waving to. Her body stiffened like she'd been bound to a plank. The man looked across the road from the harbour where he was balanced on a low wall alongside several piled up lobster creels and coiled ropes. With a wave, he hopped down and jogged across the road.

'Sorry, didn't mean to keep anyone waiting,' he said, running his fingertips across his crewcut. A flush of heat flooded Kirsten's neck as he stepped up beside her. He was tall, broad-shouldered, and his tight navy t-shirt revealed sharp musculature. Kirsten's heart skipped. *This guy is handsome. Wow, is he!* Just as well Roddy didn't have access to her thoughts, she'd be fired. She nursed an urge to hide behind the car, out of sight. How could she look at this man, and how could she not! A horrible high school memory clouded her mind. When she'd fancied the guy who served in the chip van and always hid behind her school friends because she was too scared to talk to him. Only the night before, she'd had a message from her friend, Ann-Marie, saying: *Remember your October mainland trip, only two months away! Bring your brave pants, I've got loads of nice guys for you to meet.*

The thought filled Kirsten with dread. She was so naïve when it came to guys.

Right now, she had to keep calm. 'If you want the car to open… I mean, if you can get to the car, or in the car. I'll open it, please… eh, thank you.' *Seriously. Ground open, swallow me now.* Training her sightline on the car, she fumbled with the door handle and yanked it open. A tingling sensation fluttered up her neck. Fraser was watching. Kirsten could sense it.

Mrs Baxter and her husband got in first, taking the 'boot' seats. Craig and Shelley were next. There was plenty of room in the backseat for a third person. Kirsten turned to check why Fraser hadn't got in. Her shoulders trembled as she glanced up. Oh no, he was too gorgeous to be real. *And he's on my trip. Help.* 'Are you, em, getting in?'

'Sure. I just wondered…' He strained his neck to look over Kirsten into the backseat. 'Can I go in the front?' The corner of his mouth tweaked up and Kirsten flattened herself against the car door as he leaned a little closer. 'I'd rather not sit next to my brother and Shelley. I feel like the world's biggest gooseberry already.'

'Um, right. Well, eh, yes, that would be fine, yes.'

'Cool, thanks.' He gave her the thumbs up and a cute little smile. Kirsten's misbehaving eyes fixated on the way his teeth grazed across his lower lip.

After realising she'd chewed an ulcer into her own inner lip, she took several deep breaths, and headed for the driver's seat, almost tripping on the uneven carpark. The controls suddenly looked like they'd been designed for a space rocket. What was she meant to do with them? Her palms slipped as she took hold of the steering wheel and wrestled with the gearstick, before she realised she hadn't started the engine.

Shit. Glancing in the mirror, she squinted at herself. *I look like a tomato with huge glasses.* This was a disaster. Why did she blush so much whenever vaguely attractive guys were around? And this guy was a lot more than that. So much for her lucky day. Flicking her gaze to the side, she saw Fraser casually leaning on the window ledge, rubbing his thigh and making no outward signs of amusement or scorn at her idiocy. 'Right, ok, we're off.' Engine finally running, Kirsten pumped the gas a little hard and shot into the road.

Fraser's head turned towards her. Kirsten kept her eyes ahead. *Please look away. Nothing to see here.* What would he see anyway? A nerdy girl who couldn't remember half the stuff she was supposed to be saying? 'So…' She collected herself. 'It's quite hard for everyone to hear me when we're driving, so if there's anything important, I'll pull in and tell you. It'll take about half an hour to get to our first stop. I have a CD that I'll put on, with some general information about the island.' With shaky fingers, she fiddled with the CD player.

'Here, let me.' Fraser's hand brushed over hers as he slid the CD in place. Kirsten nearly put the car off the road. Only as Roddy's tedious tone droned from the speakers did she regain some control. She chanced a glance at Fraser, and he returned it with a wink. How she avoided crashing was anyone's guess.

As Roddy's commentary ended, Kirsten turned it off, aware she hadn't listened to a single word. Having heard it several times before, it wasn't surprising, but it had nothing to do with that, and everything to do with the man on her left.

It was a relief to pull in roadside a few minutes later. 'Ok, if we get out here, I can explain why we've stopped.' With a dry throat, Kirsten waited for them to congregate beside the low shore she'd stopped at. Why did this feel stupid? A burning desire to do something reckless gripped her. But what, and why? No reason other than to show off to this guy. But what was the point? He was on holiday, so going away any day. And seriously, he was far too attractive to be interested in her. All good reasons to stay impartial and unemotive, just like Roddy. 'So, this is the least populated area of Mull on a main road. It's the ideal place to see one of our most elusive and spectacular birds, the white-tailed sea eagle. There's an eagle hide further along, and we can use it if necessary, but sometimes patience is the key. We'll stop here for half an hour and see if we get a show. There are spare binoculars in this box if anyone needs them.' She rattled off the speech, barely pausing to draw breath until she grabbed the box of binoculars.

'Are there many sightings here?' asked Mrs Baxter.

'Yes. If we walk a little further along the beach, there's a good chance we'll see one. They have fledgling chicks just now, so they need to hunt a lot.'

Kirsten marched towards the beach, but had hardly gone six feet when Fraser caught up with her. 'Hey, tell me, what brings a girl like you to be doing tours like this?'

'Oh. Um, well.' How to explain without sounding ridiculous? 'I was born here, and I live here. I like telling people about the island.'

'Wow. And you've always lived here?'

Kirsten's jaw stiffened. She wasn't going to mention her few dreadful months at college to a guy like him. 'Mostly.' Even the one word sounded defensive.

'Hey, I didn't mean that to sound rude. I think it's great. I had a bit of a nomadic upbringing; I don't feel tied to any place. I guess I'm a bit jealous.'

'Oh… well.' *Here's the part where I say something charming, or kind, or sympathetic.* But she couldn't think of anything.

Fraser thrust his hands in his pockets and kept in step with her. His feet crunching on the shingle vied with her heart's manic pounding. She swallowed. He seemed happy just to be silent, but every protracted moment sent Kirsten's core temperature up a notch. 'Is this, em, this visit, your first to the island?' she asked, finding her voice even though it sounded like Alvin from the Chipmunks.

'Actually, no, my brother and I came here as boys, well, me more than him. He's not normally overly fond of Mull, but he just got engaged. He wanted to show off his heritage. We have relatives here, that's why we came, but what's the first thing Craig does? Goes off and books an island tour. It's great for your business, but kind of defeats the point of visiting our family if we up and leave them the second we get the chance.'

'I guess. Oh, look!' Kirsten pointed skyward and all eyes followed. Everyone raised their binoculars. The mighty sea eagle flew into view, circling above them, putting on a spectacular display. 'Imagine being up there,' said Kirsten. 'What a view they must have.'

'Mull is pretty spectacular from the air, but then everything is.'

Kirsten lowered her binoculars. 'You've flown over Mull?' She'd never been on a plane and never wanted to.

'Yeah, sometimes, though usually too fast to have a good look.'

'Oh?'

'Here we go,' said Craig in a long-suffering voice. 'He's a freaking jet pilot with the RAF. I'm surprised he hasn't told you already, it's how he gets all the girls.'

Fraser's eyelids dropped slowly, and he smacked his forehead. 'My tactful brother.'

'You're a jet pilot?' Kirsten's heart missed several beats as she recalled her clumsy driving. What must he think?

Raising his binoculars, Fraser nodded. 'Yup, I am.'

Kirsten twirled her hair around her finger and swallowed, uncertain if this information made him more attractive or just downright terrifying.

After half an hour watching the eagle soaring above, gliding on the thermals, and putting on a majestic show, Kirsten drove them to the next destination. Her knuckles were white on the wheel. She mustn't make any more mistakes. Sitting next to her was someone with precision training, and she felt about two feet tall. But when she caught his eye, he didn't look judgemental. He just kept smiling or gave her a little raise of his eyebrows. Oh god, she couldn't stop stealing glances at him and he was always looking back. Every time. Something was happening. But what? *I know nothing about guys, nothing, oh help.* All her previous dates had been disastrous setups, she'd never met anyone organically, and never gone further than a terrible kiss with a guy which had felt more like being slobbered over by a bull. She chewed the raw spot inside her lip until it bled.

'Ok, next stop is Eas Fors.' Again, Kirsten pulled in roadside and waited for them all to assemble before she spoke. 'This place is one of the most beautiful hidden gems on the island.' Her eyes caught Fraser's, and he winked. 'So, well... I was saying, um, yes. Eas Fors is a very interesting name. Eas meaning waterfall in Gaelic, and Fors meaning waterfall in Norse. Some locals say it's so good they named it twice.'

'Or even better, how about the Eas Fors waterfall?' said Fraser. 'Too much?'

'Shut up, you idiot,' said Craig.

'You stole my next line,' said Kirsten softly. The base of her neck tingled as she locked eyes with him again and he gave a *sorry-not-sorry* smile. 'Now…' She coughed. 'If you'll walk this way.' She began the descent. 'The falls come from way above. You can climb right up to see the source and there are spectacular views. If you don't feel up to that, we can go down this way and there's a hidden pool.'

'Cool. Can we go for a dip?' asked Fraser.

Kirsten was glad she couldn't see the colour of her face. The idea of him going for a dip was too much until she remembered what Roddy had said. 'Eh, no. Our insurance, it doesn't cover, well, anything.' She looked him up and down. Nothing on him needed covering. The t-shirt only accentuated his chest and arm muscles. His jeans encased strong legs. And shit, he flew jets. He was a daredevil. Swimming in a pool would be nothing for him. 'I mean, it doesn't cover any accidents from swimming or diving or… other stuff.' Her eyes wouldn't budge. Fraser didn't break the connection either. He just stared back, his teeth grazing his lower lip as he smiled. A butterfly storm erupted in Kirsten's lower tummy.

'Ok, I'll behave,' he said.

No, she didn't want him to do that either. When he moved away, she tugged at the neckline of her shirt, trying to cool herself.

As they approached, the rush of the falls got louder. Kirsten remembered swimming here and shrieking with laughter as her dad and Beth jumped in from high above. Kirsten didn't have the nerve, even now she wouldn't. Some days, she wanted to break out of her comfort zone and do something amazing, but did she have the guts to do anything extraordinary? Wild ideas of things she could do with Fraser whizzed before her, but she dismissed them. A fun fantasy, maybe, but it wasn't going to happen.

'Wow.'

Kirsten wasn't sure who said it. The group gathered in a clearing at the bottom of the twisty path and looked over the cascade of water falling into the pool below.

'So beautiful,' said Shelley. 'If we weren't engaged already, you could have proposed here. This is amazing.'

'Yeah,' said Craig.

'It's magical.' Fraser approached the pool's edge and stood on a shiny wet boulder. Kirsten watched him. He placed his hands on his hips, gazing around. Kirsten remembered a story her granny had told her about the falls, one she used to love hearing as a child, but it was a fairy tale, not something Roddy would want her telling guests. But why not? They were so mesmerised, they'd love it and Roddy would never know.

'There's a local legend about these falls.' She'd started, now she had to finish. Though she wasn't sure if it really was a legend or just something her granny had made up. 'It tells that if you dip your fingers in the pool, then trace the shape of a love heart on your forehead, you'll fall in love with the next person you see. My granny told me it had worked for her, but local people in times gone by were afraid to do it, in case the next person they saw was a selkie.'

'A what?' said Craig.

'A legendary creature that can change from a seal to a person by shedding its skin.'

'Weird.'

'Have you never heard of a selkie?' said Fraser. 'Where have you been?' He smirked at Kirsten and said aside, 'He works in a bank. If selkies were like goblins and had pots of gold, he'd have heard of that.'

Goosebumps erupted all over her. Fraser was so close. A waft of manly scent floated into her lungs, making her light-headed. Oh god, she was quivering. *If only I wasn't so inexperienced.* Slipping her hand into the pocket of her shorts, she fingered the coin she'd found that morning, her own little pot of gold. She rubbed it frantically, like it was a talisman. If she could just say something funny or do something interesting. Instead, her legs trembled, and the inside of her lip was about to burst.

Fraser cocked his head. 'Here, I have an idea, let's try something.'

'What?'

He walked towards the pool, crouched down, and ran his fingers through the water. Kirsten's pulse raced. No, he wouldn't, would he? Slowly, he raised his hand to his forehead and drew his finger across it. *Oh, my god.* Kirsten froze, her knees ready to give way. Fraser stood up, turned around and trained his sight on her. Kirsten stared, feeling a surge of desire. She wanted this guy. Really wanted him with her body and soul. Nothing could shake it and the most terrifying part was she knew he wanted it too. He wanted her, and he looked like a man brave enough to get exactly what he was after.

Kirsten broke eye contact, but as soon as she looked away, she turned back. 'Did it work?'

Fraser was still looking. 'May-be.' He enunciated each syllable. 'Stranger things have happened.'

'Hmm, funny,' said Kirsten, hoping she sounded carefree like an experienced flirter, though she was anything but. Her heart hiccupped erratically and she blinked. Fraser's gaze intensified and his smile increased like he was sussing her out, gauging her from head to foot, and admiring what he saw. She'd almost forgotten there was anyone else on the tour until she heard voices.

The moment splintered and Fraser took a deep breath, tugged the collar of his t-shirt and looked away. 'Can I climb to the top?'

'Yes,' said Kirsten. 'Just don't fall.' She was torn about whether to go with him or stay with the rest of the group. As he looked extremely capable, it seemed sensible to wait with the others. But without Fraser, Kirsten's chest ached with impatience. If he would just come back so she could see him again.

A jolt of reality struck. In a couple of hours, she'd never see him again anyway. *I need to stop.* Why couldn't her friends set her up with a guy like this? Life just wasn't fair.

When Fraser returned to the glade, he stretched his arms behind his head and looked up into the falls. He was so drop-dead gorgeous, the only way out might be to actually drop dead. How would Roddy square the paperwork on that one?

Chapter Two

Fraser

Fraser glanced over and saw Kirsten checking her watch. Time was almost up. A tingle of uncertainty brushed up his spine. In a different setup, he wouldn't have hesitated, he'd ask her for a drink and take things from there. But Kirsten was different; bright-eyed, fresh and unsure of herself. It wasn't fair. He'd enjoyed a bit of a flirt. They could leave it there. He'd just ignore the completely alien – but wonderful – sense of familiarity and warmth he felt in her presence. Or he'd try.

Back in the car, he took his seat next to her and smiled as she fumbled with the controls. Her hand shook and he reeled in the urge to place his over hers and tell her she was doing just great. It might have the opposite effect to the one he intended. Why was she still so nervous? She'd done the tour. The twisty roads must be second nature to her. *Which leaves… Me?*

Fraser rested his head back and sighed. *Is she nervous because she's afraid of me or because she likes me?* He chanced a glimpse, guessing she'd look back. Her lashes flickered, and she gave a twinkling smile as she hit play on the CD. *She likes me, I can feel it.* A twinge of impending loss crept over him. He didn't want this meeting to be over so soon. Tightening his lips together, he stared out the window. The dull summing up speech droned from the speakers. He didn't hear a word, his brain was too busy ticking over impossibilities, reliving everything he'd felt as they'd looked into each other's eyes.

Possibly the most stupid thing he'd ever thought kept running through his head: *I'm going to marry this girl.* He gave himself a mental shake. What had got into him?

Lost in his thoughts some time later, it was a surprise to look up and see the Argyll Hotel. The car crunched into the car park, Kirsten pulled on the brake and jumped out. Fraser followed, joining Craig, Shelley and the other couple.

Kirsten fiddled with the ends of her hair and her gaze darted across the road to the low wall piled with lobster creels where two men were talking. One of them waved to her.

'Are we going straight to Gran and Granpa's?' asked Craig. 'I'd rather not, I'm knackered.'

'Let's go later then,' said Fraser, still side-eyeing Kirsten.

'Thank you for choosing Hidden Mull. I hope you all enjoyed it,' Kirsten said.

'Yes, and thank you,' said the older woman, speaking for the group.

'Yeah, thanks.' Fraser joined in with the others. Kirsten fixated on Craig's shoulder, a bit too deliberately. 'I'm going to hang out here,' Fraser muttered to Craig. 'I'll catch you guys later.'

Kirsten had her fingertips on the driver's doorhandle. Jogging around, Fraser thrust his hands in his pockets as a self-restraining technique. 'Hey, would you like to go for a drink? We could chat for a bit.' Well, it was out now, though he knew there was ninety per cent chance of a no. Kirsten turned with a start, her brown eyes widening behind her round glasses. With just the slightest flicker, she looked him over.

'Oh, well, um. I would, but...' She glanced across the road. 'I'm not really supposed to. My boss doesn't let me socialise with guests. I shouldn't.'

A weight fell on Fraser's chest. Ouch. Curse his arrogant mind. He didn't like being turned down, but it was more than that. The tingle in his stomach was new. Through the mental fuzziness clogging his brain, he couldn't make himself believe this was it. 'Pity.' He looked away, running his hand over his bristly hair. 'But, yeah, best do what the boss says.'

'Thanks… and—'

'Hey, don't sweat it. It's fine.' Of course, he respected her wishes, but his insides felt empty. With a half-hearted shrug, he gave her a gentle pat on the upper arm. 'I enjoyed your company today. You're very knowledgeable. In another life, I can see myself doing this kind of thing, maybe in about forty years when I'm retired.'

'It's not that easy, you know.'

'Yeah. I bet you get some real corkers on tours.'

'Well, I've only been doing this a few months and there have been one or two.'

Fraser beamed. The passion in her eyes had sprung to life again. She was bright and eager, and still here.

'Listen.' Kirsten glanced sideways. 'I'd get into trouble if my boss found out I was socialising with clients and news travels fast on the island. I know lots of people here.'

Fraser put up his hands. 'That's quite all right. I get it. I'll go.'

Kirsten swallowed visibly, and her eyes wandered across the road to the two men. 'Maybe we could go for a walk around the shore? I can just say I was showing you something as part of the tour.'

Warmth infused the emptiness in Fraser, knocking him momentarily speechless. 'Wow, eh… sure. That sounds great.' He raised his eyebrow and motioned with his hand for her to lead the way. Kirsten gave a little nod and a wave to the two men as she and Fraser passed, hopping onto the rocky shore, separated from the road by a low stone wall.

'Sorry, if I'm being ridiculous. It's just, well, those two guys back there, I know them.'

'I used to visit here a lot as a boy, I remember the island grapevine. What was the old joke? If someone broke wind in Tobermory, the people in Fionnphort knew about it ten seconds later.'

Kirsten shook her head and pressed her fingers to the bridge of her nose. 'Yeah, something like that.'

'Sorry, trust me to lower the tone.' Fraser took a few quick steps to draw up beside her and they walked together in pleasant peace, their feet crunching on the rocks. A few cars passed on the road beyond and a distant sheep let loose a prolonged bleat; other than that, there was just the gentle lilt of the sea.

Stopping abruptly, Kirsten looked up at Fraser and untangled a long lock of hair from her face. Fraser stopped just short of walking into her. 'Today…' Kirsten's voice was quiet, almost lost on the wind.

Fraser waited, watching the jumble of expressions on her face, but nothing else seemed to be coming. She rolled her lips and looked about. 'Are you ok?' he asked.

'Yes.' She swallowed, pushing a thick twist of hair behind her ear. 'I really enjoyed today, but I'm not good at things like this.'

'Things like what? I don't expect anything from you. I enjoyed today too, but it would be stupid to think anything could come of it. I mean, I'm only here for a few days and you… Well, you're younger than me.' *Valid, very valid.* And he had to keep reminding himself.

'I'm twenty-two.'

'Exactly. I'm nearly thirty. We had a good laugh today, but it's not fair to start something we know can't go anywhere.' Because here was a girl not like any of the others; not someone for a quick fumble to be tossed aside as soon as it was over. No, she deserved better, and he couldn't do any better.

'I know, it's just… I feel like I always miss out.' Kirsten looked out to sea, as the wind twisted her hair out behind. 'I love living here, but sometimes it just feels like all the fun passes me by.'

'What kind of fun do you mean?' Fraser stepped up behind her and gently placed his hand on her shoulder. She glanced up at him as he scanned down her face; her eyelashes flickered. Fraser raised his hand and removed her glasses like he was in an old-fashioned film, and he'd transformed the gawky librarian into a glamour model with just one move. Kirsten stared, rooted to the spot. 'Maybe I could kiss you? Just once? For fun,' he whispered.

With a tremulous nod, Kirsten tilted her head and Fraser dipped in. Their noses bumped and Kirsten let out a nervy giggle. Fraser smiled before placing a featherlight kiss on her mouth. She responded with surprising intensity. It took his breath away before he got into it, wrapping his arms around her, and savouring the softness of her lips. Her hands rested flat against his chest. She was quivering all over. Instinctively, Fraser rubbed her back, letting her know she was safe with him. She could walk away at any time. But he really didn't want that. A desire to protect her burned inside him along with a swelling warmth in his chest and a lightness in his head.

'Fraser,' Kirsten whispered as he gently pulled away. Her eyes were still closed; it was adorable. 'Maybe just one more.' She opened her eyes. 'Or two.'

'Ok.' He ran his hand down her arm. 'Sit down.' He gestured to a flat rock.

Kirsten giggled as she did so, and he sat beside her, gently sweeping a strand of dark hair from her forehead. She shuffled closer, brushing her lips against his, looping her arm over his neck. His stomach tightened. He inched in, spreading his hands over her spine. A groan escaped him as she brushed her fingers over his short hair, anchoring her grip behind his head. Kirsten responded hungrily to his kisses. Time evaporated as they sat, entwined together. Fraser savoured every mind-blowing second, delving deep inside Kirsten's mouth.

Trailing her hands down his chest with a moan, Kirsten slipped them under his arms and into his waistband.

'Jesus,' he muttered, breathing fast. 'Maybe we should take this somewhere else.'

'How do you mean?'

'No, nothing. I'm sorry.' Fraser ran his hand across his hair. 'I just got carried away.'

'I want to,' said Kirsten.

Fraser's jaw fell slack, and he probed her face; she didn't flinch. 'You want to what?'

Kirsten shivered. 'Go somewhere, you know, more private. I don't want this to stop here, but I'm... Well, I'm a little bit afraid.'

'Of me?'

'No. I know I should be. You could be anyone.'

'I could, Kirsten, and there's no way for me to prove otherwise. But if you want to come with me, I swear I won't do anything you don't want. I don't want this to end either.'

With a beautiful smile, she stood up and held out her hand. Fraser's heart leapt. Jeez, he had to make this special. Because it was. Whatever was going on here was a beautiful thing not to be wasted. Adjusting his neckline, he took her tiny hand in his. Would she notice how sweaty his palms were?

Checking the two men were looking the other way, Fraser and Kirsten crossed the road to the hotel. Giddy sensations fogged Fraser's head as they ran up the stairs. The key jammed in the lock to room four and Fraser wrestled with it. Seriously? What was wrong with him?

As it sprang open, he led Kirsten into the room. 'Are you sure?' His eyes bored into her, probing every inch of her face, checking for signs of anything amiss.

'Never more so.' Pulling off her glasses and throwing them onto the dresser, she pushed onto tiptoes and swung her arms around him. As their lips sealed, Fraser felt an inferno ignite inside him.

'Jesus Christ,' he mumbled, as Kirsten's fingers played up the nape of his neck. The words falling on her soft lips. 'This is just…' His breathing was so ragged, he could barely force out the words. 'Incredible.'

In one swift movement, he swept her feet from under her. 'Fraser.' She squealed as he carried her across the room. 'You're so strong. Oh my god, don't drop me.' Her arms locked around his neck and her wide brown eyes sparkled. Curls rioted around her face and fell behind her.

Dipping in for a kiss, Fraser let the taste linger on his lips before saying, 'I won't drop you. You're too precious for that.' He placed her on the bed and sat down beside her, tucking a lock of her hair from her forehead. His eyes feasting on her; the cute snub end of her nose and the smattering of freckles. 'Are you still sure?'

She sucked in her bottom lip and gazed at him. 'Yes.' Shuffling closer, she brushed her mouth against his. He was ready for her, meeting her intensity, letting his tongue seek hers. A surge of electricity stunned him. All thoughts went out the window as she chased him into another delirious kiss. He just wanted to feel this moment, prolonged and deep. Pulling back to breathe, he edged onto her neck, kissing down towards her shoulder blade.

'Oh, my god. I love you,' Kirsten whispered mindlessly, throwing back her head.

'You what?' Fraser stopped, resting his lips on her shoulder. A wave of uncertainty filled him. Normally that would have been a real mood killer, but for some reason, it just increased the rush of endorphins to his brain, making him giddy.

'Oh shit.' Kirsten pulled back, clutching her cheeks in her hands. 'I didn't mean to say that. I just meant… I don't know what I meant…' She looked on the verge of tears. 'Oh, god. I don't know what possessed me. Shit.' Her cheeks glowed fiery red.

'It's ok.' Fraser pulled a one-sided smile and ran his hand down her cheek. 'Don't sweat it.' Leaning in, he pushed her hair out of the way and enfolded her in his arms.

No one had ever said those three little words to him before, ever. Not even family members. He wasn't from a demonstrative family, they never talked about feelings.

'Do you want me to leave?' Kirsten asked.

'Hell, no.' Fraser released her to look into her eyes. 'You're free to go if you want to, but that's not what I want.'

Taking a gulp of air, Kirsten leaned forward and placed the most delicate of kisses on his lips. Fraser almost died. It was so tender; it set everything on fire again. When she broke away, he sat back, just looking at her. Well, if she was feeling affectionate, he'd give her something to love. He ripped off his t-shirt and eyed her. Kirsten looked on; her pupils wide and her cheeks red. Taking hold of her again, he lowered her onto the pillow and smiled. 'You're a beautiful girl. Let's make this special.'

He'd done this kind of thing countless times in seedier places than this, but those three little words had changed everything. Nothing he'd ever done had induced a verbal outburst like that and whether it was the heat of the moment or not, it made him feel more wanted than he'd ever been.

*

Fraser opened his eyes. Daylight streamed in the window. *Where am I?* Drowsy and contented waves stopped his brain answering for a few seconds, then he looked up. Kirsten was sitting on the edge of the bed, fumbling with the buttons of her shirt.

'Hey.' Fraser sat up. 'Sorry, I must have fallen asleep.'

'I did too.' She didn't look at him.

'Where are you going?' He edged towards her until he was next to her and took over fastening her buttons, adding a kiss for good measure.

'I can't stay. I'm so late. I'm going to get into so much trouble.' She looked stricken, like she might cry. 'Look at the time… Oh my god, I should have been back hours ago.'

'Oh, jeez. I'd like to come and sort out this boss of yours. It's your life. Blame me. Tell him I was very demanding and wanted to explore all the sights intimately.' Fraser raised his eyebrows with a cheeky smile. It spread as Kirsten mirrored him.

'I can't say that.'

'Really?' Fraser swept her long dark hair behind her ear. 'You have a hidden tigress. Don't take any crap.'

Kirsten stood up and retrieved her glasses from the dressing table. She fidgeted with them, her eyes not settling.

'Kirsten. How about we meet up again tomorrow?'

'You really want to?' Kirsten replaced her glasses in front of the mirror and looked at herself with a quizzical expression.

'Yes. Don't you?'

'I have a tour, and you're on holiday.'

'I know. And I've got a few more days. So how about you come here after your tour tomorrow? I'll wait out the front at what, about six?'

'Ok, yes.' Her smile returned, brightening her face. Fraser stood to embrace her. Who cared he was buck naked? Though maybe he should have covered up before she saw how much the kisses were getting to him. One last kiss – he made sure it was a long one – and she was gone. Grabbing a towel, he wrapped it around his waist and watched her from the window, getting into the black Alhambra and whizzing off. Wow. What a day, and it wasn't over, not yet. As he showered and got ready to go with Craig to his grandparent's house, he couldn't think of a time he'd wanted to see someone again as badly as this. All sorts of previously unknown possibilities whirred through his head.

The following morning, when a call came from his commander, Fraser couldn't believe his ears. He had to return to his unit ASAP. Seriously? Talk about bad timing. That had never happened before. And hell, Kirsten. He hadn't taken her number. Still, he knew how to get in touch with her through the business.

Leaving his family should be a wrench, but Fraser had always been able to detach, maybe because he didn't count anywhere as home. So why was his stomach cramping like he'd eaten a vindaloo followed by a jar of piri piris? Because of Kirsten. Why? He tried to shake her from his head. She was a fling. Not the first, probably not the last. But something so much bigger rumbled away in the back of his mind. *Come on, Fraser, get with the programme.* He had to be back and ready to fly a Typhoon jet in a few hours. He couldn't afford any distractions. There was no way he'd be recalled like this unless it was an emergency.

Three and a half hours after leaving Mull, and making sure Fraser knew how annoyed they were, Craig and Shelley dropped him off at RAF Lossiemouth.

Knowing, once he was back at the base, he wasn't likely to have time for anything other than digesting his orders,

Fraser had called Hidden Mull on the way and spoken to a man called Roddy, asking him to get Kirsten to call him. Presumably, this was the tyrannical boss that Kirsten was so worried about. Not wanting her to get into trouble, Fraser hadn't said why he was phoning, only that she needed to call back.

By midnight, he was briefed and ready to fly. No word from Kirsten.

*

Three days later
August 31st
To: Kirsten@HiddenMull.me.com

Hi, Kirsten. Did you get my phone message? I'll put my number in this email, please call me, or reply to this. I found your email address on the website. I have to apologise for not meeting you. I had an urgent call back from my commander. I'd always said they could put me top of the recall list as I don't have as many ties as some of the guys. Ha! Typical bad timing. Please get in touch. I didn't want to leave like that, but I didn't have a choice. Hope to hear from you soon.

Fraser X

*

Seventeen days later
September 14th
To: Kirsten@HiddenMull.me.com

Hi Kirsten. What's happening? Are you mad with me? I've sent so many messages. Should I assume you're not getting them (which is a stupid question if you're not!)? I just wanted to say, you really had an impact on me. I've been in the RAF since I was seventeen. I've devoted myself to it, and I never really thought about relationships. But something changed in me when I was with you. I don't know how anything could work, but it feels wrong to throw it away. Please, please,

get back to me.
    Fraser XX

*

Thirty days later
October 1st
To: Fraser54321@ymail.com
Dear Fraser
Regarding the emails you persist in sending, I demand you stop now.
Do not take advantage of me. I want no contact with you. Do not
harass me further.
    Kirsten

*

With barely a second to breathe between operations, Fraser took his chance when he got it, calling the Hidden Mull phone number. He drummed his fingers on the table in his paltry quarters in his encampment in Afghanistan. The tent flapped in the first breeze he'd felt in days, and he listened to the muster of vehicles as he waited for the call to connect.

'Hi, is that Roddy?'

'It is, how can I help you?'

'Listen, my name's Fraser Bell, I've called before, I need to talk to Kirsten.'

'You,' said Roddy in a sharp tone. 'Yes. Well. Now, I know all about you. When will you leave Kirsten alone?'

'Hang on, it isn't like that. I'm not harassing her. If I could just talk to her, I could explain.'

'Absolutely not. In fact, she's left the island.'

'What?' Fraser stared at the screen. Kirsten had left Mull? A month after telling him how much she loved it. *Because of me?* Surely not. *Have I really been harassing her?* Fraser hit the end call button and put his head in his hands. He'd been so sure, so certain this was different. A chance for something new. *What have I done?*

NOW

Chapter Three

Kirsten

Kirsten clung to the passenger seat of the Land Rover. 'For heaven's sake, Beth,' she snapped at her sister. 'Slow down.' A greenish-blue blur of the sea on her left whizzed past as Beth screeched around a corner. Takeover day had arrived. Kirsten's insides prickled with excitement alongside a pang of anxiety.

'You just said we're going to be late,' said Beth.

'I know, but I need to be alive when I get there, otherwise what's the point? If I'm late Roddy might still sack me.'

'What? A few seconds before he retires?'

'I wouldn't put it past him.' Kirsten opened the window, breathing in the salty sea breeze.

'I'm glad he's going,' said Beth. 'I think you'll be better off without him. From what you've told me, he's lost touch with what people want from tours.'

'That's true. But it's such a responsibility. I hardly know anything about the bookings, accounts, the website, the minibus's MOT or anything. It's only recently I've felt more confident about even guiding the tours. And it'll only be me. I won't have anyone to bounce ideas off or talk to.' Being alone in her personal life was one thing, being alone in business quite another. It wasn't as if she could shut the door and pretend everything was ok.

'You can talk to me. I don't know about running tours, but running the farm is similar. People don't get how much hidden admin there is. Sometimes it's just muddling along day to day.'

Kirsten raised her eyebrow. 'Yeah, you're hardly a muddler.' Beth had run their family sheep farm for seven years and was tough, strong, independent and capable.

'Don't you believe it. But Roddy and Linda must think you can do it. And I agree.'

'Well, I don't exactly have experience doing anything else.' And mostly, she enjoyed it. There were occasionally tricky customers, but on the whole, she had fun, taking people around her beloved island and showing off its hidden gems.

Beth rattled the Land Rover over the cattle grid and into the driveway at Roddy and Linda's house, slamming on the brakes as they pulled up beside a blue minibus gleaming in the morning sun. Sea and hills provided the backdrop, and Kirsten reminded herself not to take it for granted. This was a special place, her special place.

Roddy stepped out from behind the minibus, checking his watch and frowning.

'Grumpy bugger,' said Beth, shooting a cheeky little wave at Roddy. 'We're two minutes early, nothing to complain about.'

'Thanks.' Kirsten unbuckled her belt. 'But you know Roddy, if he can find something to complain about, he will. I won't miss that.' Kirsten jumped out, waving to her sister.

Beth reversed out the gate onto the seaside road.

'All yours.' Linda Hunter sidled up and patted Kirsten on the shoulder. With a teary smile, she dropped the minibus keys into Kirsten's palm.

'Passed the MOT, and she's going great,' said Roddy. 'So you shouldn't have any problems.'

Famous last words! An uneasy spasm gripped Kirsten's tummy. Wouldn't it be just the thing, she'd drive out and hit a deer or crash with a tourist who hadn't worked out island etiquette and passing places? Roddy whipped shut the minibus doors. The words Hidden Mull aligned neatly. The sea eagle logo twinkled.

'I can hardly believe it.' Kirsten swallowed and her fingertips tingled, itching to get behind the wheel and own it.

'Take care of her.' Roddy ran his fingers through his wispy grey hair.

'I will.'

Roddy coughed and glanced at Linda. 'Ahem... there's um, something else you should know.'

'Oh?' Kirsten pressed her lips together. Her head bulged with the weight of information already stored in it. On top of the island facts, there were spreadsheets, booking forms, review sites, email enquiries. If she'd moaned before about the time Roddy took doing paperwork, she took it all back. How was she going to do it plus keep the tours going? Her brain burned just thinking about it. What else could there possibly be?

'We heard there's someone else doing tours this year too.'

'Who?' Kirsten's eyes darted to Linda.

Linda placed her hand on Kirsten's shoulder. 'Don't worry, as far as we know it isn't Derek.'

'We don't know anything about them really, but I doubt Derek will be back. Silly man,' said Roddy.

Silly man? Horrible, sleazy man, more like. But as long as it wasn't him, that was a relief. Still, the idea of competition struck a chord of dread in Kirsten's stomach.

'You'll be fine,' said Linda. 'You're the ideal person to take over. You have an impressive memory for facts and you've shown us your dedication over the years.'

Taking on the business was a whole new level, especially as Roddy had kept the admin strictly his domain. He'd even seen fit to allocate an account to Kirsten's name because he *was designated five free email addresses with the business account and it seemed a shame to waste them*, but he hadn't bothered to tell her. Kirsten had known a moment of panic when she'd discovered this, just over a month ago, and demanded to see it, imagining somewhere in the dregs of the account, floundering beneath the spam, she'd unearth a message from Fraser. A light breeze shifted a cloud over the sun, and Kirsten shivered, a few raindrops tweaking her button nose. Why had she dragged up his memory again? It belonged locked up in the darkest chasm of her mind.

'Just keep on the straight and narrow,' Roddy said with a slight frown. 'Rule number one: the clients are not your friends. And rule number two: stick to facts and don't indulge in anything fanciful.'

Kirsten chewed on her lip. She'd heard those rules spouted more often than her own name. The survival of the business had been a source of frequent worry. Roddy had lost his grip on what people wanted from tours. If visitors wanted cold hard facts, they could look them up online. At least now Kirsten had the chance to change things before it was too late. 'Yes, I remember.' The words were only to appease Roddy because she'd already irrevocably broken those rules five years ago. She'd never told a soul and now wasn't confession time. The whole thing was a cringeworthy embarrassment. A nervous laugh escaped her. Sometimes she wondered if she'd dreamt it all. Only the pain in her heart reminded her it was real. The rain got heavier. Kirsten followed Roddy towards his bungalow to collect the final paperwork while Linda ducked under a tree and fussed over one of her cats. Roddy reappeared with a box file and coughed.

'I've tidied the email and booking systems, and I think you'll find the accounts sheets easy to follow. This is the only actual paper, the rest is online. The top sheet has all the passwords. Don't lose it. There are no tours booked for today, so you'll have time to check through everything. I should also remind you, it's traditional for me to make the closing speech at the Midsummer Party. You'll do it this year.'

'What?' Kirsten gaped. She had to make a speech? *Ok, somehow, I need to get out of that.*

Linda sidled up, cuddling a big fluffy grey cat, and rolled her eyes, then turned them cross-eyed. 'Don't worry.' She patted Kirsten's arm, and the cat scrambled off under a bush. 'I'm sure it's not compulsory. And, Roddy, you've retired. So quit panicking her.'

'That's not what I'm doing. Now, on Friday there's a group that looks tricky, take extra care with them, nothing too extreme. There's also the tour tomorrow.' Roddy tugged at the collar of his beige shirt as the rain subsided.

'There isn't one.' Kirsten racked her brains. She'd checked the diary and blocked off the day to get her head around everything else.

'It's the monthly community tour,' said Roddy. 'I have a group of six people from the south of the island lined up for you.'

'You have?' Kirsten summoned a smile, not caring if it looked fake. *Seriously?* Her worst nightmare gift-wrapped and handed to her on a plate.

'Don't worry.' Linda placed her firm hand on Kirsten's shoulder. 'You'll be fine.'

A twinge of sadness pricked. Losing Roddy and Linda was the end of an era. They'd given Kirsten the big break when she most needed it; after her father had died and she'd given up college. Despite Roddy's authoritarian ways, the structure had given her purpose. 'I'll do my best.'

'Listen.' Linda took Kirsten's arm and led her away from Roddy. 'I'll always be at the end of a phone if you need any pointers or just to talk. This job can be lonely.'

'Thanks.'

'It's harsh meeting so many people but never getting to know them.'

Kirsten coughed and observed her feet, reminding herself she needed a new pair of walking boots before the season heated up.

'I've seen you grow into a strong young woman,' Linda continued. 'You didn't think you had the confidence to do tours on your own or drive the minibus. Just look at you now. You're the one in charge.'

With a deep breath, Kirsten nodded. *Yes, I have the strength to do this.* Five years ago, she'd never have believed it, but now she was ready.

'I heard about the other thing,' Linda whispered, turning her back on Roddy, blocking him with her lurid floral top.

'Oh?' Kirsten tugged her long plait over her shoulder and twisted the end. What had she heard?

'Well, I understand you were interested in Carl Hansen, lovely man. I'm very friendly with his mum. He's moved in with someone though, hasn't he?'

'Oh, that.' Kirsten twirled the plait's end into one neat curl, watching as the light rain dripped from it. Yet another thing she needed to forget. *I made such a fool of myself there.* 'Yeah, Carl moved in with Robyn Sherratt.'

Carl Hansen was a good guy. But despite being handsome, single and lonely, he'd never been the man for her. She'd forced herself to believe she was in love – she wanted to be. He was her ideal man on paper; nice guy, similar age and best of all an islander born and bred. Because never again would she be duped into pursuing mainlanders who loved the island just long enough to con her. So, yes, she'd been devastated when Carl had gone off with someone else, though not for any of the right reasons. She was convincing. Sometimes she even fooled herself. Sitting at home alone in her little bothy with a tub of ice-cream and the TV on was quite respectable for a jilted twenty-seven-year-old.

Linda patted her arm. 'Being rejected doesn't mean you're inferior or inadequate. He just wasn't the right man for you.'

'Thank you. I'm ok, honestly.' She drew in a breath and let it develop into her biggest grin yet.

'Well, in you hop.' Linda beamed. 'Let me take some photos. Roddy can upload them onto the website, and that's the last thing he'll ever put on there. It's all yours from now on and I insist you change the password, so there's no chance of him breaking in and meddling with it. I know what he's like.'

'But don't change too much,' Roddy said. 'We have our regulars and they expect our good traditional values.'

'I know.' Kirsten climbed into the minibus, her hands trembling. Change would be necessary to survive, though how to bring it about? She'd been spoon-fed Roddy's regimented philosophy for so long, the temptation to change everything straight away was strong. But that could be disastrous. One step at a time or she'd drown in the overwhelm, exactly like she'd done in her disastrous college experience.

Pinching out the neckline of her white poplin top, she shook out the damp and smiled for Linda's photos.

After their farewells, which Kirsten was glad they kept brief, she turned out of the drive onto the winding road north, following the shore for several miles. Her hands gripped the wheel tightly to stop them shaking. She'd driven this minibus countless times since they'd bought it three years ago, but suddenly it felt priceless, like she was driving a truckload of diamonds.

As she drove towards her home at Creagach farm near Calgary, her phone rang through the hands-free and she jumped a mile, glad she was on a straight part of the single-track road. Seeing the name of her friend, Georgia Rose, she hit the accept button on the dashboard.

'Hi, lovely.' Georgia's chirpy voice crackled. Patchy island reception was a nightmare. 'Are you coming to the meeting on Friday about the Midsummer Party?'

'Er.' Kirsten would rather not. There was so much admin to learn, but maybe she should go and make sure someone else got volunteered for the closing speech. That was an extra pressure she didn't need. 'I'll try.'

'Well, just a heads up…' Georgia's voice dropped and Kirsten pushed up the volume. 'Carl and Robyn have just announced their engagement.' Georgia's top volume voice rang through the minibus.

Kirsten punched down the sound before processing the words. 'Oh.'

'Yes,' said Georgia. 'They'll want to tell you themselves, but I thought it would be kinder to forewarn you. I know it's a sensitive subject for you.'

'Yes. I see.' Of course, they were happily moving on with their lives, everyone was. *Except me.* 'I'll try and make it, but I have so much to do.'

'How about you—'

Reception cut, leaving Kirsten feeling slightly sick. Not because of Carl, no. He was lucky to have found his love. But because of her own part. The way she'd acted was ridiculous. Even when she'd known he wasn't interested, she'd made eyes at him, dressed up and all but thrown herself at him. She cringed. All she wanted was companionship; a friend, and someone who loved and understood the island as much as her.

That was all in the past. She pushed her shoulders back. Carl was behind her. So was Fraser and every other annoying man she'd ever met. Her new role as company director was the chance to make the break. Time for something new. A fresh start. She could and would do this. A new Kirsten was about to emerge from the ashes of wasted dreams.

*

Thursday dawned with another cracking blue sky for the monthly community tour. Kirsten had spent the previous day cramming her brain full of admin and attempting to update the website with photos Georgia had taken of her. As a professional with an artistic eye, Georgia had made an amazing job of them. Even though Kirsten had found the experience uncomfortable, she was getting better. After getting contact-lenses and watching numerous makeover videos on YouTube, she'd almost shaken the dowdy island girl look, and Georgia had a way of putting people at ease.

Today's trip wasn't the way Kirsten fancied spending the day. Taking a group of elderly people to a café for a cuppa every month was an honourable venture, and Roddy and Linda may have been of an age when they enjoyed that kind of thing on their day off, but it wasn't exactly Kirsten's idea of fun. What would they talk about? Nerves jangled in her tummy. She'd prefer a tour of twelve demanding Americans to this.

The six invitees were located towards the south of the island. She headed directly for Bunessan for the first two couples. Mr and Mrs Brady, and Mr and Mrs Foster were waiting at the bus stop close to the Argyll Hotel. Kirsten dropped her head. The hotel's prominent roadside position meant she passed it frequently, but never without a stab of memory. With cheerful smiles and excited chatter, the four guests got on board. Kirsten relaxed a little, tentatively glancing at them in the mirror. 'I've got two more people to get. Agnes Ogilvy in Uisken and Mary McLean in Fionnphort,' she said.

'Oh good, I like Mary. I haven't seen her for a long time,' said Mrs Foster.

'And Agnes is coming. That's nice. I heard she's got a bit wandered,' Mrs Brady added.

In the rear-view mirror, Kirsten caught Mrs Foster flicking Mrs Brady a sceptical look.

'Sharp as a needle if you ask me,' said Mrs Foster. 'She just likes to play daft. Then she gets her own way.'

Kirsten giggled. They sounded like naughty kids in a playground, but they were lucky. They'd found their island partners and were still together.

The drive to Uisken was narrow, twisty and beautiful. The sea glinted beyond Agnes Ogilvy's croft and the wide sandy beach. Dressed in a green tweed outfit that reminded Kirsten of Miss Marple, Agnes hobbled out, clinging to a walking stick. 'I'm quite capable,' she said, refusing assistance into the minibus. 'And where's Linda?'

'She's retired.' Kirsten hovered as Agnes teetered up the fold-down step. 'She and Roddy are moving to Inverness to be near their daughter and their new grandson.'

'Oh yes, I remember now,' Agnes said. 'Speaking of grandsons,' she continued as she took her seat. 'My grandson's coming to see me later. He's going to camp in the field behind the garden.'

'Aw, that's sweet.' Kirsten shut the door and returned to the driver's seat. Cosy memories fluttered into her mind of camping in their granny's garden when she and Beth were children. Even though her granny had only lived a few miles away, it was always an amazing holiday.

The collection of white houses in the village of Fionnphort gleamed against the emerald channel of sea separating Mull from the holy island of Iona. Mary McLean, the final guest, sported the fluffiest hair Kirsten had ever seen. She resisted the urge to pat it.

'This is lovely,' said Mary, limping to the minibus, allowing Kirsten to take her arm. 'Such a treat. I love good tea and cake. And what's your name?'

'Kirsten.'

'Oh, what a beautiful name. And it goes with a beautiful girl, and so clever, you can drive a bus. You must be very brave.'

'Thanks. I'm braver than I used to be.'

'Well, I'm eighty-two and haven't got to bus driving yet, so you're quite far up there.'

With a smile, Kirsten helped her aboard. As soon as they were comfy, Kirsten switched into tour mode. As they were just at the end of May, high summer wasn't yet in full flow, and although she'd done some tours already, this was the ideal opportunity to brush up on her facts. She always panicked she'd forget everything over the winter. Roddy had taught her every fact possible. Sometimes she felt like a walking, talking Mull encyclopaedia, though some of it was dry as dust. How could she change it up? What would she tell people if not the facts? She needed a way to jazz it up without getting too tacky.

As the group were happy chatting, Kirsten only interjected a few facts when necessary in the hour's drive between Fionnphort and the café at the ominous stonewalled fortress of Duart Castle. She didn't bother with Roddy's CD. It was going in the bin. If she got the chance, she'd attempt one of her own, or better still get a microphone.

The castle's position on the side of a cliff next to the raging sea was dramatic, if somewhat vertigo-inducing.

Kirsten wasn't bothered, but Mary shook her head and said, 'Oh, no, I'll stay well back from the wall.'

Many times, Kirsten had been inside and climbed to the roof where the views were even more incredible, but with today's group, the teashop was a safer bet. The Bradys and the Fosters sat together at a neat round table with a frilled tablecloth and a small vase of flowers in the centre. Kirsten sat with Agnes and Mary. Mary was full of fun chat, her voice twinkling over the clatter of dishes and the clink of spoons. There was a neat little gift store and Kirsten picked up another history book. Like she needed it; her bothy was crammed with them. But the book looked intriguing with black and white photos of the Hebrides in a time gone by. 'It's amazing to think some of these people might be my ancestors,' she told Mary. 'Or yours.' How she'd love to keep the tradition going by raising island-born kids of her own, but the possibility of that was getting smaller all the time.

Agnes checked her watch regularly in between sips of frothy coffee. 'When do we leave?' She scratched her scalp through her thin layer of hair. 'My grandson will be on his way. I wouldn't like him to arrive at the house when I'm not there.'

Kirsten finished her chocolate chip cookie and brushed the crumbs from her lips. 'I'll pay, then we can head back.' At the till, she leaned on the oak counter, smiling at the two old ladies while the cashier rang up the bill. Agnes's chat about her grandson made it sound like a little boy was making his way to the island on his own. Presumably, he had parents, but their importance was zero next to him. No doubt Agnes had a cupboard full of treats, waiting.

So, I've done my good deed for the day, thought Kirsten, as she drove them back home. Actually, the month. It wouldn't be so daunting from now on, though she still had heaps of work to do. Still, their companionship had been cheerful and comforting. Now, she just had the tours to worry about and the unknown quantity of the rival company. Hopefully, whoever they were, they'd be pleasant and cooperative, not an utter sleazeball like the last one. Even the thought of oily Derek sent a shudder down Kirsten's spine. *Ugh.* Roddy's great idea that the two companies help each other out hadn't gone to plan. Derek had taken it as the green card to come on to Kirsten.

As she opened the door for Agnes in Uisken, Kirsten said, 'I hope you have lots of fun with your grandson.'

'I hope so too. He always eats me out of house and home, he's such a big lad now. I think you'd like him.'

'I'm sure I would. He sounds wonderful.' Kirsten waved her off. Only Mary remained as they took the long winding road back to Fionnphort. Aware of her scrutiny, Kirsten blinked in the mirror. 'I hope you enjoyed the trip.'

'I did indeed. You know a lot about this island,' said Mary. 'Goodness, when I was your age, I don't think I knew half those things. I still don't.'

'I hope it was interesting.'

'Oh, yes. But why don't you tell me your story before we get back?'

'My story?' Kirsten sucked on her lower lip. 'I'm just what you see. An island girl who does tours.'

With a flicker of a laugh, Mary said, 'I think there's more than that.'

'Not really. I just moved into a bothy close to the family farm. I wanted to move out so I could be independent, but sometimes I'm so lonely. But I needed to try. I've always relied on people when I should have done my own thing.'

'Well, I'm an old lady. I know all about being lonely.'

'I guess. I just hoped. Well, a few years ago, I met a guy I really liked. It was silly.'

'What happened?'

'We clicked.' Kirsten had mistaken Fraser's actions that day as love. How naïve she'd been. If nothing else, it was a life lesson. 'I arranged to meet him, but he never showed. He'd already left the island, and I never heard a thing from him again.'

'I wonder. I hope nothing terrible happened to him. But don't give up. One day your man will turn up when you least expect it and it'll feel like magic.'

As Kirsten helped Mary into her house, a breeze picked up straight off the sea. Maybe Mary was right, but sometimes it felt hopeless. *I'm an island girl through and through.* She knew everything there was to know about Mull, but nothing about real life. And it didn't seem like the two could be combined. She'd learned the hard way never to put her faith in *island magic.* Or love. And definitely not men.

Chapter Four

Fraser

Uisken Bay was an hour's drive from the ferry port at Craignure. Fraser Bell carefully manoeuvred his repurposed Ford SUV off the ferry. After piloting Typhoons at dizzying speeds, this thing was lightweight despite its size. But still, he didn't want to knock the paintwork or do anything silly. It'd cost him to have it customised, and now he had to keep it good for at least three months. After that, all going well, he'd be completely recovered and a new man. This venture would keep him fit, keep him busy, and possibly make some money as a bonus. With a string of dates already in his Google calendar, he was ready to make a go of it. And if it all went pear-shaped, so what? Since his discharge, he needed a place to indulge in some R and R and where better to do that than here, job or not. Despite the uncertainty of the next few months, Fraser's shoulders hung loose and free. A broad smile split his face. Nowhere was home, but this place always had a special pull. Something about it tugged his heartstrings more than anywhere else in the world.

With the sun cascading through the clouds, he zapped down the windows and drove south, adjusting his sunglasses in the visor mirror, still not sure about his hair. Air Force habits die hard. As soon as the hair got slightly too long, he had it clipped, but he wanted to ditch that look, so he had to leave it alone.

He breathed the fresh air. After flying the world and back again, it was sublime to see familiar sights passing by. A few new houses had sprung up in the villages, but nothing to rock the perfect natural beauty. Already the island's therapeutic effect had started to work. Any remaining tension ebbed from Fraser's body with every twist in the road, leaving a hopeful excitement.

As he reached the winding open road through Glen More, he drew in a sigh. There was sadness here too. His grandpa had died two years ago. But there were other haunting memories and demons. Wherever Fraser went, he attracted them. Kirsten had been the first in a string of muck ups. Meeting her had opened him to the possibility of a new world. She'd touched his heart in a way he couldn't explain, but then he'd messed up bigtime, trying to drag it out into something she clearly hadn't wanted. And it didn't stop there. Not until his ultimate cockup last year. Now he needed to hide in the wilderness where he was free to fall in love with the sea and the sky, the mountains and the river. No one could take them away or break them apart.

The sun had started its descent behind the peaks and the journey whizzed by. He flicked on an upbeat and chill-out playlist, watching the birds flying home to *Lovely Day*. With a deep sigh, he passed the Argyll Hotel in Bunessan. His gaze wandered to the window of room four. Memories of what had passed there and what might have been seeped into his mind. He was still mulling it over ten minutes later when he pulled up outside his gran's little croft in Uisken.

As his gran peered out the door, Fraser's eyes widened. How had she got so old and stooped? A tiny wisp. Leaping out of the car, he stepped up and hugged her briefly, afraid even his gentlest of touches would crush her, and knowing she didn't really do hugs. None of his family did.

'Dear, dear, put me down. My heavens, you've grown again,' said Agnes Ogilvy, straightening herself out.

Like everyone else in Fraser's family, Agnes disapproved of *PDAs* (as his mother called them). Public displays of affection were frowned upon in the Ogilvy-Bell-Hamilton mishmash clan.

'I don't think that's possible, Gran. I'm thirty-four, I stopped growing about sixteen years ago. Maybe you've shrunk.'

'Nonsense. Now, in you come. I've got food in for you. I haven't had much time to get it ready. I was on a trip today with some friends. A very pleasant young lady took us on the bus. We had some tea at the castle. I only got back about an hour ago. I've put some potatoes on, and I have pork chops. Do you still like them? They used to be your favourites.'

'Yes, I love them. I'll eat anything, but listen, Gran, I don't want to put you to any trouble. I told you. I've brought lots of food and I'm happy to cook. All I need is the use of the shower, a plug, and if you're on Wi-Fi, I'll use that too. If not, I'll get it fixed up. I'll need it for the business, but I'll make sure it doesn't cost you a penny.'

'Oh, Fraser, I haven't a clue what you're talking about. But you're not actually going to camp, are you? You're a bit big for that. I've sorted the spare room for you.'

'No. That's kind, but I don't want to. I've made up my mind. I need to be on my own. I have a lot to think about. I'm happy to be here and give you company whenever you want it, but the tent will give me the space I need.'

'Dear, dear. Are you hiding away in a tent because of the business with the baby?'

'Please, Gran, I don't want to talk about that.' It was the prime reason he didn't want to stay in the house. Minimising opportunities for his gran to quiz him was necessary. There were some subjects he would not enter into. He was done thinking about the past. Only the day to day. He had to, for his sanity. Since PTSD had entered his life, the world had become a changed and unfamiliar place, and dwelling on the negatives didn't help.

'Oh, have it your way.'

'Thanks. Now, what have we here? Something smells good, must be the chops.' Diverting Agnes to the galley kitchen, Fraser sat with her until after dinner while she told him about everything he'd missed in the last five years. Obviously forgetting she'd had several communications from him in other ways in the interim, she filled him in on every minute detail.

After saying goodnight, Fraser returned to his SUV. Placing his hands on his hips, he surveyed its shiny silver exterior. As he opened the boot, he caught the newly valeted smell intensified by the heat. Lifting out his backpack, he placed it on the ground and dragged out another kit bag. Moments later, he was saddled up and carting his gear along a stony track, past an overgrown field towards the rocky hillock behind his gran's house. Midges clamoured him. He shook his head and grunted. Finding a flat area, he opened the kit bag and began pitching his tent.

It was still light and would be for a while yet. It barely got dark here in the summer. Only for a few hours, and if the moon was high, it was almost as good as daylight. Stopping, he stretched and looked into the distance. The curved silver expanse of Uisken beach lay beyond. In the stillness, the sea lapped against the shore and foamed around the rocky outcrops. The rising whistle of a curlew blended with the chatter of dancing crickets. A light breeze rustled the grass and rippled the newly erected tent. Here was life. Unadulterated, pure and free.

Kirsten had left the island years ago, according to Roddy. There was always the chance she'd come back; this was her home after all. But the chances of meeting her now were slim. Those few hours Fraser had spent in her company could stay buried. He almost wished he hadn't wasted his time trying to get in touch. She'd made her position quite clear, and he'd stopped trying; exactly what she wanted, splintering his heart and his dreams at the same time.

Used as he was to life in the field, Fraser's tent bordered on a five-star hotel. As he rolled out his sleeping bag and lounged back on its soft padding, he remembered doing this as a boy, his gran shouting at him to check he was ok and making sure everyone in the nearby village knew if he needed the toilet or not. Grinning at the recollection, he picked up his book and his clip-on light. The utter bliss of no noise, no phones, and no Wi-Fi was like a cool cotton blanket of calm. Whatever had been stressing him before, he blanked it out. This was why he was here, and nothing was going to get in the way.

Chapter Five

Kirsten

Heat radiated through the minibus's gleaming windows, and Kirsten fiddled with the air conditioning. The satisfaction of leading her first tour as company director was lost in the stifling heat. Twisting around the island roads, she sped to their first destination; the bus packed with guests. A day like this was optimum weather for viewing the scenery, not sitting on a bus, or worrying about the paperwork back at the bothy.

Watching the guests fanning their red faces in the rear-view mirror, Kirsten was relieved to pull up roadside twenty minutes later. She peeled herself off the seat. *Why did I wear my walking trousers?* Sweat clung to her, and she felt sticky. A huge silver Ford SUV was parked on a nearby verge. A rental car possibly? Had some random tourists stumbled upon the Eas Fors, her private beauty spot? Tugging at her neckline, she wished she'd donned a cool dress. As she opened the door for the clients to exit, a gentle breeze caught her. She welcomed the cooler air and adjusted her sunglasses. Her fingertips trailed over her sizzling cheeks. Squinting at her reflection in the sparkling window, she saw red blotches blossoming. *No way.* The gorgeous blue sky was great for tours, but she was burning. She raked in her emergency backpack. No sunscreen! Again. It was the same every year. The first hot day, she burnt like a crisp and stayed that way for the rest of the summer. Last year she'd gone out in ballet pumps with a narrow strap and spent the next two months trying to hide the white line across her foot.

Her face would have to wait. Nothing was going to hamper her first tour as Hidden Mull boss. She grinned at the thought. *Me in charge!* Making a mental note to grab a bottle of fizz at the village shop on the way home, she turned to the assembled group of tourists and smiled. 'If we walk down the path here, there's a waterfall, and a hidden pool named Eas Fors.' She launched into her patter, explaining how it got its name and adding. 'It's a perfect place for a day like this. There's spectacular scenery and we can have our picnic there. I've known locals to take a dip in it but, by and large, it's undiscovered. There are some brilliant photo opportunities looking out to the small islands and they'll be visible today.'

'We don't have to swim, do we?' an American woman asked, adjusting large sunglasses.

'I wouldn't advise it. But you could dip your feet.' Kirsten was sorely tempted to plunge in her cheeks.

'I wouldn't mind a dip.' A burly man with thick black hair and bushy eyebrows gave her a leering smile. 'But I doubt anyone wants a close-up of this.' He shook his large belly.

Kirsten looked away. *I certainly don't.* 'That's the Isle of Ulva in the near distance. I can tell you about it when we get down.' She kept her eyes away from the man's midriff. 'There's a great view, and it has a fascinating past.' And she was off. 'If you'll walk this way.'

Leading the way down the hill, she took the winding path through twisted, gnarly trees in the start of their summer burst. Every time she came here, memories slapped her like a wet fish in the face.

After Fraser had left, she'd returned frequently, hoping, praying even, that she'd walk into the clearing and Fraser would be standing there with a credible story for disappearing. It still opened a gash of pain in her chest. What a gullible fool. An echo of the trepidation lingered on every visit, but she'd abandoned hope years ago.

As she dropped onto flat ground, a man's voice rose above the rush of the falls. A jolt of abject terror hit her in the gut. She couldn't move. As she breathed the rich, water-saturated air, her rational brain took hold. Ok, someone was there, but nothing to be alarmed about. Just the SUV owners. But she'd never met another soul here except the ones she'd brought with her. Raising her hand to stop the others, she frowned. It sounded like someone giving a sermon, maybe a marriage ceremony. Her pulse raced a little too fast. Something about the low sonorous voice was unsettling.

'What's going on?' the burly man asked.

'I'm not sure.' Kirsten moved out of his way and lifted a trailing branch, revealing the pool. A small group huddled around the waterfall. A man in a kilt was talking. 'It looks like a wedding,' said Kirsten, but no one else was dressed for it. Then again, if you came out here to get married, high heels and fascinators wouldn't be much use. Maybe the bride hadn't arrived. Was she about to show at any second? Kirsten's group assembled behind her. 'There's not normally anyone here. If it's a wedding, I don't want to disturb them.'

'Sounds very romantic,' said the sunglasses woman. 'Can we have a peek? I'd love to see the dress.'

'There isn't one.' Kirsten crept into the clearing and tuned into the deep, soothing tone. Her heartbeat quadrupled.

'There are many local legends relating to the pool,' said the kilted man. 'Some claim it has links to fertility. But my particular favourite tells that if you trail your fingers in the pool, then trace the shape of a heart on your forehead, you'll fall in love with the next person you set eyes on. So take care.' With a low laugh, the man crouched and dipped his hand in the water. As he drew his finger over his forehead, Kirsten froze. She scanned upwards over his hefty walking boots, his kilt, and the white shirt clinging to every muscle on his broad back. A surge of adrenaline stabbed her. She staggered back, colliding with the burly man.

'Whoa, look out there, Princess. You ok?' he said.

Get me out of here. The heat in her cheeks had nothing to do with the sun any more. 'We should go somewhere else.'

Too late. In a sweeping gesture, the kilted man turned from the waterfall. Somehow his glance missed the group huddled around the pool. With a shaky breath, Kirsten fiddled with her sunglasses. Within a nanosecond, his gaze landed on her. If her legs had collapsed, it wouldn't surprise her; she couldn't feel a thing. But even from this distance, she knew those eyes were olive green because she'd seen them before. He was older, more rugged than she remembered, the dark hair a little longer, but there was no mistaking who it was. Fraser. Him. Here. How? Why?

A tidal wave of emotions surged in her stomach, putting her on the verge of retching. Blood pounded in her ears. Gripping the straps of her backpack tight, her knuckles turned white. She gaped, frozen and speechless.

Fraser slid his hand round his shirt collar, and his brow furrowed. The colour drained from his tanned face. Kirsten realised her sunglasses wouldn't disguise her. Despite her attempts to ditch the dowdy, she'd barely changed in five years. A seedling of curiosity poked through her terror. How would he handle this? *God, how will I?* Her chest cramped like it was caught in a vice. But what did she have to fear? He'd used her, then abandoned her. *I did nothing wrong, except being taken in like a fool by a hotshot pilot.* She swallowed, forcing each breath out one by one.

'Hi.' He shuffled forward. 'Kirsten?' Rubbing the back of his neck, he furrowed his brow.

'Excuse me?' She kept her focus low, examining the broad curve of his shoulder, trying to sound aloof. 'What's going on here?' Zeroing in on his group, she gestured around. Her heart hammered like Thor on a mad rampage. *Keep cool, just keep cool. Act like he's a stranger.* Easier said than done. His very presence set a fire ablaze in her soul. Memories of how he'd kissed her, touched her and whispered sweet words in her ear soared into her brain. She wanted to scream.

'Oh.' His voice faltered. 'I'm giving a tour.'

'A tour?' Her eyeballs almost popped out. 'What kind of tour? A family tour or something?'

His teeth grazed his lower lip. 'Well, no. I'm doing an island tour. It's my new business, Discover Mull Tours. Are you—'

'What?' He was her new rival? He had the balls to do that? If she was just a bit taller, she'd take a swing at him. She folded her arms to stop them shaking. This was not happening. The utter nerve of him sent her already buzzing brain into furious overdrive. Breathing very deliberately, she sized him up. The kilt! Seriously? What a gimmick. A cheap draw and totally below the belt. *Pun subconsciously intended.* The man who'd once been her guest, chatted her up, joked with her, made love to her, and filled her foolish brain with false hope had set himself up as a competitor? 'If you're running tours, it would have been polite to get in touch.' Somehow, she forced the words from her dry throat.

'Well… I thought Hidden Mull had finished. I read the owners were retiring. And I understood you'd left the island.' He rubbed his hand on his stubbly chin. Avoiding looking at him, Kirsten stared fixedly into the middle distance, making it quite clear she had not left the island. Where did he get that idea? She'd only left for a holiday with her friends a couple of times. What was he doing here, running tours when he was supposed to be flying jets? This was beyond weird. 'My group are almost done,' he said. 'I'll gather them together.'

'Good.' Kirsten kept her arms folded over her raging heart. 'We'll wait here.' She needed to sit down, otherwise she'd collapse.

With a brief backward glance, Fraser returned to his group and spoke to them.

'I apologise, everyone.' Kirsten steadied herself. 'This has never happened before.' She moved them into a clearing while they waited for Fraser to usher his group towards the path. After setting them on their way, he marched back to Kirsten.

'So, how can I best contact you so we can avoid this kind of thing in the future?'

'The email address and phone number are on the website, as they have been for several years.' She couldn't help saying it. He could have contacted her a hundred times. Fraser's eyes widened, he opened his mouth wordlessly, then backed off. Kirsten took a steadying breath and led the group to the pool.

'He was a real hunk,' said the woman with the sunglasses. She took them off and peered after him. 'The kilt is hot, like Jamie from *Outlander*.'

Oh, please. Kirsten tried to hold on to her eye roll. Why was everyone so obsessed with that show? *Gratuitous, historically inaccurate nonsense.* Sheesh, she even sounded like Roddy. 'If you'll walk this way.'

'Any way you wish, Princess,' smirked the burly man, waggling his thick brows.

Kirsten forced a smile, but her mind was racing like the infinity machine on steroids. *What the hell just happened? Fraser is here, running tours!* Without so much as a word in five years. Not a message, a call, a letter, nothing. *And now he shows up! Where did he get the idea I'd left the island?* A story to ease his conscience, maybe. Sparks of rage, frustration, shame, panic and dread flared inside, making her head ache.

She began her spiel about the Isle of Ulva, but it was robotic. She'd rather sit on a shard of glass than see Fraser again, let alone talk to him, and try and compete with him. Everything she'd dreamed of was about to go up with a bang.

*

It was late when Kirsten arrived home after dropping her tourers back at their accommodation. Taking a moment to breathe in the warm air as she got out of the minibus, she bit her lip. Seeing the bus neatly parked in a space beside her little bothy should have filled her with pride, after her first tour as company director, but she felt sick. The distant sea rushing and the low hum of insects filled the air. Behind her, set on a hill, was Creagach Farmhouse, where her mother and Beth lived. A blue Audi gleamed in the courtyard. Beth's new boyfriend, Murray, must be there too. Kirsten didn't begrudge her sister the happiness, but it made her feel lonelier than ever. Despite the heat, a shiver coursed through her. She opened the door to the bothy and former holiday-let that was now her home.

Throwing back her head, she groaned as she surveyed the beautifully tidy living area. The bedroom was equally clean and fresh, the white wrought iron bed gleamed and the pretty floral cover was neatly made. It even had a fluffy white towel folded on it. *Mum!*

Gillian McGregor hadn't quite grasped this wasn't a holiday home any more. She still popped round to clean and tidy. Kirsten grimaced. *I am more than capable of doing my washing and making my bed!* But Gillian enjoyed 'looking after' her daughters. Kirsten had moved out to get some space. She'd craved alone time; now she dreaded it. And Fraser was back. What had possessed him to return? Crossing paths would be unavoidable. Five years ago, when she'd been in his arms, she'd felt like she could do anything. 'Why did I have to meet him at all?'

She poured herself a glass of wine. She'd forgotten the fizz and celebrating was the last thing on her mind. Pulling out her phone, she googled Discover Mull Tours.

There he was, beaming back at her. It wasn't the best quality photo, but it jolted her, and she wrinkled her nose. Her fists balled as she read his blurb, only releasing when a ginger furball jumped onto her knee.

'Hello, Jellicle.' Kirsten stroked him until he purred like a jumbo jet taking off. 'You are one seriously noisy cat. And what do you make of this?' She scrolled down the page. 'Call Fraser to book your tour directly. And look at all the places he claims to go. Stolen straight from me.' She slammed the phone onto the side table and threw back her head. Jellicle flexed his claws. 'So, he's put himself out there in direct competition with everything I've worked for. You know, five years ago, I fell for him so hard. I wish I'd known better.' With a huge gulp of wine, Kirsten smacked the glass on the table. 'Well, I'm ready for him this time, and I will not be lying down for the competition.'

Chapter Six

Fraser

Fraser would have taken a punch to the gut, even a bullet. At least it would have been over quickly. But the lingering unease in his stomach wouldn't settle that easily. Something, somewhere, had gone wrong.

Kirsten's parting message five years back had made her feelings brutally clear and told him she wasn't open to listening to what he had to say. Did she think he was here to stalk her or harass her? Just like she'd accused him of before. Nothing could be further from the truth. Despite getting the idea for island tours from Kirsten, there was no way Fraser would have done this if he'd thought she was still here. What a mess.

After dropping off his clients at their hotel, Fraser drove the SUV into the car park at Garmony, a grassy picnic area by an estuary, with a view east over the shipping channel towards the mainland. It also had good 4G. Back in Uisken, there was occasionally a signal on the hill behind his gran's house, but it was too unreliable to bank on and it was too late to use the community centre Wi-Fi.

Fraser took his phone and sat at a wooden picnic bench, resting his forehead in his hands. He'd never believed in fate, but that day with Kirsten had felt significant and so real. But what had it really been? A kiss on the beach? Late afternoon sex? To him, it had been so much more. It had ignited fireworks in his soul and lit the touchpaper of possibility in his heart.

With a sigh, he switched on his phone and opened the browser, waiting. His phone was brand new and state of the art; he needed it so much for business. Still, no one had told the 4G. It didn't care how new and shiny the phone was; it wasn't in any rush. Pressing his hands together in a gesture of prayer, Fraser leaned his chin on his fingertips and breathed slowly. Whatever happened, he had to stay calm. That was number one. He'd never beat the demons if he lost control. Finally, the browser opened, and the bar flashed, ready for him to type in his search. He drummed his finger on the edge before tapping out the words Hidden Mull.

Expecting the familiar landscape picture to open, it surprised him to see a different setup on the homepage. He scrolled down, reading. Gone was the bio of Roddy and Linda Hunter and the newsflash where they had announced their impending retirement. Fraser clicked the *about me* page, tapping his finger as he waited for it to load. Glancing up, he watched an enormous oil tanker sailing down the strait.

Another screen loaded more stunning photographs. This was a lot more professional than the previous site. Lifting the page with his thumb, he rested on a vivid photo of Kirsten sitting on a boulder with her trim legs crossed at the ankles and her knees pulled up for her hands to rest on. The blurry turquoise sea glinting behind was the perfect backdrop. Brown eyes stared directly out of the picture. Her smile was welcoming if a little forced.

Tour guide and Mull expert Kirsten McGregor has lived all her life on the island and has a wealth of facts and knowledge to share. 'Wow,' he sighed. Why hadn't he considered this? Granted, this venture had been rushed, but he hadn't given any thought to the possibility of what to do if she was still here. The feelings were too big and too sudden. A surge of helplessness made him want to throw the phone into the sea. What must he look like, turning up here like this when she'd asked, or demanded, that he kept his distance? A total git.

With a cleansing breath, he contemplated her picture, her cute button nose pointing out at him. Long chestnut hair rolled over her shoulders, ending in neat coils. She'd ditched the quirky glasses and looked calm and sophisticated. Her face was a riot of freckles. With a sigh, his hand hovered over the screen. What now? Email her? Or pack in the whole damn thing and leave her alone?

'Come on,' he muttered. They were adults. They could put the past behind them and work in harmony. Couldn't they? Or would Kirsten see this as more harassment? Christ, all he'd done was attempt to explain the truth. Why had he bothered?

Well, he had to try. Hitting the contact button, he thumbed out a professional sounding email, proposing a strategy where they would agree on itineraries and perhaps help each other out on rare occasions or busy times. *Yeah, may as well scratch that.* He guessed her reaction already. But why not? He left it in and after checking the email several times, hit send. There was nothing offensive. It was perfectly friendly and accommodating, with no mention of anything which had passed between them previously. In fact, a stranger could have written it. And right now, that was exactly how he felt. Like a stranger. And she'd made it quite clear, as far as she was concerned, that was all he was, if not worse.

Chapter Seven

Kirsten

Kirsten parked outside the two-storey stone-built Glen Lodge Hotel, ready to collect her first customers. She was early. Despite the hotel being newly done up and looking very swish with the bright floral displays outside the entrance, a lingering queasiness filled her tummy every time she did pick-ups from here. The dark green shutters were flung wide, inviting the sunshine to make an appearance. So far it hadn't obeyed; thoroughly annoying because this was the tricky group Roddy had warned her about. Well, bring it on. It wasn't like she hadn't done tricky tours before.

To the left, down a short path, was an old log cabin where Carl Hansen had lived before moving in with Robyn. Kirsten stared through the raindrops. Only a few months ago, she'd dreamed up a life for the two of them, though it was nothing like the dreams she'd cherished for Fraser. Carl was an old school friend – safe and reliable. Fraser was the untouchable, the daredevil, the what might have been. Now he was back, the feelings mounted up too. Kirsten couldn't ignore the twinge of desperate hope and desire, but it didn't change facts. He'd been unreliable five years ago, leaving her without a single word. Was there any reason to think he'd changed? She checked through her messages. She'd added the Hidden Mull email account to her phone. And what was this?

One new message.

Fraser Bell – Hi

So there it was. Only five years late. Fraser Bell. That explained why she'd never found him on social media. He'd been booked on the tour with his brother, Craig Hamilton. She'd assumed they had the same name. Apparently not. Presumably they had different fathers. She read through the email, her frown growing. A business arrangement. *Who does he think he is?* There was no way she would ever come to any kind of arrangement with him. How could she trust him? And how curious, he'd managed to contact her so quickly, what prevented him doing that the first time round?

She glanced up and saw the guests standing outside the hotel door, pulling on waterproofs as the rain started to fall. She shoved the phone into the tray; she would attend to it later.

Wet days were always tricky and on Mull, they happened a lot, every two or three days at least, even in high summer. Somehow, she needed to make the island the most beautiful place on the planet, even under a thick layer of black cloud. But it didn't feel beautiful right now, and she wanted to hit someone, preferably someone whose first name was Fraser and whose surname was Bell.

Carl strolled out, chatting to a couple of guests. Kirsten slunk behind the wheel. *What's he doing here?* He and Robyn had moved to a new cottage and didn't live here now, though Robyn's mum owned the hotel. Turning his curly blond head towards her, Carl gave a cheery wave. Kirsten raised her hand slowly before stepping out to welcome her guests, flinching as their wet boots touched the slick carpet she'd have to get used to cleaning. Another job Roddy always did and was very precious about. Someone tapped her shoulder and Kirsten spun around.

Tugging up his hood, Carl beamed at her, his blond curls falling across his eyes. 'Hey,' he said. 'I was hoping to catch up with you. So, you're in charge now. I think that calls for a party.'

'Yeah, maybe.' Kirsten squinted through the rain.

'Leave it with me. I'll see if I can organise a wee celebration.'

'Oh, thanks, that sounds great.'

Carl scanned around like he was steeling himself to say something else. 'We're looking after the hotel for a few days,' he said. 'Maureen's gone to see Liam. She wanted a break. It's not been an easy year for the family. Speaking of which, Robyn and I—'

'I heard you're engaged. That's great. Congratulations. We can talk at the meeting tonight. I need to get this tour going.' *Did that sound enthusiastic enough?* The last guest had boarded the minibus.

'We might not bother with the meeting, but we should definitely talk soon. Come down to the cottage.'

'Thank you. I can't wait to see it.' Kirsten jumped in and waved to Carl. In her rear-view mirror, several faces scowled at the dismal weather. 'Welcome, everybody.' She closed the door and took off a little too fast. A rabbit leapt out from the side of the path and she slammed on the brakes.

'Whoa,' said a voice. Kirsten glanced in the mirror, observing a passenger rubbing his neck. 'We wanted to see the wildlife, not kill it,' he muttered.

'Apologies,' Kirsten said. 'Sometimes they come out of nowhere.'

Driving very carefully for the next half hour, she squinted through the rain, keeping her commentary to a minimum while she concentrated on the road. Now, she realised the value of a CD, but no way was she ever listening to that dire recording of Roddy's ever again. As they reached their first destination near an off the beaten track village named

Croggan, Kirsten sent up a prayer the sun would break through soon.

Dragging open the door and lowering the step, she indicated for the guests to get out. Most of them looked like they'd rather not.

'Why are we here?' asked a shrew-faced woman in totally inappropriate ankle boots. Heels? Seriously? On a wildlife trip. Kirsten didn't even have a chance to reply. 'Are we walking here? It's far too muddy.'

'Will we be able to see anything?' another passenger asked. 'I can hardly see my hand in front of my face. I think I'll wait here.'

'We need to walk to the best location,' said Kirsten. 'I can't take the minibus up the track. And the best place to view wildlife is in the quieter areas.'

After much eye rolling and sighing, she left with only half the party. The rest chose to stay on the minibus. Not a good sign. High-Heels Woman had decided to try. Kirsten smiled and encouraged her, though she wondered after a few metres if it would have been easier if she'd stayed behind too.

'This weather,' muttered the woman, 'someone told me it was like the tropics here in summer. It's nothing like.'

'Just a bit of rain.' Kirsten tightened the hood of her black waterproof jacket, biting back the reply she wanted to give. *It's an island off the west coast of Scotland. Wet weather guaranteed!*

After half an hour waiting, getting more saturated by the second, it was obvious nothing was going to show. The sea eagles, otters and deer were safely nestled away somewhere out of the rain, sensible creatures.

Gritting her teeth, Kirsten attempted to explain how to capture the best seascapes in the mist, but there wasn't even a great surge of breakers. The sea was flat and dull, much like everything else.

A shriek. Kirsten spun.

'Oh, my god! Help!' High-Heels Woman screamed, ankle-deep in a puddle.

Kirsten ran over and grabbed her. 'I've got you.'

'My boot!' the woman yelled.

'Oh hell,' muttered her partner.

Kirsten's hand flew to her mouth. The woman's ankle boot had slipped off and was still in the puddle, stuck in the gloopy mud. Her blackened sock dangled as she hopped, clutching Kirsten's arm.

With a gut-wrenching jolt, Kirsten hit the ground and a heavy weight slammed on top of her. Wet mud slopped over her waterproofs, grit stuck to her palms as she raised them from the ground and tried to get a hold of the hysterical woman, flailing above, her bulk pinning Kirsten into the muck.

A couple of other passengers dragged her up, and Kirsten scrambled to her feet. A few people turned away to hide their sniggers.

Resembling someone who'd just lost a mud-wrestling competition, Kirsten tried to smack off the dirt. 'Let's get back to the minibus, we can sort this.'

'Sort this? Have you seen me?' The woman balanced on one foot, clinging to her partner and gesturing over her body. 'And my boot. How can I walk?'

Kirsten pulled the boot out of the puddle between her finger and thumb. 'Just put it on for now. I'll help you back.'

'Put it on? It's ruined.'

'This was a terrible idea,' muttered her partner.

Every negative remark was like a slap. *I'm not God! I can't change the weather to suit a tour.* 'Right.' Kirsten frowned around, trying to think up a plan. 'I should take you back.'

'Haven't we got more places to see?' a man asked.

'We do, but this lady is soaked and so am I. Half of the group are still on the minibus and you all look frozen.'

'But we paid for the trip,' said another woman.

'I know.' Kirsten gnawed on her lower lip. There was no back-up. She couldn't phone Linda and ask for a bright idea. She'd have to conjure up something herself. 'I don't want to diddle anyone out of a trip. I just want to make sure you're all comfortable.' Though getting rid of them all was the most appealing idea.

'Then take me back for dry clothes and we can continue.'

Kirsten closed her eyes, pulling in a deep breath as she sank into the driver's seat. No chance of keeping the minibus clean now. It looked like a pig with diarrhoea had been set loose.

Back at the Glen Lodge Hotel, they waited while High-Heels Woman went in to change. It was forty minutes before she returned and the other passengers were not happy. Kirsten was wet and cold. Her fact supply ran dry and her teeth chattered. As the weather had seriously mucked up the day another change couldn't hurt. Calgary Bay was always a beautiful place, and the woodland trail could be done in the rain. She set off directly, hoping to lift their spirits. On the way, she told them some of the history. An annoying man behind her kept throwing his wife smug looks and shaking his head. 'Do you have a different version?' Kirsten asked, regarding him in her mirror. Eek, she hadn't meant it to sound quite so aggressive, but the mud seeping into her backside was distracting.

The man searched around and pointed to himself. 'Do you mean me?'

'You were shaking your head. I just wondered if you knew a different story,' Kirsten tried to clarify.

He shrugged. 'I don't know what you mean.' The muttering with his wife continued all the way there.

Kirsten pulled up the sharp slope into the bumpy car park. Her heart pounded manically at the sight of a silver

Ford SUV. Too late to change her mind; if she drove off now, the group might lynch her. As she shut the door after them, she spun around to see Fraser striding across the *machair*, the wide grassy plain between them and the silvery beach. His legs extended like great tree trunks under his kilt. It swirled in the wind; any more and they might get a glimpse of the crown jewels. Kirsten blanched. Fraser seemed unperturbed by the wind and rain, sporting only a lightweight jacket. His dark hair clung in wet strands to his forehead, making him warrior-like. If he'd been attractive five years ago, double it, treble it now. But whatever she'd felt back then had been crushed. His good looks just added fuel to the vengeful fire simmering in her stomach. Not satisfied with notching up a wide-eyed island virgin then ghosting her for five years, he had the nerve to swan back here and take her on in business. Kirsten glared at him. But her mind detoured. What had happened to his career? Why would someone with such a high-flying life pack it in to guide tours out here? *Surely not just to annoy me.*

Stopping midway, Fraser spoke to his clients. They beamed at him and laughed. His arms waved in a sweeping gesture, then his hands sprang in front of him like he was telling a dramatic story.

Kirsten ground her toe into the gravel. Maybe it was the kilt that had them smiling. If she donned something equally clichéd would her clients laugh in the face of the dreadful weather? Maybe she should get into a highland dance dress or go the full hog and wear a Flora MacDonald gown and white cockade. What wasn't to love? She screwed up her lips. Roddy's doctrine blended with her love of the island constricted her to geographical facts, real history and human stories. Not claymore-wielding, ginger-haired haggis, Claire and Jamie tack. The beating heart of the Hebrides without the tartan and shortbread. If adapting her tours meant changing to this kind of display, she'd rather pack it all in.

'Excuse this.' Kirsten folded her arms, waiting for Fraser's tacky tour to come through. 'We'll let them leave first. I'm very glad you chose Hidden Mull.' Some foot shuffling followed and a few people studied Fraser with interest. Why couldn't he be an average bloke with a hygiene problem, instead of looking like the ad for Scottish Beef? All he needed was a can of Irn-Bru and a deep-fried Mars bar, and he'd be set to tackle the Loch Ness Monster.

'I like this guy,' said High-Heels Woman, now in trainers. *Why didn't she wear them originally?* She ogled Fraser. Her partner rolled his eyes.

Another woman chipped in. 'He's very rugged.'

'We should have gone with that tour,' her husband muttered, 'would have kept the ladies happy and that's half the battle.'

The first woman's partner agreed.

What? Kirsten's ears burned. Her feeble marketing strategies evaporated in the sight of Fraser. Her brand of honest island tours, focusing on natural beauty, deep cultural history and wildlife was about to be trumped in an *Outlander* style ravishing of their values.

Fraser spotted her as he led his group to the car park. He gave her a brief nod, and his eyebrow raised as he took in her mud-splattered outfit. Kirsten flicked him a slaying glance before looking back at her clients. 'If you'll walk this way. And stick close to the edge. We don't want to damage the *machair*. That's what we call this low-lying grassy plain. It's one of the rarest habitats in Britain and home to some unique flowers and a type of bee found nowhere else but the Hebrides,' she said loud enough for Fraser to hear, before he crushed it with his outsized *Braveheart* boots. *What a typical ignorant mainlander.*

Kirsten couldn't help checking over to see his reaction. Fraser's left cheek bulged like he was trying to hold in a smirk.

As she escorted her group forward, Kirsten caught a movement. A woman from the party leaned over and touched Fraser on the arm. He turned rather theatrically. 'Yes?' He grinned.

'You look gorgeous. I love the kilt,' she said in her Texan accent, patting him on the forearm. 'Just what I wanted to see. It's made my day. And sounds like you're having a great time. Our tour is so dull. We're here until Friday, maybe we could get on yours before we leave.'

'Eh, sure,' said Fraser. 'Drop me a message, I'll see what I can do.'

'Thanks, handsome.' She winked and followed on.

Kirsten observed the whole thing. A flush crept across her cheeks. She clenched her fists. Despite the heated tension bubbling inside, a lump rose in her throat. Nothing made sense for a moment or two; her brain was muddy and clogged. *What now?* Did anyone care anyway? The sickening pang reminded her of when Derek the prat had run tours. How he'd always tried to outdo her, make out he knew heaps more and was so much more popular. Even Roddy had thought he was wonderful, until he'd done the dirty, stolen some of their best clients, tried it on with Kirsten, then left the island for his next dodge. Now, Fraser, the man she'd dreamed about for years, was doing the same. How long would he last this time? Hopefully, he'd live up to his track record and vanish quickly. *I want my island back to myself.*

The trouble was, a part of her also wanted Fraser. Her heart fractured just knowing he was back because the version of him she'd brought to life in her head wasn't real.

The clouds drifted slowly west across the bay as the group reached the tip of the bank. Miles of sea sprawled in front of them. The white sand sparkled, and the sun put in an appearance. Too late to salvage what was possibly the worst tour ever.

Kirsten couldn't wait to get rid of the group. Her head and her heart were too full to concentrate, but she still had the meeting about the Midsummer Party to attend. With no time to go home first, she arrived at the pub still in her filthy clothes.

'What happened to you?' Georgia glanced up from the table as Kirsten slumped into a seat opposite.

'Don't even ask.' Kirsten ran her hand over her wind-matted and mud-clogged hair. 'I've just done the tour from hell and I don't want to talk about it.'

The main door opened, and some other members of the organising committee arrived, heading straight to the bar. Georgia leaned across and whispered through her wide red lips. 'Don't look now, but wait until you see the barman.' Kirsten held the urge to turn and stare. 'He's Australian and over here for the summer, I asked him if he'd like to help us out. He said he'd check in.'

Kirsten scanned the room casually, travelling across the assembled punters until she got to the bar. A tall, handsome man with a great tan and dark spiky hair pulled a pint, laughing along with the committee members. Kirsten sized him up. 'He looks nice.'

Georgia drummed her fingers. 'Nice? Is that all you can say?' Her mouth curved into a smile. 'I thought you and him might get together for a date.'

'What?' Kirsten gaped.

'Shh, he's coming over.'

'Oh my god, no. Look at me, I'm covered in mud.' Kirsten blinked, forcing a smile as the barman grabbed a chair and pulled it to the table end between her and Georgia.

'Hi, ladies.' He grinned.

'This is my friend Kirsten,' said Georgia.

'Matt.' He extended a tanned hand, his azure blue eyes twinkling.

Kirsten shook his hand and blinked. 'Hi, excuse the state of me. I was on a tour and well, things got messy.'

'It looks fine. I like a girl who doesn't mind getting down and dirty.'

'Seriously?' Kirsten arched an eyebrow.

'Aw man.' Matt dropped his head into his hands. 'That bad, huh? I'll try harder the next time. Listen, I can't hang about, I'm supposed to be working, but if there's an exciting event at your fair, put my name down. Nothing with glue.'

Kirsten laughed and shook her head.

'Ok, craft it is,' Georgia said.

'I mean it, I hate glue. Mud is fine, but glue, no. Now, I better go, I'm getting some filthy looks from the bar.' He jumped up and replaced the chair. Kirsten watched him as he took orders from the awaiting punters, and he glanced back with a wink. Her cheeks burned.

'He's only twenty-four.' Georgia waggled her eyebrows. 'You could have a toy boy.'

'Seriously? How do you even know what age he is?'

'He told me something about when he graduated, I worked it out.'

'Right,' said Kirsten. 'I hardly think it's going to lead to a budding relationship. He's a twenty-four-year-old from Australia. Not exactly my type.'

'Who knows?' Georgia smiled. 'Maybe you'll fall in love and he'll stay here for you.'

'Ok, let's not get carried away.' Kirsten shook her head.

'Uh oh.' Georgia tucked some wayward strands of her blonde tousled bob behind her ears. 'Here come the rest of the committee.'

'Well, before we start.' Kirsten checked no one else could hear her. 'Do I have to make the closing speech? I've been attempting to bake, and I said I'd help my mum on the cake stall. Can I do that instead?'

'Yeah. I don't see why not. I think Carl might do the speech, but he's not coming tonight. I need to remember to ask him.'

Two dull and tedious hours followed. After the day she'd had, Kirsten wanted a long soak in the bath, then to curl up and sleep. Totally unfocused on the conversation, her mind returned to Fraser and how she now faced the impossible task of competing with the kilted wonder as he dashed about the island, making the ladies swoon.

Matt's parting shot, 'Remember, Kirsten, mud bath this weekend. Be there!' gave her the only reason to smile all day.

*

Kirsten deliberately avoided replying to Fraser's email. Was there any point? She'd tried working alongside Derek two years ago and look at what had happened. A few days later, however, she decided she should probably say something. She began thumbing a reply.

I would appreciate it if you stayed away

It wasn't unreasonable to ask him to stay away from some of her particular places, especially at times she'd be there. As she pondered, a notification pinged from TripAdvisor.

YOU HAVE NEW REVIEWS

Have I? Without thinking, she pressed send on her unfinished email and opened the reviews. *Please let them be good.*

TWO STARS

Her heart slipped into her sparkly pink toenails.

So, the weather wasn't great, but it was made worse by the guide, whose grim face was worse than a black cloud. She scowled at us all day, rolled her eyes and made sarcastic comments. For a tour that calls itself 'Hidden Mull', we saw nothing other than the mundane. The highlight was when the guide and a passenger fell into a muddy puddle. At least it was a bit of light relief. All in all, I would not recommend this tour.

Kirsten pressed her hand to her forehead, wishing she hadn't checked. Using about the only part of her brain that was still working, she stopped herself from being physically sick, and sending a rage-filled reply. Then she noticed the next one.

ONE STAR

The tour started badly and continued in that vein. The guide arrived early but instead of welcoming us she sat on her phone until the exact time then opened the bus. By this time, we were already cold and bored. The places she took us to all looked the same (covered in mist) and she tried to fob us off by saying black and white photos would look great. I accept the weather was out of her control, but we expected some entertainment. Other than a few local, and frankly dull, stories, she didn't seem to have much knowledge about the place, other than what we could guess, such as it rains a lot. When it brightened up, instead of rushing us to one of the hidden beauties the tour claims to provide, she took us to Calgary Bay. This was a beautiful beach, but it was also filled with other people, including another tour! Hardly hidden! What seriously ticked us off was that the other tour looked to be having a great time; their guide was clearly entertaining. We spent half an hour on the beach wandering about while the guide stood with her arms folded, looking bored. A complete waste of a day and money!

A rush of nauseous panic flooded through her veins. *I have to do this again tomorrow and the day after and forever.* She wanted to jump off a cliff or never get out of bed again. A feeling which had plagued her before: at college, when her dad died, after Fraser left, when she'd been pursued by Derek. She didn't want to succumb to that kind of despair again. *I can deal with this.* She held her breath, then let it out slowly. *Yes, I can.* But nothing could quite quell the urge to throw up or the desire to crawl into hibernation for the rest of the season.

Chapter Eight

Fraser

I would appreciate it if you stayed away

'Right.' Fraser stared at the message from his position atop the hill behind his gran's croft. 'That's it?' The same bluntness he'd experienced in her only email five years ago. How could he stay away though if he didn't know where she'd be?

He scratched his chin. Kirsten's tours seemed quite random. He'd read the blurb on her website and she offered flexibility. Maybe he should do the same. He wasn't in the RAF now, he could loosen up a bit. He'd planned itineraries with little variance, but nothing was set in stone, not now. Being free was part of being on this island; untamed and wild.

Today would be a test of his strength in stepping out of his comfort zone. No tours, but the appointment in his calendar gave him a stabbing pain in his gut every time he thought about it. In the SUV's boot, he lined up the three different kilt outfits he'd purchased. Each day, he chose the one that suited the tour. For the history tours, he wore the Bonnie Prince Charlie, for the wildlife tour, his traditional number. And for the romance and mystery tours, he pulled out the more modern, unconventional one, with a tweed-style kilt and linen shirt. Which would work best today? Maybe he'd need all of them. He decided to start with the traditional. Squirrelling it into his gran's house, he emerged fully dressed some twenty minutes later.

Agnes followed him to the doorstep. 'Are you sure I shouldn't iron your shirt?'

'I already did it.' Fraser brushed his fingers over it.

Agnes raised a wispy eyebrow.

'Thanks for the offer though.' He bent down and kissed her crinkled forehead. With a slight headshake, she waved him off.

Turning on the music, Fraser cruised north through the glen towards the ferry port at Craignure. When he arrived, he strolled towards the promenade, adjusting his watch and scanning around. He'd arranged to meet a local photographer, but he had no idea what she looked like. His stomach squirmed. He hated getting his picture taken, but to make his website as appealing as Kirsten's, he was going to need some great photos, and a few cheesy selfies weren't going to cut it. Time to fork out for a pro. Who better to do it than the photographer who had done Kirsten's pictures?

A tap on his shoulder. He turned to see a pretty, young woman with a tousled blonde bob and a broad, shining smile. 'Are you Fraser?'

'Yes, I am.'

'I'm Georgia Rose, the photographer.'

'Nice to meet you.' Fraser put out his hand, and they shook. Her cheery expression put him at ease. The nerves he'd felt about the process ebbed temporarily. 'How did you know who I was?'

Georgia checked him up and down. 'Well, the outfit. You've already got yourself quite a reputation.'

'Oh, really?' He appreciated what impact a uniform could have on people, and this was no different.

'Yeah. And I can see why. It's seriously hot.' She gave him the once over.

Once, he'd have taken that as a green light, ditched the photoshoot and found the nearest hotel, but he'd grown out of all that. Heat burned in his cheeks. 'I'm not sure how to reply to that.' If he gave the answers his brain was primed to give, he could land in all sorts of trouble. This woman seemed nice, but his days of quick flings were over, and with everything going on in his head, he wasn't in a place for anything else.

She grinned. 'It's not a dodgy pick-up line, if that's what you think. It's just an observation. You hired me to get some photos for your website and I can see you've really thought about the look.'

'Well, yeah. I guess it's a bit cheesy, but it gets people talking.'

'Absolutely.' Georgia nodded. 'It's exactly what tourists want. So, we just have to get photos which reflect that. I'd say you're already there with the image, now I have to work out where best to shoot you.'

'Sounds terrifying.'

'You have no idea.' She smiled.

Fraser rubbed the back of his neck. He'd faced dangerous times in his life; flown jets into warzones at breakneck speeds, intercepted foreign warplanes, carried out recce missions in enemy territory, disobeyed his commander and ended up with a court martial. None of these had produced the kind of nerves currently rankling his gut. He drove Georgia to a beauty spot with stunning sea views, cliffs and wind likely to knock down trees, which explained why there weren't any. Bare and rugged coastline spread for miles.

'I hope this is safe.' Fraser approached the cliff edge and peered over.

Georgia frowned and flicked him a puzzled glance. 'I didn't have you pegged as someone who'd be bothered.'

'It's not the drop, it's the kilt. There are certain things I'd rather not have captured for posterity.'

With a laugh, Georgia raked in her camera bag. 'Don't worry, I'll get you looking suitably windswept without compromising your dignity.'

Flexing his hands, he nodded. 'So, you tell me what you want me to do.'

He didn't realise quite what he'd let himself in for. Georgia was relentless, manhandling him like a piece of meat, setting him up in poses, and snapping him from every angle.

'Turn so you're looking towards the sea, just your head.' The camera clicked. 'Keep your chest facing me. That's it, nice.' More clicks. She moved her position. 'Now, put your left foot on the boulder in front of you.' Click. 'Now look at me.' Another click. Fraser looked over Georgia's shoulder and burned hot around the neck, tensing. Georgia shouted. 'Relax, drop your shoulders a bit, don't hunch them.'

He tried, but he was aware of the Hidden Mull minibus approaching.

'Eyes on the sea, Fraser.'

They wouldn't obey. The minibus had parked. Kirsten was helping a group down. Her face was filled with kindness and concern for each passenger. Fraser watched, and she glanced back, her expression flickering. She halted for a moment, stared at Fraser, then pointed to something in the distance. Her group took out binoculars and looked seaward.

'Fraser!' Georgia's voice cut through the wind. 'What are you looking at? Eyes that way.' She pointed to the wild ocean.

Fraser blinked and turned but Kirsten was stalking their way, her cheeks red, brows drawn together. A stream of clicks. Fraser glanced back. Kirsten tapped Georgia on the shoulder. Fraser didn't have time to warn her. She jumped. 'Oh, my goodness. Kirsten! You gave me a shock.'

'What are you doing?' The wind carried Kirsten's hushed words to Fraser.

'I'm doing a shoot.' Georgia glanced over as Fraser approached. 'This is Fraser Bell. I'm getting some publicity shots for his business. Actually, he's in the same line as you, maybe you know him.'

'Yeah, I know who he is.' Kirsten stepped back, almost tripping over a rock. 'I can't talk now. I'm on a tour.' She turned with a flick of her long dark curls and muttered, 'I just can't believe this.'

'Believe what?' Georgia followed her and put her hand on her shoulder.

'I'll tell you later.' Kirsten marched back to her group and started talking to one or two of them. Georgia watched her with a puzzled expression.

'Let's leave. I don't want a fight.' Fraser rubbed his hands together.

'I hope she's ok; she looked annoyed.'

'Let's get to the car. I'll explain.' But what to say? He wasn't sure how much Georgia knew, and he didn't know her well enough to tell her what had happened five years ago. Did he even want to? The fewer people who knew, the better. Island gossips would have a field day if they discovered the two rival guides had a history like theirs. But what a change in Kirsten. Words in an email could always be misread, but seeing her like this for real was disturbing. She'd been sweet, funny and affectionate, not this tyrant.

He led the way, taking them a route that didn't pass by Kirsten's tour. As soon as they were in the SUV, Georgia folded her arms and stared. 'What's going on? Kirsten's my friend. I don't want to do anything to upset her.'

Fraser rubbed his forehead. 'She thinks I'm muscling in on her patch. Which I suppose I am. But it was unintentional.

I read on the Hidden Mull website the owners were retiring, I hadn't figured that anyone was taking over.'

Georgia took a deep breath and tapped her knee as Fraser started the engine. She didn't reply until they reached the main road. 'You should talk to her.'

'I've tried.' Fraser threw up his left palm. 'She told me to leave her alone.'

Without removing his gaze from the road, he couldn't study Georgia's reaction. Kirsten was her friend. Maybe she'd told Georgia herself.

'This isn't the first time something like this has happened,' said Georgia.

'What?' He clenched the wheel.

'I'm not sure of all the details. I haven't known Kirsten that long. I only came to the island last year. But the rumour mill works overtime around here. There was someone else who ran tours a few years ago, and well, I heard he harassed her almost to breaking point. I think he was a real sleazebag by the sounds of things. I guess she's worried you'll be the same.'

'Right.' Had the guy harassed her or was that just Kirsten's favourite story? 'Listen, did she leave the island some years ago, then come back?'

'She went to college.'

'But she hasn't left since she started doing the tours?'

'Maybe for a few holidays with friends, but that's all, as far as I know.'

So she'd lied in her email. Why? To throw him off? How had he misjudged her so fully? 'Well, whatever she might say, I'm not like that, I don't go around harassing people and I'd much rather we worked alongside each other peacefully.'

'It isn't me you have to convince,' said Georgia. Fraser tapped the steering wheel. 'This is a big island in landmass.

But it's not big enough to hide when people fall out. Pull out your charm and call her.'

'What charm?'

'You don't dress like that by accident.'

The words made him squirm; his temper rocketed. He breathed slowly. Stay in control. 'Look, I'm not trying for some porno image here. I hope that's not the kind of pictures you've taken.'

She laughed and held her lips in a smile before continuing. 'No, don't be ridiculous. But you better get used to the idea some people are going to look at you irreverently. Still, what I meant was, you must have some self-awareness. You have a good body, you want to flaunt it, why not? We've been chatting a few hours and you seem a friendly, level-headed, smart kind of guy to me. There's no reason why you can't make Kirsten see that. Give it a go.'

'Ok.' He leaned one elbow on the window ledge. He'd been oh so successful with that previously.

Georgia's pleas helter-skeltered round his head for the rest of the day, making his brain ache. If he'd been a newcomer to the island, a stranger to Kirsten, then Georgia's ideas would make sense. But how to even look Kirsten in the eye without being made to feel like a mad stalker? This was going to need a whole new level of courage, something he'd never doubted in all his years of military life.

Chapter Nine

Kirsten

Staring in the mirror, Kirsten clamped her straighteners into her hair and pulled them down. Normally she didn't bother, letting her long dark tresses tumble about in wavy tendrils. Up until two years ago, she hadn't even owned a pair of straighteners. On tours, the wind played havoc with her hair, so it was easier to let it stay natural or plait it out of the way, but today called for poise.

She flicked out her sleek tresses. Not bad. Carl and Georgia had organised a Sunday lunch celebration at the Craignure Inn in honour of Kirsten becoming Hidden Mull boss. They were kind friends, but Kirsten really hoped they hadn't visited Trip Advisor recently. It put a dampener on the desire to celebrate.

Taking the short track from her bothy to the farmhouse where her mum and Beth lived, Kirsten admired Beth's wood-carved animal sculptures that lined the way. Things were changing on the farm now Beth was dating Murray Henderson. Kirsten wanted her sister to be happy and settled, of course she did, but seeing her all cuddly and close with Murray made Kirsten painfully aware of her own singledom.

Straightening her daisy patterned chambray dress, she opened the door to the side porch. Today she was not going to think about anything annoying, just happy things.

'Oh, hi.' Beth turned as Kirsten entered the kitchen. 'I haven't seen you for ages. The tours must be busy.'

'Yeah.' Kirsten stretched. 'I had a lot of pre-bookings.' It was just as well. With Fraser dashing around and those crap reviews up there for all to see, it was amazing she was still in business. She might die of embarrassment if her family read them, and if Roddy or Linda saw them, they'd be horrified. 'I'm still trying to shake things up.'

'Good. The sooner you ditch Roddy's nonsense, the better.'

'Yeah, it's not exactly that simple.'

'Is that because of this other tour guide? Is he causing problems?'

Kirsten pulled a face. 'I just wish he'd go away. I could do without this when I've just taken over the business. He's got the looks to make him instantly popular.'

'Hmm. It's a tough one. Maybe best to just keep out of his way.'

Ha! If only that were possible. But he had a way of turning up. Kirsten gave a wry smile.

Gillian McGregor came into the kitchen, beaming. Her expression dropped as she scanned her younger daughter. 'Ready to celebrate? Are you all right? You look a bit red.'

'I'm just tired.'

Gillian stepped forward and wrapped Kirsten into a hug. 'You're exhausted. Maybe we should hire someone to help with the paperwork. You're doing this job on your own when there used to be three of you.'

'Murray would help you with paperwork,' said Beth. 'He's good at that. I've got him doing the farm admin. I can't stand that side of things.'

'Well, maybe.' Should she admit defeat and agree? Was it defeat or just accepting help?

Murray bounded in a few seconds later, running his fingers through his fair hair. Lucky Beth had landed a man who resembled a catalogue model and doted on her too.

Kirsten took the front seat in the Land Rover so they could hold hands and make eyes at each other in the back. Murray wasn't an islander, but he'd pledged his desire to stay. Kirsten hoped it was true, and something told her it was. If only she could be so fortunate. She had a bizarre mental image of herself dressed like Elizabeth Bennett with her hair in ringlets, telling Beth that even if one hundred other Murray Hendersons came along, she could never be as happy as her.

The beer garden looked very inviting with its rustic picnic tables and huge blue parasols, but when Gillian parked at the front of the Inn, Kirsten groaned. *Here we go again.*

'What's wrong?' Gillian asked.

A silver SUV gleamed outside. *Sometimes this island just isn't big enough.* 'Nothing.'

Dreading what she was going to find inside, Kirsten let Beth and Murray lead the way. They were both about six foot two and with Kirsten pitching in at five four, she was able to keep a low profile.

Murray ducked under the low beam at the door, and Kirsten stayed in his wake. The Inn was quaint with a mixture of little seating booths, round tables and a couple of leather sofas near a large empty fireplace. Kirsten squinted over at the bar. A pair of azure blue eyes gleamed back. Matt gave a cheeky wink, looking dazzlingly out of place in his Hawaiian shirt amongst the oak panelling and raftered ceilings. Kirsten tried to smile. Gillian tapped her on the shoulder. 'Georgia's over there waving.'

'What? Oh.'

Georgia stood at the garden door gesturing for them to follow her outside, her floaty pink shift dress ruffling in the breeze. Murray, being his chivalrous self, put his hand out for

Kirsten and Beth to go first. Flattening her lips, Kirsten snuck forward. As she passed the bar, she flicked a glance at Matt.

'Hi, Kirsty, nice to see you again.'

'It's Kirsten,' she said.

'Of course it is. And I knew that. I just thought Kirsty sounded a bit jaunty for a Sunday afternoon.'

'Funny.'

'Seriously?' said Beth.

As Kirsten got to the end of the bar and the room opened out further into another area beyond two wooden pillars, her smile slipped. Sitting in an oak-panelled booth was a hulking muscular figure with strong tanned arms. Without doing an obvious stare, she couldn't see who he was with for the pillar, but he was chatting to someone. She'd almost made it when he glanced her way. Willing her legs to keep going, she tried not to look back, aware he was watching.

Outside, Georgia led them to the octagonal picnic table. Carl, Robyn and Robyn's mum, Maureen, were already seated. Maureen, the proprietor of the Glen Lodge Hotel, scanned over Kirsten and the others before waving to Gillian.

'It's so hot,' said Gillian. 'A bit too hot for me.'

'Let's go inside and leave the young ones to talk,' said Maureen.

Beth took a seat next to Robyn, and Kirsten walked around, sitting next to Georgia.

'How's everything with your mum?' Beth asked Robyn.

'Getting much better.' Robyn smiled.

In the harbour, beyond the garden and the road, sat the ferry with its nose up ready for boarding. Cars bumped on and gulls let out shrill cries from the lampposts. Kirsten focused on the sounds while examining Robyn's elegant profile and long blonde hair. She knew Robyn had always had a tricky relationship with her mum, and since the winter, they'd been reconciliating. Having Carl as her partner must make things a lot easier. Kirsten glanced at him, but his smile was trained on Robyn.

'I thought she'd come round,' said Beth. 'Your mum can be quite scary, but I'm sure she appreciates everything you've done for her.'

'Hey.' Georgia tapped Kirsten and whispered, 'What's up?'

'What do you mean?'

'You don't look happy.'

Kirsten fiddled with her fingers and glanced at the door. The windows were too dim to see inside, but Fraser might be able to see out. 'I'm fine.'

Georgia leaned in as the others carried on chatting. 'The other day, when I was doing a photoshoot, what were you going to tell me?'

Kirsten tapped the table. 'About Fraser. You realise he's like my rival? He's popped up and taken over the island. He doesn't need any more help. Your photos are really good – you'll have him looking like an advert for Visit Scotland – who wouldn't choose that tour over mine?'

Georgia smirked. 'Lots of people enjoy your tours. This island is crawling with more than enough tourists for both of you. I think you should talk to Fraser. There's no reason why you can't work something out. He's a nice guy. He's inside just now, go and chat to him.'

'I really can't.'

'Honestly, I know he looks, well, I guess quite intimidating.'

'What do you mean?' The comment stung. Kirsten's island friends had always ribbed her about her shyness around boys at school, and sometimes she still felt it. If Georgia only knew – once Kirsten had been bold enough to sleep with Fraser! The urge to blurt it out was overpowering. She'd since braved some dates and hook-ups with random tourists, doing nothing for her self-esteem, or her nerves. If Roddy had found out, she wouldn't be sitting here celebrating the takeover. And of course, she'd been brave with Carl, and shoved her foot right in it there. Would the cringy memories ever stop? If she could just strike a happy balance between being brave and downright idiotic.

'Nothing bad. He's just got a larger-than-life air about him when he's dressed in his kilt.'

'Don't I know it.'

Matt sauntered out, grinning as he approached their table. 'So, what can I get you, lovely people? Kirsten, shall we start with you?'

Hoping the sunburn would cover her on the blushing front, Kirsten ordered. Matt's blue eyes never left hers except to stray towards her lips and her neck. Totally exposed, Kirsten clamped her hands to her elbows and blinked. If she wanted to settle for quick flings all year round, she was quids-in with guys like Matt, but there just wasn't the possibility of anything more concrete.

Kirsten checked the menu and ordered.

'Perfect.' Matt scribbled on his pad. 'And you, beautiful?' He turned to Beth. Kirsten cringed. Beth might throttle him for calling her that; everyone knew she didn't suffer fools. Matt's gaze widened at the expression on her face. Murray lifted his hand from Beth's knee and folded his arms.

'Well, handsome,' began Beth. Everyone sniggered. 'You can get me the hunter's chicken and no more cheap chat up lines.'

'Gotcha.' Matt smirked.

'Kirsten.' Georgia tapped her shoulder again. 'Let's not fall out over this. I didn't mean to upset you. I have to take work where I can get it.'

'Sure, I understand.' Kirsten smiled and happened to catch Matt's eye, only for him to wink at her.

'He likes you,' whispered Georgia. 'But he's shameless, so watch out.'

'Stop it,' Kirsten said through gritted teeth. 'I'm not interested anyway.' Seasonal workers came and went. Matt would be gone by the end of August.

'Now, my lovebirds,' Matt said, as he reached Robyn and Carl. Carl's hand gripped Robyn's.

Georgia patted Kirsten's arm gently. 'I'm all right,' Kirsten said, a little louder than she meant.

'I know you are,' said Georgia. 'But I also get how tough this is for you.'

Yes, it was tough, but only because of the way friends threw pitiful looks at her or tried to set her up with any man who could draw breath. Kirsten hated the way Carl walked around her on eggshells or when he and Robyn attempted to be over-nice. Kirsten had used him in a pathetic attempt to move her life along. She hadn't felt the all-consuming love for him that she'd pretended to. That was reserved, and she'd only known it once with the man just a few metres away through the thick stone wall. He was the one who'd caused the biggest trauma to her heart. They'd had a few hours of bliss, and the connection she'd felt to him had been stronger than anything she'd felt since. But it was stupid.

Who was he with now? Someone from a tour he was just having a chat with? Was that why he'd chosen this job and this image? To provide him with a steady stream of drooling women. Kirsten's fingers tensed. There was every chance Fraser had settled with someone. Did it matter? One way or another, he was nothing but a memory. Though one Kirsten couldn't quite leave behind.

Matt reappeared with a tray of drinks some moments later. He came to Kirsten last. Leaning over her shoulder, he said, 'Here's a little extra for you, try this on the house. It's a cocktail of my own making. I think you'll like it.'

Kirsten considered the shot glass of pink liquid, complete with a strawberry and mini parasol. 'I've heard about guys like you, drugging unsuspecting girls like me.'

'Nothing dangerous in there,' he smiled. 'And this lady has your back, so I wouldn't dare.'

Beth raised an eyebrow. 'That's the most sensible thing you've said yet.'

Matt quirked a grin. 'Just a little taster for my favourite Kirsten.'

Unable to suppress her smile, Kirsten lifted the glass, raised it to him and drank it. He watched closely. 'Actually, that's really good. What is it?'

'I call it the Sexy Berry, trade secret.' He gave them a salute and headed back inside.

'What a twit.' Beth sipped her beer.

'Shall we drink to the new Hidden Mull boss?' Georgia raised her glass, grinning.

'Cheers!' They all said together.

'Thanks, everyone.' Kirsten felt the heat in her cheeks.

'I heard there's a new guy doing tours too,' Carl piped up. 'It isn't affecting the business, is it?'

Georgia coughed into her drink and shook her head.

'Well... If you want the Disneyland version of Mull; all flashy lights and razzle-dazzle, and none of the island's real heart, then he's got it.'

Robyn set down her glass. 'Maybe he's just trying to give the tourists what they want to see. He's branded himself and it's a hit. If he goes for the razzle-dazzle to draw them in, he can add authenticity later. It's brilliant.'

Kirsten wished she'd kept her mouth shut. Of course, Robyn's background was in marketing. Kirsten felt about three centimetres tall. She looked around. What could she say? Everyone loved Fraser and his glitz.

'Your tours are great,' said Georgia. 'And don't think otherwise. I know what a bitch imposter syndrome can be, so don't you go thinking there's something wrong with what you're doing.'

'Of course not,' said Robyn. 'You don't have to market your tours the same way, even though your end goal is similar. Your ideal client won't be the same as his. They may both be looking for tours, but they won't necessarily want the same experience on a tour.'

'I'm sure Robyn could help you out if you need any pointers,' said Carl.

'Sure, any time.' Robyn smiled across the table.

'Thanks.' Who else did she need to help her? First Murray, now Robyn. Maybe they could run her business and her life better. Maybe she should just kick back and let them try. Or better, just accept the help and stop being so stubborn. 'Maybe we could meet and chat about it sometime?'

'Of course,' said Robyn.

Kirsten took a sip of the Sexy Berry and smiled. Yes, if accepting help was the way to win, then what did she have to lose? Because this felt like a war and she needed to win.

Chapter Ten

Fraser

Fraser opened all the windows and the sunroof in the SUV, but it was still roasting hot.

'Close the roof.' Agnes clung to her wispy grey hair. 'I might get sucked out.'

Obeying his gran, he did so, hanging his arm on the open window ledge. 'It's like an oven in here. Did you enjoy your lunch?'

'Yes, very nice,' said Agnes. 'Though far too much. I'm not sure what size of people they're trying to feed.'

'You ate most of it,' Fraser observed. It was pleasant to keep talking. The whole experience would have been enjoyable if he could've removed seeing Kirsten. No words were necessary to convey her feelings. The disgust in her eyes was enough. It sickened his heart. Once three little words had escaped Kirsten's lips and flipped Fraser's world on its head. Now he couldn't imagine anything kind coming from her.

He'd enjoyed a brief chat with Georgia, but she'd seemed edgy. Had he put her in a tough position with her friend? A guilty knot formed in his gut.

'Who was the nice young lady?' Agnes asked.

'Georgia Rose. She's the photographer who took the pictures for my website.'

'And will you date her?'

'No, Gran. I'm not here to date anyone. I want to get away from all that. I'm happy on my own. That's how I work best.'

'But you were with someone before. The woman who had the baby. I still don't know the whole story about that, Fraser. One minute you were writing saying you were going to be a father, next thing is, it was all a mistake. How can something like that be a mistake?'

'Because it was. I explained before.' Fraser tugged at the neck of his pale green shirt. *Just breathe.* 'I don't want to talk about it.'

Steering Agnes's chat wasn't too difficult, but she liked to rehash the same subjects, and Fraser found it hard to concentrate. When they got back to Uisken, he set a chair outside for her in the shade where she promptly fell asleep. He lay down on the neat square lawn in her back garden and opened up his laptop. Now he'd got her up and running with broadband, it was easier to conduct business.

The browser was open on the Hidden Mull site and he noticed a link to a new Facebook page. That was a good idea. He made a mental note to make one for himself. He opened the instant messenger icon. Should he send one? Just something professional. Nothing she could complain about or take umbrage at. He tapped out some words, hoping they sounded friendly and sent it. What hope of a civil reply this time?

Agnes woke with a start. 'Fraser.' She sat up.

'What is it?'

'Have I missed the party?'

'What party?'

'The Midsummer Party at Dervaig. I'd like to go. Netty Foster is going. I've missed it for a good few years. Is it tomorrow?'

'No, tomorrow's the seventeenth. If it's midsummer, it must be on Friday or Saturday. I'll find out. I don't mind taking you.' He really didn't. In fact, it surprised him how many things he was enjoying a lot more than he'd imagined. Escaping here was one thing, but he hadn't expected to feel so at ease. If the Kirsten part of the equation was removed, life could be almost perfect. How could he change things? He didn't suppose she'd appreciate flirting this time around, so what else?

As he drove through Dervaig most days on his tours, he was able to check the village hall noticeboard after he'd finished the following day. He noted down the party details for Agnes. It went on until midnight; if she lasted that late, it would be a miracle.

A grey-haired man came out of the hall door, scratching his head. He glanced at Fraser and frowned. 'Are you the new tour guide?'

'Yes. Fraser Bell.'

'Ah, yes, your reputation precedes you.'

'Does it?'

The man furrowed his brow. 'Well, we've all been wondering how you managed to build such a steady client base so quickly when we'd never heard of you.'

'I organised it when I lived in Glasgow. I took a stand at the national tourism EXPO.'

'Oh, you're very organised indeed.' The man thrust out his palm. Fraser shook it, not bursting his bubble by confessing he'd done it all in the space of a few months. It was nothing short of a miracle what had happened. 'I'm Donald Laird,' the man continued. 'I'm organising the Midsummer Party, but my goodness, this year, we have too many chiefs, I'm afraid. I'm happy to have new blood, but sometimes it feels like the right hand doesn't know what the left is doing.'

'Oh? It's not cancelled, is it? I was just getting the details.'

'No, it's not cancelled. But every year we get someone to close the festival with some well-chosen words. The chap who used to do it has left the island and nobody remembered to ask anyone else. I didn't either, but I will say in my defence, it wasn't my job to do so. I'm trying to take a step back. Oh, I do apologise. Here I am telling you all this when it's nothing to you. Please, come along, we'll be happy to welcome you.'

'Would you like me to do the speech?' Fraser asked, uncertain exactly where the words came from. A face clouded his vision. Joseph Sloane, the padre he'd served with, an inspirational man Fraser had been devastated to lose. His words of wisdom had seen Fraser through many a dark night. He'd have been the ideal man for a job like this. Fraser became aware Donald was scrutinising him.

'I wonder…' Donald rubbed his chin. 'Yes, that would be good.'

'So, just a thanks for coming type thing.' Now Fraser wished he hadn't volunteered.

'Yes, that kind of thing. A midsummer blessing. Wear your kilt, it'll be very fitting.'

Fraser adjusted his sleeve. 'Sure, no problem.' As he spent all day everyday talking and thinking up ways to engage customers, he was certain he'd manage something. 'I wonder, do you know where Kirsten McGregor lives?'

'Yes, I know Kirsten very well, been friends with the family for years. And she's a guide too, of course. Now, it's not far from here, just past Calgary at Creagach Farm. You can't miss it. Kirsten's in one of the bothies at the track end. I can't remember which one, but her mother and sister live in the farmhouse, they'll help you out.'

'Cheers, thanks.'

Following the winding road around the coast, past the beautiful beach at Calgary and onwards, Fraser saw the farmhouse from some way off. What a stunning place. He pulled onto the verge and skimmed over the wide-open landscape of rolling hills, stunted trees and scrubland heading in a vast sweep towards the sea far below.

If Kirsten wouldn't reply properly to his messages, how else was he going to talk to her? But if she was here, the minibus would be here. Should he wait? Sunbeams baked the SUV and now he'd stopped, no air was coming in the roof. The kilt was too warm, but it was part of the package. And he had a shiny new website with some photos of him looking like a movie star. Georgia might be a chatterbox, but she was a brilliant photographer. Even Fraser's mum had messaged him saying she could hardly believe it. Whether or not that was a compliment, he wasn't sure. Especially when her messages were accompanied by ones from Craig, filled with gripes such as:

Please don't think just because you're staying with Gran it means you're going to get her cottage. It should be sold, and the money shared evenly, that's what Mum wants. She says Gran's quite wandered now, and she doesn't want you trying to get her to change the will. I'm sure you won't, and you'll be fair, but I want to ease my mind. Especially as I've got two kids of my own to worry about. I'm in a position where I'll always need an extra bob or two. Sure you understand, Bro.

Yes, he understood. Loud and clear. His coming back had nothing to do with a sordid attempt to cajole Agnes into leaving him anything. He'd much rather have her alive. He was here to regroup and refocus his life. Maybe it was the closest place he had to a home. It was at least somewhere he felt attached to. As a child, he'd learned to live without a father, then to be second best to the brother who had his mother and a natural father. Here he'd known some kind of stability and belonging, even if it was only for a few weeks each summer.

As he started the engine, he saw a blue glint snaking up the road in the other direction. The Hidden Mull minibus. He waited, uncertain. Its indicator blinked, and it pulled across the road into a space next to the bothies. Kirsten jumped out. Turning towards him, her eyes flashed dangerously. The desire to explain himself burned strong and Fraser leapt out.

Before he was close to the house, the door slammed. A nervous tension crackled in Fraser's chest. He had to do this, even though his throat burned. Right now, he'd rather attempt the cobra turn at two-thousand miles per hour. *Come on, Fraser. What's the worst that can happen?* He adjusted his shirt and rapped on the green door. What to say now he was here? The door swung open and Kirsten stared at him, her jaw set, her arms firmly folded across her middle, her shoulders, appearing to shiver even though it was roasting. 'Why are you here?'

'Well, eh.' He scratched his jaw and took a deep breath. 'Your reply to my email wasn't exactly helpful, though from your track record that isn't unexpected.'

'I beg your pardon? What are you talking about? And why were you parked on the verge out there? Are you stalking me?'

The words stung. The vaguely intact part of his heart shrivelled a bit more. He rolled his lips as he considered, but he maintained eye contact. If she wanted a fight, she could have one. He'd seen the sensual side of the tigress and lived with the devastation she'd caused his heart, but he wasn't going to back away. 'No, not stalking you,' he said. The innocence she'd once used so effectively on him was replaced by a steely glare. 'I just want to talk.'

'Well, I don't want to talk to you.' She moved to push the door shut, but he stuck his foot in it.

'Hold on a minute.'

Red in the face, she looked ready to slam the door several times onto his foot if that was what it would take to shut it. Her knuckles clung to the door, and she glared. 'Get out,' she said.

'I haven't even come in.'

'And you're not coming in.'

With an exasperated sigh, he stomped back and raked his hair. 'Can you spare me three minutes? That's all. Three minutes. Let me say my piece and I won't trouble you ever again.'

'Ever?' she asked with a sarcastically hopeful expression.

'Ok, ever is a long time, but maybe for a while. Please, can I talk?'

'Well, hurry up. You've already wasted several seconds.'

He resisted the urge to yell. 'Ok. So, like it or not, I'm here. I'm not just going to go away.' He ignored her contemptuous snort. With only three minutes and the certainty she was timing him, he had to stay focused. 'I realise this is an inconvenience for you, but I didn't set myself up to rival you. I thought you'd left the island, and the company was finished. But I'm here now and I'll be here until the season ends. I have bookings up to the end of August, and I don't want to disappoint anyone. But in every job, there's competition. I don't want to be your enemy. I'm not saying we have to be anything else. Can we just function alongside each other?'

'Stop,' she said. Did she have a stopwatch? 'And you're right, we're not going to be anything else. But how can we function together if you keep coming along, flaunting your kilt, and making me look like a clueless country bumpkin?' Her cheeks reddened. 'My tours are meant to be about the hidden heart of the island, not the flashy trash you provide.'

His eyebrows darted up. *Wow*. How to pack an emotional punch. That hurt. 'Actually, this island doesn't have much flashy trash. It's unspoilt, you taught me that, and I want to keep it that way. We just approach things differently.'

Kirsten leaned on her doorframe, pouting, and scrutinising him. 'Oh, I know all about your approach.'

'No, I don't think you do. You've made up an idea of me to suit yourself. You don't know me at all.'

'Tell me then. Where are you from?'

'What's that got to do with anything?' He frowned. She glared, and he gave in. 'I was born in Glasgow, but I've lived all over.'

Her head bobbed and her eyes glinted like she'd uncovered treasure. 'I thought as much.'

'I don't follow.'

'You think I know nothing about you. Well, you know nothing about this island. You're a typical mainlander, prancing about making stuff up as you go along. It's ridiculous.'

'I do no such thing.' He moved closer. A surge of energy crackled between them.

'Is this why you're here? To argue with me? Or what?'

'No.' He loosened his shoulders and pulled himself tall. Kirsten was several inches smaller, but she folded her arms and hardened her stare, looking like she meant war. 'I came to discuss a compromise.'

'Such as?'

'I'll back away from the hidden places, like the Eas Fors and rig my tours for the popular sites and more obvious places. That way I won't infringe on any of your places and we can keep out of each other's way.'

She glanced around. 'Is that it?'

He nodded.

'Fine,' she said.

He flicked a half-smile in her direction. 'Good.'

'I'm going to give you a list of my places,' she said, 'and you better keep away.'

'I will. And in return, I'll give you my itinerary, so you can avoid those spots when I'm going to be there. Then we can keep safely out of each other's way.'

'Fine.' She leaned on the doorway, her eyes travelling over him.

Fraser rolled his neck. 'Right. Well, I have different itineraries depending on weather and things.' *Stay composed.* It was difficult; her stare was causing all sorts of disruption to his mind and body. 'I'll send you the most up-to-date one, but I do change them so I can't guarantee they'll stay the same. But I'll let you know if anything drastic changes.'

'Ok.' Kirsten moved inside her tiny hall to a cabinet piled with books and pulled a typed list from a drawer. 'This is the list of hidden places I use.' She passed it to him and their hands brushed. The tell-tale prickle of electricity coursed up his arm. It was a struggle not to jump back. *No, no.* He didn't need that again. He'd been so badly burned the first time his insides were charred. But it was there. Her stiff neck and rigid jaw told him she'd felt it too.

He didn't shake her hand, not just because she would probably refuse anyway, but he didn't want to give the pheromones anything else to play with. She was still at the door as he drove off, watching through narrowed eyes. He wasn't sure he'd achieved anything other than unsettling himself some more.

Chapter Eleven

Kirsten

Although Kirsten was involved in the initial planning of the Midsummer Party, as her tours got heavier, she'd lost touch. She'd heard nothing further about the speech, so she assumed Georgia had arranged for Carl to do it. A special cake for the raffle, shaped like an island map, sat boxed in her kitchen. It had seemed like a good idea when she'd started decorating it; now it just looked amateurish. She pulled a face at it before setting off on her tour.

It was a typical wet start to the longest day. Maybe an omen? *Do I believe in such nonsense? No.* The tour group for the day comprised of some alternative hippy types, who fell hook, line and sinker for Kirsten's back to nature, no-frills tour and loved all the hidden places. At Eas Fors, the raindrops played in the water, and she listened to the tourists making wishes. Most of them took off their socks and shoes to dabble their toes. Here was the ideal opportunity to branch out. Why not? Roddy's silly rules no longer applied. Sticking to facts was a bore. What was wrong with a bit of magic, even if it hadn't worked for her?

She'd already begun making inroads on some new ideas; a shiny new microphone adorned the minibus, and she'd relinquished the accounts to Murray who had added them to the admin he now did for the farm, freeing up Kirsten no end.

This group would appreciate a legend and she was glad she decided to tell it as they all enjoyed running their hands under the water, tracing hearts on their foreheads and taking care the first person they looked at was their partner so they could fall in love all over again. If Kirsten needed some local legends, she could drag them out. She was an island girl with a wonderful heritage. Why hide from the stories of her ancestors when she could embrace them? A brief laugh escaped her lips and her shoulders relaxed. She was in charge here; she could do what she wanted. Her dad and her granny had told her so many weird and wonderful tales. Even if they were only one or two generations old, they were still important. It was Roddy who'd been stupid not to see it. *But I'm not Roddy, I'm Kirsten McGregor and I can do what I like.* She flicked a bug off her arm, imagining Roddy's face.

Arriving home that afternoon, Kirsten was buoyed by the words of thanks and praise from her guests. They'd promised five-star reviews, and as she stepped inside the bothy her fingers were still crossed and she bounced on her toes. Please let them do it, please!

Her phone pinged. And again, then vibrated with more pings and notifications. 'What the…?' "The Four Mullsketeers" chat group popped onto the screen. Sixty-three unread messages! Seriously? Weeks could go by with nothing, then suddenly this. The bothy Wi-Fi couldn't always keep up. Kirsten frowned as she read the messages from her three old school friends: Ann-Marie, Cha and Rhona. Notifications were still coming thick and fast, interspersed with gifs and laughs, making it impossible to read the whole thing. But she got the gist. Ann-Marie was engaged. Kirsten added a heart to the news. *What?* Her eyes almost popped out at the next message.

ANN-MARIE: What about we have a hen party back on Mull? I can't manage the wedding there, but wouldn't it be a laugh!

Kirsten's jaw slipped open. Before she could respond, three dots appeared. Ann-Marie was typing again.

ANN-MARIE: We could go on Kirsten's minibus.

CHA: And she could show us the sights!!!!!!

RHONA: Cause we've never seen them before.

CHA: I bet she has some new ones.

RHONA: Kirsten? Are you there? Are there any new sights on the dear old island? How are the tours going? My mum told me there's a new guy doing tours too, I looked him up... he looks like a hottie.

Seriously? Well, ok, Rhona had a point, but how come every time tours were mentioned these days, up popped Fraser I'm-too-sexy-for-my-kilt Bell?

ANN-MARIE: Does he? How about we do his tour too?

That did it. Kirsten started typing.

KIRSTEN: I'm really busy in the next few weeks. If you want to do a tour, I'm not sure I can fit you in. It's my most popular month. But don't you dare go on the other tour!!

ANN-MARIE: Oooh! Intriguing. Is the other tour guide a sleaze?

KIRSTEN: Let's just say, he has enough women going gaga about his tours already.

The more they pressed the idea of coming back, the more Kirsten wasn't sure she wanted to see them. Not when they were all sophisticated. Did she really know them anymore? Their favourite sport was so often the dissection of her private life. But nothing was enough to fob them off. For the first time in two years a date was set up in less than half an hour and she couldn't do a thing about it. There was no time to press the point further as she needed to get ready for the party.

Dressed in jeans and a coral jersey, Kirsten nipped up to the farmhouse and found Beth in the kitchen. 'You look great,' Kirsten told her, admiring her new red top and white three-quarter-length trousers.

Beth adjusted her hair. Although she suited being smart, she didn't always seem comfortable with it. 'Murray bought me this stuff. I like it but I feel a bit odd.'

'Beth, I've been a bit mean.'

'Why?'

'I was resentful about you and Murray, but actually, I'm really happy for you both.'

Beth smiled through a frown. 'That's ok, I knew you were. I know it was bad timing, but I didn't exactly plan it.'

'It wasn't bad timing. You probably won't believe this, but I never really fancied Carl. I just liked the idea of him.' Kirsten bit her lip and looked around.

'I believe you if you say it's true.'

'Thanks. You know, I'm worried about seeing Georgia tonight. I hope she's still speaking to me. I overreacted when she took photos of Fraser.'

'What is it with him? Is he bothering you? Because if he is, I'm not kidding, I will lamp him.'

Kirsten grinned. *Boy, would I love to see that.* 'I just wish he'd go away.'

'Just wait until the end of the season and he'll vanish like douchebag Derek. And don't worry about Georgia. I've never known her to fall out with anyone. It's just a pity none of your old friends stayed on the island.'

'I think I get on better with Georgia, I just hope I haven't blown it. And my old friends are coming back to visit.' Kirsten sighed. Mull had a relatively small population, and she'd been lumped together with a group of girls she wasn't sure she'd have chosen if there were more options, and they'd stayed in touch but sometimes seeing their antics on Facebook filled her with shame. There they were in the big bad world, abroad or working in cities, attending functions, and looking a million dollars. What would they have to talk about?

The weather was still dire when Kirsten arrived at the soggy field with Beth and Murray. The planned outdoor activities would be a washout, and they'd end up squeezed in the hall. The first thing Kirsten saw was Georgia dressed in a bright yellow raincoat and polka dot wellies, laughing with Matt at the games stall beside the hall. Matt grinned as he invited people to have a go at throwing wet sponges at their loved ones for a pound.

'Come on, it's wet anyway,' he smirked. 'Time to get revenge on Dad?' he asked a small boy.

Georgia could power the lighthouse in her coat. It was belted around the middle and fanned out in a wide skirt. Kirsten approached, hoping everything would be ok.

'Hi, anyone want to get wet?' Georgia asked with a cheesy grin, seeming quite her usual self. A wave of relief washed over Kirsten.

'Are you going to start singing?' Kirsten beamed.

'What?'

'You just need a brolly and you could give us a bit of *what a glorious feeling, I'm happy again!*'

'Maybe later, after a few drinks, you never know.' Georgia winked. 'We could duet if you like.'

'Ha! No way. My cat sings better than me.' Kirsten breathed a contented sigh as Georgia giggled.

Matt returned to the table from the stocks where he'd just clamped in an unsuspecting father. A sloshy wet sponge smacked the man in the face, much to the delight of his young son. His wife turned away in an attempt not to laugh too hard.

The man's cry of, 'You'll be next!' was lost in another splatter.

'How about it, Murray?' Beth asked.

'Eh.' Murray drew back, running his fingers through his immaculate feathered hair. Kirsten smirked. Was this a test of their new relationship? Even if it was a silly one, it was funny watching him sweat. 'Sure, I've got a great aim. You put your head in and I'll show you.'

'Bugger off,' said Beth quickly. Murray and Georgia laughed.

Kirsten checked around. 'I should go and find Mum, see if she still needs help with the baking stall.' As she crossed the small grassy area, passing a few rather dismal stalls, she glanced towards the car park, doing a double-take. Not again. Fraser opened the back door and helped out an elderly man. Going around to the other side, he appeared moments later with two elderly ladies. Kirsten's jaw dropped. Seriously? All three of them had been on her community tour. Was Fraser muscling in on that now too? And no doubt they loved his chivalry.

Sidling over, she ducked down behind her mum, opening boxes and pretending to be useful, but her senses were alert, checking the field, scanning over the various stalls with their holders wrapped up in heavy waterproofs. There was Fraser. She caught his eye. He met her gaze, a slight smile dimpling his cheek, and he raised his eyebrow. Her heartbeat revved a notch. He looked utterly delectable. More edible than any of the goodies on the stall.

'Can you cut some more tiffin,' said Gillian. 'I didn't have time to cut it before we left. There's a knife in that Tupperware box.'

Kirsten found it in a crate behind the stall. From her position, she could see down the hill, across the village and to the sea. She stabbed into the chocolate with satisfaction. 'Fraser bloody Bell,' she muttered. All his smarmy words the other night about having a friendly professional relationship. Like she believed a word of it. She stabbed another slab. His jibe about answering emails was particularly cutting. *My track record!* What bloody track record? It wasn't as if he'd sent her anything to reply to. Funny how he'd found the knack of contacting her using every way known to man when five years ago it had been impossible. Heat bloomed in her cheeks. She'd been young and naïve, handed herself to him on a plate, and enjoyed every second. That made it even worse. If he'd been awful, she'd have been happy to forget. Now he was back all kilted and godlike, and her starved body ached for him again, but this time her brain knew better. She grimaced and slit the last piece of tiffin. Turning to put it on a tray, she quickly wheeled back. The three elderly people from Fraser's party were at the stall table chatting to Gillian. Not wanting to hear their effusive praise for Fraser, Kirsten pulled the foil from a tray of millionaire shortbread and started butchering it. When she was sure they'd moved on, she placed the trays on the stall.

Through the drizzle, she saw the beacon that was Georgia across the field, talking and laughing with Fraser. *Is she after him?* Kirsten rubbed her forehead. *Please no.* Not when she'd finally found a friend she related to. How would she bear it if Georgia started seeing Fraser? They looked ideal, both smiling and attractive. *Maybe I should warn her about him.* But what a lot of cringy confessions that would mean. And would Georgia even care? She maybe wouldn't mind a short-term fling. For all her fun, cheer, and interest in everyone else, she didn't give anything away about her own love life.

'Hey, you got anything tasty over here?' A pair of sparkling azure blue eyes confronted Kirsten. Matt grinned.

'Take a look,' Kirsten said.

'Well,' he said quietly, 'I see something I like.'

Kirsten's cheeks burned, and she glanced at her mum, who was happily busy with another customer. 'Are you always this forward?'

'I am if I like what I see. There's a dance later. Fancy it?'

'I guess.' Though strictly speaking, Matt wasn't the partner she wanted to imagine herself dancing with. 'You know it's ceilidh dancing?'

'Sure, I can handle it.' His Australian accent twanged.

'It might be cancelled, even though the rain's going off.' Kirsten held up her hands. 'The field's a bit muddy though.'

'Dancing is going ahead inside, but if it stays dry, we can have the late evening conclusion outside, so says Miss Georgia.'

*

Packing away the stand just after seven-thirty, Kirsten and Gillian were ready to go inside for the dancing. Kirsten scanned around for Matt, but he wasn't there. The music started and people took the floor. Bottled Woo Woo in hand, Kirsten hovered at the edge of the tiny hall, crammed in beside Beth's friend, Will Laird, and a couple of other locals. As the dance began, Beth skipped by with Murray, ducking under the next couple's raised arms and almost knocking them over. Carl and Robyn were twirling round too. Kirsten lowered her chilled bottle and sucked her lip as Georgia and Fraser danced by, looking like a match made in heaven.

Kirsten wanted to leave, but she'd come with Beth. It was miles too far to walk, and even if she nicked the Land Rover, she'd probably be done for drink driving. Pushing her way outside into the cool air, she still couldn't see Matt. The musical buzz from inside the hall was muffled. Down the hill, the sea lapped at the bay as the sun finally started its slow descent. The heavy rain had blown away, leaving a clear night and a velvety pink sky.

Turning, she saw a tall figure pacing outside the hall, talking on a phone. Matt. Finally. He waved apologetically and dropped the phone to his shoulder. 'Sorry, it's my mum, back home. She never remembers what time it is over here. She's having a crisis.'

Kirsten wandered to the edge of the field close to the car park and squinted towards the village of Dervaig, the sea in the distance and rocky silhouettes of islands cut out against the sun's glow. For several minutes, she just stared, enjoying the cool breeze playing on her cheeks.

'Hey, are you ok?'

Kirsten turned swiftly to see Fraser striding towards his car. 'Oh, it's you. I'm fine, not that it's any of your business.'

He acknowledged his interference with an eyebrow lift. 'Ever the charmer. Oh, by the way, I won your cake.' He held up a white box. Kirsten cringed and heat spread up her neck. What an embarrassment; the cake was like something an eight-year-old might make. 'It looks quite remarkable,' he said.

'Right.' She side-eyed him as he went to his SUV with a slight smirk playing on his lips. Was he being serious or sarky? He opened the car boot. Maybe he was looking for a new kilt. While his back was turned, she ducked out of sight to the side of the hall.

Matt hung up his phone and greeted her with a one-armed hug. 'So sorry. Have I missed the dancing?'

'Probably.' Kirsten pulled away from his hold. 'It's too hot in there anyway. I'd rather stay out here for a bit.'

'Sit here.' Matt tapped some empty crates, and they sat together while he explained his phone call. Kirsten dipped in and out, her mind only half listening. She simultaneously wanted to scream and cry. Something inside her ached. What was her problem? Turning her head from Matt, she scanned about for Fraser. Where had he gone? Why was it so important? Maybe he'd snuck out with Georgia for one of his *chats*. The music had stopped. Voices chattered outside.

'Time for the ceremony thingy,' said Matt. 'Let's go see what it is.'

'It's just a boring speech,' she muttered. 'I hope Georgia remembered to ask Carl.' A skirl on the bagpipes tore through the air.

Matt smirked. 'Ah, you don't get more Scottish than that.'

A piper led the partygoers to a hillside beside the hall. Kirsten and Matt fell into step with the others in the chattering crowd. The pipes stopped and Donald Laird took centre stage, holding up his hands for attention. 'Thank you, everyone, for coming to celebrate the Midsummer Party. It's been a marvellous success. Now, I'll introduce you to someone who's going to say a few words to close the ceremony. Please welcome Fraser Bell.' There was a round of applause as Fraser burst into the group's centre.

'You have got to be kidding,' Kirsten said. Why couldn't she have been brave enough to do it? Now he was going to be the star attraction again.

'So, it actually does get even more Scottish.' Matt smirked at the kilt.

'Unreal.' Kirsten gaped. He *had* changed his kilt for a muted down one, with earthy colours. Its style was unusual and with it, he wore a loose shirt, open very low. Leather thongs crossed over his broad chest. Kirsten's jaw fell slack. This was the reason she'd fallen so hard five years ago. Unadulterated lust. He was insanely hot.

He leapt onto a boulder, so he was above them, and threw his arms wide. 'Friends,' he said, his voice clear and commanding. Dropping his arms, he smiled. Kirsten frowned, what a show-off. 'Earlier, I overheard some words of concern that this festival may be deemed pagan and therefore unchristian. Let me tell you something to put your mind at ease. Be you Christian, Buddhist, pagan, atheist, agnostic. None of the above, all of the above. Whoever you are, this party has brought you here to celebrate the beating heart of the island. This wonderful island that unites us. We are the people who belong here. Together we sustain the land and in return it sustains us. The perpetual cycle of nature and nurture. It filters through us all. Midsummer is celebrated profusely by our Scandinavian neighbours. They make the most of the long days and the warmth, knowing winter is never far away.'

He lifted his gaze to the rosy sky, and many eyes followed. But Kirsten was transfixed on Fraser. Power resonated from him. He was alluring, enticing, and so annoying. What utter guff, making it out he cared about the island while making up all sorts of crap, but she couldn't look away.

'Together we've felt the might of our great island this evening,' continued Fraser, looking back at the group. 'We've worshipped and thanked her. It has been a night to remember. May you all feel the warmth and blessing of love in your hearts as you return home.'

His attention fell on Kirsten; her cheeks seared. Before she could do anything else however, Matt tugged her towards him; his lips touched hers.

'Matt.' She drew back.

'Sorry, I couldn't resist; you looked so cute.'

Glancing back at Fraser, Kirsten wrapped her arms around herself and listened as he continued. 'May you all benefit and prosper from the kindling of this love, and the bounty it brings to the environment, our bodies and our souls.' He paused and smiled, his eyes flickering towards her. 'Thank you for coming and safe onward travels.'

His conclusion was met by a bracing round of applause, and as he jumped down from the boulder, several people patted him on the back and shook his hand.

'Who does he think he is? Bloody Jesus?' Kirsten muttered.

Matt leaned in and whispered in her ear, 'How about we go back to my flat?'

'What?' Kirsten swallowed. 'Oh, no. I can't. I have a tour first thing tomorrow. And, oh god.' She spotted Gillian frowning in her direction. 'I need to go.'

'Another time, then,' smiled Matt.

'Eh, well, maybe.'

Gillian watched Matt with an arched eyebrow before turning her scrutiny on Kirsten. 'He's a bit of a flirt,' she said.

'Yeah, just a bit.' Kirsten frowned as Matt sidled into the crowd and struck up a conversation with some young women dressed in hiking gear.

'That Fraser Bell has a lovely voice,' said Gillian. 'Is he the new guide?'

'Yes.'

'Well, his speech was much better than any of Roddy's,' said Gillian. 'Roddy was a fuddy-duddy and a windbag.'

With images of Fraser swirling around her head, Kirsten was halfway home before she remembered Matt had kissed her. It should have been all that was on her mind, but the only thing she could think about was Fraser; his shirt gaping open, his arms spread wide, standing atop the boulder. It was locked on repeat. *Why can't he just go away!* But try as she might, Kirsten could not stop the slideshow of swoon-worthy images her brain insisted on showing her.

Chapter Twelve

Fraser

Sitting at his tent door, Fraser listened to the wind flapping the canvas in the fresh morning breeze and pressed his hands together, looking heavenwards. His speech at the end of the Midsummer Party was done and had gone ok. One thing to lift from his mind. 'Cheers, Padre,' he said.

Padre Sloane had succeeded in taking a bunch of hard-as-nails servicepeople and teaching them to believe in themselves. Despite his obvious Christian faith, he'd never made distinctions. Everyone was important. Fraser's love and respect for the man burned deep. *I miss you.* Fraser had never known his real father, but Padre Sloane had been there through tough times. *What would he make of my life now? I've let him down in so many ways.*

Fraser's departure from the RAF had been dramatic and humiliating. He'd let himself down while trying to do good. After leaving, he'd gone into counselling for his PTSD. But a one-night stand that ended in a counsellor getting pregnant wasn't his smartest move, especially when he'd discovered she was married. It had flipped his world into an even bigger web of chaos and entanglement.

Burying his face in his hands, he tried not to dwell. He had to keep up the positives and his tours were going well. *Focus on that.* He prided himself on being an intelligent guy, he'd been given coping strategies and he was going to use them. So far it wasn't going to plan, mostly because of Kirsten. Her very existence created confusion, questions and irritation. The Kirsten he'd met five years ago didn't tally with the narky emails. Though after their standoff the other day, he realised there was venom in her. He couldn't account for it.

Stretching beside the tent, he admired the tranquil beauty and the mesmeric quality of the sea beyond the grassy hillock; it calmed his wayward thoughts. Today was a day off. After a midnight speech, he thought he'd need it. This was all part of his recovery plan. Yes, he was working, but that didn't mean stretching himself to breaking point. Days off were a must.

However, at the party, he'd bumped into a local man named Iain Beaton who ran tourist boat trips. They'd got talking, Iain did tours to the smaller isles off the coast of Mull, and was happy to work in conjunction with main island tours. Somehow, Fraser had got himself an invitation on today's trip to try it out. He supposed there were worse things he could do on a day off than enjoy a lazy sail.

Heading to the island's west side, Fraser soaked in the peaceful beauty of Mull as the sea twinkled all around. Once at the harbour in Ulva Ferry, a middle-aged, bald man with a bushy white beard greeted him.

'Hi, Iain.' Fraser shook the man's hand.

'Hello, hello, let's get you aboard the Dòbhran.'

Fraser moved onto the deck of the shiny black vessel as Iain chatted away. 'This is cool,' said Fraser. 'I quite fancy getting a boat.' Maybe after all the years in the air, the sea should be his next venture.

'Come up to the cabin, you get a magnificent view up there.'

Standing on the small bridge, Fraser looked down at the comfortably fitted out boat. Wooden benches lined the edge and life jacket storage pews in the middle doubled as more seating. Across the narrow strait between Mull and the small island of Ulva was the Boathouse Café and an old croft now set up as a museum; quaint reminders of a bygone age.

Iain left him to go and welcome his guests aboard, and Fraser did a recce of the controls. *I could do that,* he thought, running his fingers over the switch panel. Hearing voices below, he turned back to observe the passengers on the creaky gangplank. His heart skipped a beat. Kirsten was here. *What the hell?* He looked away, pinching the bridge of his nose. How could he square this one? She'd flip out if she knew he was here, and why was she here anyway?

Iain returned a few moments later.

'Why, em, is Kirsten McGregor here?' asked Fraser, trying to sound casual.

'She's doing the tour today. Well, I'm taking them to Gometra and she's leading it from there. That's what I explained last night.'

Fraser's eyes widened. *You did?* Racking his brains, he couldn't recall that part.

'I work with local tours, that's why I thought you'd like to come along today.'

'Right.' Fraser hadn't picked up on the fact he was going to be gatecrashing a tour. He thought he was just getting a trip on the boat.

'Yes, Kirsten's a frequent user, I also work with a couple of hiking tours. Is everything ok?'

'Yes, fine.'

Iain fired up the engine. 'I do the intro and boat commentary, but if you want to do a tour with me at any time, we can work out how you want to play it.' He put on the microphone and it crackled into action. 'So,' he said, his voice resonating around. 'Welcome everyone to the MV Dòbhran.' Waves slapped against the hull as they moved off slowly. Fraser contemplated the undulating sea as the boat headed up the channel between Mull and Ulva, trying to keep out of sight. If Kirsten glanced up from the deck, there was the chance she could see him through the small window, and she'd be furious.

The intercom crackled as Iain went on. 'What I'm going to do is take you to the tip of Gometra. That's the island next to Ulva, which Kirsten will tell you all about. I'll land there and you'll have two hours ashore. Gometra is difficult to access by land. You can take the short crossing at Ulva and walk the eight miles to the bridge that joins the two islands. There are no cars or roads on either island, so this is a wonderful opportunity to discover a truly remote part of the country.'

Fraser watched Kirsten stand up and talk to her guests. How much more confident she looked these days. With an indescribable feeling in his chest, Fraser tilted his head, fixating on Kirsten's mesmerising dark hair. Long wavy tendrils drifted in the breeze. With a slight smile, his eyes wavered out of focus. Once, five years ago, he'd spent a tour watching her and he hadn't been able to drag his eyes away. He'd played out the librarian fantasy, pulling off her glasses, setting her hair free, and unleashing her inner goddess.

Now, she'd managed the transformation on her own and it was a thing of beauty, resulting in a confident and shining young woman. Fraser continued to watch as she led her guests to the side and showed them a group of puffins. From her animation, he could see her knowledge and excitement shimmering through.

'You should go chat to her,' said Iain. 'She's very experienced, even though she's just a young lass.'

'Yeah, I know her. We don't always get on too well.'

'Ah, I'm sorry to hear that. I'm glad she's taken over from Roddy though. You know it was him that usually made the end of the Midsummer Party speech, don't you?'

'No, I didn't. I hope mine was up to scratch.'

'It was, but no offence, a flatfish could do a more entertaining speech than Roddy Hunter. His speeches were dire. Roddy's dull as dishwater. Total die-hard Christian, he always used to give a long-winded reasoning behind the festival to make sure everyone knew it wasn't pagan.'

Fraser recalled the dreadful conversations he'd had with Roddy. After Kirsten had been so insistent about not letting him discover what had happened, she obviously had a change of heart, telling Roddy instead that Fraser had been harassing her. *Right*. She had some funny ideas. Maybe it had been her age, or maybe she was too much a hardened islander, set in her ways. Was what had happened between them just a step too far out of her boxed-in island comfort zone? Was sleeping with a near stranger a punishable offence in the Hebrides? Maybe she was just embarrassed. Though Fraser wasn't sure why she would be.

'I wondered. Someone asked me about the pagan thing, I thought they were taking the mick.'

Iain rubbed his chin. 'I grew up with Roddy. He was older than me, but we all knew each other. I knew your mum too. Didn't she ever mention Roddy?'

'No.' Fraser's mum was always worried he would ask about his father, so she rarely spoke about Mull. Fraser hadn't even considered that his mum might know Roddy.

'Roddy was a prude. He didn't appreciate your mum having you without being married first. I think Roddy had a bit of a thing for your mum before he met Linda. Honestly, the way he went on, you'd think poor Marion had reincarnated the devil when she got pregnant with you. You know about your dad, right?'

'Yeah, he was a logger from Greenock who worked on the boats one summer.'

'I knew him too.'

'Did you?' Fraser looked away, unsure. Did he want to know? Did he need to?

'Aye, but nothing you'll want to hear. Your mum always wanted to leave the island and running off with your dad was her ticket out. I reckon she'd have come back after he left her if it weren't for Roddy. Agnes would have helped her out, but Roddy wanted her head on a spike.'

'I didn't know.' Fraser scratched his forehead. 'She doesn't talk much about those days.'

'How is she keeping? You have a brother too, is that right?'

'Yeah. Mum's fine.' Fraser supposed, but his contact with her was minimal. He couldn't live up to his brother's standards. Seeing the sparkle in his mum's eyes when she saw Craig, followed by the flat disappointment when she looked at him, was unbearable. As his mum was short with strawberry blonde hair and pale skin, Fraser assumed his looks came from his father. Maybe that didn't help, and it wasn't something to be proud of. The man had given him nothing except his surname and a bad gene. Fraser had followed in his genetic footsteps. Always letting people down.

'I hope I haven't offended you,' Iain said. Fraser blinked, lost in thoughts. Thoughts he was supposed to be putting away. 'By speaking about your father.'

'No. I knew he wasn't a nice man.'

Iain shook his head. 'He wasn't all bad, just misguided and very young. My wife saw your gran a while back. Is she all right?'

'Yeah, she's doing ok.'

'We thought she might be getting a bit muddled. She told my wife you were having a baby, but you don't have a family yet, do you?'

Fraser drew in a sharp breath through his nose and rubbed his tense jaw. 'No.'

'I wondered if she'd muddled you up with your father or maybe your brother. Though it's always possible my wife got the wrong end of the stick.'

The boat chugged through the channel, trundling around the beautiful shore of Ulva. Fraser stepped outside, keeping out of sight from the lower deck. He could hear Kirsten pointing out notable spots and wildlife; the enthusiasm for her homeland poured from her voice. No matter how much glitter he threw at his tours, Fraser wasn't sure he could ever match her passion.

As they rounded the head of Ulva, it joined almost imperceptibly to Gometra. The wind picked up and a lot of the passengers moved into the sheltered area towards the front. Twenty minutes later, they skirted into a sheltered bay. The sea twinkled emerald green as the sun poked through the clouds. As they edged closer to the shore, fish darted beneath the rippling water. On the far side of the bay, a bright white cabin cruiser dazzled, bobbing up and down.

'Wow, that's the way to do it.' said Fraser. 'It's like something from Monte Carlo.' *What must that be like?* Moored on the world's edge surrounded by these glorious waters. A sudden urge to be there seized him. Maybe he should sell the SUV and get a boat.

'You can have a go steering if you like,' said Iain. 'After your jets, this must be a cinch.'

'Cool, let's have a go then.'

Fraser grinned as he settled the Dòbhran alongside a jetty which had seen better days. If Iain intended to bring regular tours here, he'd need to make an investment or health and safety inspectors would have a field day.

'Very good,' said Iain. 'You're a fast learner.'

'I just like driving. Anything really.'

'Well, the beach is just a few minutes' walk away, you could head ashore if you like or if you'd rather stay aboard, that's fine.'

Iain went below to set the gangplank, and Fraser watched Kirsten lead her group ashore. They trudged around the bay and Fraser's eyes followed; the peace, tranquillity and beauty called to him. 'I think I will go ashore for a bit.'

'Yes, go and enjoy yourself.' Iain smiled.

Walking a good way behind Kirsten's party, Fraser followed them around the other side of the beach where a grassy headland climbed up, close to where the Monte Carlo cabin cruiser was moored. Kirsten led them along a narrow path at the edge. At a jutting corner, she stopped and let them walk ahead to an open flat area. Fraser couldn't see what they were looking at but guessed it was a colony of puffins. The tourists were kneeling, taking pictures.

Fraser broke into a jog and caught up with Kirsten, who was standing back, letting her group get in close for their photos.

'Kirsten.' Fraser tried to pitch his voice low so he wouldn't startle her. She spun around, eyes wide with shock. *Ok, the pitch thing didn't work.*

'Oh my god,' Kirsten mouthed through gritted teeth, walking away from her group. 'What are you doing here? Seriously? Here? There's no way—'

'I came on the boat,' said Fraser.

'The Dòbhran? You were on that boat? What is going on?' Facing him, she folded her arms.

'Iain invited me yesterday. I didn't know you were going to be on board. But is it that much of a problem? I've enjoyed watching your tour.'

Colour rose in her cheeks. 'Are you taking the mickey?' she muttered.

'No, I'm serious. I've always enjoyed your tours.' He drew in a breath and looked around. 'Which makes me wonder… Why do you hate me?' The words tumbled out. *Shit*. Why hadn't he phrased it better? Now he guessed how she'd felt five years ago when she'd blurted out the three little opposite words. But she couldn't know how they'd changed his perspective. He'd never seen himself as someone worthy of love before. Physical gratification was one thing, but love. He knew she hadn't meant it. God knew what kind of crap people blurted out in moments like that, but those words had touched his soul and given him hope, no matter how short-lived it had been.

'You actually have to ask?' Kirsten gaped, her eyes darting back and forward to her tour group.

Fraser staggered back. 'Well, yes. I don't get what your problem is.'

'Seriously?' She screwed up her face. 'If you don't know, how can I possibly explain?'

'Ok, fine.' Why had he asked? He didn't get it. Maybe saying those words had humiliated her and after the furnace of desire had cooled, she resented what had happened. His messages obviously hadn't been welcomed. She'd decided to misconstrue them as harassment. The knife in Fraser's gut twisted a bit further. 'I don't get why you couldn't even be civil about it.'

'Civil? You are kidding, right?' Kirsten's hands tensed like panther claws; steam might billow from her ears at any second. This was how offended she was?

'Look, what we did...' Fraser rubbed the back of his neck. 'I don't regret it, but you never gave me a chance to explain.'

'You're kidding, right?' Kirsten gaped. 'Explain? Your actions said everything I needed to hear. Now please, leave me alone. I've got a tour to do.' She looked ready to shove him off the narrow path into the sea. Instead, she spun around and stalked towards her group. So much for the timid girl he'd fallen for.

Standing stock-still, Fraser drew in a long and deliberate breath. 'My actions?' What had he done other than give her his body and soul, then tried to let her know how much it had touched his heart? Seriously, what more could a guy do? 'Jesus, what a mess.' He kicked a patch of scree, sending it over the cliff edge.

'Hey, watch it.' A man's voice made Fraser jump. He hastened to the edge of the verge. The sea lapped around a cluster of rocks. Sitting on a ledge was a man clad in a wetsuit and diving gear.

'Holy crap,' Fraser said, 'you gave me a heart attack.'

The man squinted up. 'Yeah, well, you nearly took me out.'

Vaulting off the verge onto the rocky ledge, Fraser landed beside him. 'Jeez, sorry, mate. Are you ok?'

'I'll live.' The man got to his feet, standing a couple of inches taller than Fraser.

'Did you hear that conversation?' Fraser rubbed his hand down his face.

'It was hard not to.'

'Sometimes I just don't get women,' said Fraser.

'Sorry,' said the man. 'Can't help. I'm definitely the wrong person to ask. And I need to get back to my boat.' He gestured at the gleaming cabin cruiser.

'That's yours?' Shading his eyes, Fraser squinted at it. The thought of sailing away was the most appealing thing in the world right now.

'Yup.'

'Wow, she's a beauty. And what a spot for diving.'

'I don't do it for pleasure. I'm working. Though it can be enjoyable.'

'Working?'

'I'm a marine biologist,' said the man.

How amazing must that job be? Beautiful sea, peace, and a boat to boot. 'Wow.' Fraser sighed.

'I can't stop and chat,' said the man. 'I'm on a deadline and unfortunately living creatures don't always comply to timetables.'

'Yeah, no worries. Sorry about the rocks.'

'It's fine.' The man pulled on his mask, fixed up his breathing apparatus, looked over the edge and dropped in. Fraser leaned over and watched the splash below. It was quite a distance. He swayed on the edge for a moment. If he thought he could climb out again, he'd do it, but he couldn't guarantee it and it was a long swim to the lower levels. This wasn't the moment for doing anything stupid. Instead, he placed his jacket on the ledge and sat on it, closing his eyes and allowing the breeze to wash over him. Time swept away and Fraser lost track because when he opened his eyes, he saw on the other side of the bay, Kirsten's group getting back on the Dòbhran.

'Shit.' Fraser scrambled up the ledge onto the path, legged it round the headland and across the beach. If he made Kirsten's tour late, she'd be furious. He sprinted like he hadn't done for months. Perhaps not quite as fighting fit as he used to be, he still had a turn of speed. Bolting up the rickety old jetty, he reached the boat totally out of breath.

'It's ok.' Iain grinned. 'I wouldn't have left you behind.'

'Cheers.' Fraser jumped on board, panting. 'I lost track of time.'

'That was some run.' A woman smiled as he got on board. 'You're very fast.'

'Am I?' Fraser glanced around and saw Kirsten standing at the side. She glowered and her jaw hardened.

'You had our full attention,' smiled the woman.

'Don't you always.' Kirsten muttered, folding her arms.

Fraser approached her. 'Look, I'm sorry. I didn't want to hold you up.'

'I should have told Iain you fancied running back. You could have tried to beat the boat.'

'Funny.' He threw his head back, filled with a stabbing notion she'd seriously considered doing it. A vision played in his mind of a parallel universe where he stood abandoned on the beach while they sailed away, and Kirsten laughed at him. Inside his chest, his heart deflated like she'd stuck a pin in him.

Chapter Thirteen

Kirsten

Kirsten couldn't believe it. Fraser was on board the MV Dòbhran. Halfway back, the rain blew in and several people darted into the covered section. Without quite knowing why, Kirsten didn't move from her position at the back of the boat. Her eyes lifted slowly upwards. A stab of electricity jolted her as her gaze landed on Fraser, up above leaning on the edge of the bridge just outside Iain's cabin.

As their eyes met, Fraser's jaw stiffened, but he didn't budge, and Kirsten was damned if she was going to. If he could weather this, so could she. Her disobedient eyes would not focus on anything else for long before they bounced back to him. There he lolled, effortlessly handsome with his arms crossed in front of him, shapely forearms on display. Not even a jacket. He had the nerve to ask her why she didn't like him. After he'd abandoned her without a word in five years? Ok, so when they'd met, she'd been wet around the ears. Up until then, no one had ever looked at her, except the creeps on the flat-out crap dates she'd had at college, which she couldn't even bear to think about. But it didn't give Fraser an excuse. In fact, as he'd seemed so much more worldly wise than any of her college dates, his behaviour was even worse.

Completely forgetting she was staring, she stiffened as his eyes rolled back onto hers. Unflinching but holding her breath, she held his gaze. He equalled it. Her chest constricted, she struggled to get air, but she didn't look away. Who would blink first? As soon as she thought it, she wanted to. Her eyes prickled with the urge to move them. Raindrops clung to her lashes. Damp hair stuck to her forehead. Tension crackled on an invisible wire stretched from Fraser's olive eyes to her brown ones. With a glimpse heavenward and the flicker of a grin, he straightened up and went inside the cabin.

Why had she ever thought a guy like that would like her? Thank goodness she'd come to her senses. *I have.* She stood and went under the cover to talk to her guests. Rainy moments were easily filled these days with a tale or two from her childhood, but knowing Fraser was about somewhere made Kirsten tense. Still, when the guests laughed at her retelling of her granny's story of the *Wee Lost Pict Fae Ulva*, she felt better in herself.

'Wonderful tour,' said the woman who'd admired Fraser. She patted Kirsten on the shoulder as she disembarked. 'I'll recommend it to all my friends. Having a tour from a real islander with all that knowledge is quite fantastic.'

'Thank you,' said Kirsten.

'Another good show,' said Iain as the last person left. 'And I had a good helper with me today. That was Fraser Bell who brought us almost all the way home. I think I'll be out of a job if he sticks around.' Iain laughed as Kirsten got off the boat.

'You and me both,' she muttered as she jogged towards the minibus, ready to return her guests to their hotel. In typical island style, the rain had blown off, leaving bright blue skies, and Kirsten felt too warm. By the time she got home, she just wanted to get into the shower, cool down and wash out the windswept tangles from her hair. Her jaw tensed when she saw a pink van covered with outsized pink flower decals parked outside the bothy. The easily recognisable vehicle belonged to Georgia. The thought of how close Georgia had got to Fraser made Kirsten's stomach churn. She had first-hand experience of Fraser's quick work and just how very seductive he could be. And Georgia was so pretty and easy to like. Kirsten rammed the minibus into the space next to the van.

Behind the bothy, Georgia sat draped across a garden bench, sunning herself. She looked a little too at home in her floaty dress and broad-brimmed sun hat. She'd be quite fitting as the cover of a romantic book or on a notecard. Kirsten never got her outfit right for the weather, she'd have to pack a suitcase every day, but Georgia had the knack of always looking just right.

Glancing around, Georgia peered over her sunglasses as Kirsten approached. The gate creaked and Kirsten joined her on the seat. Georgia smiled and lazed back. Her tousled bob draped at her neck. Her whole demeanour asserted effortless elegance and beauty. 'It is so hot.' Georgia took off her hat and fanned herself with it. 'Have you had a busy day?'

'Every day is busy at this time of year.' Kirsten pulled at the neck of her t-shirt, feeling sweltered. 'I did the Gometra trip today. It's usually a relaxed one.' Though not this time.

'That sounds fun, but I know you're busy, so I don't want to keep you.' Georgia sat upright.

'Look—' Kirsten began.

'I'm sorry,' Georgia interrupted.

'For what?'

'For whatever I've done. I hate to see you looking so upset, you used to be so smiley and happy. I know the thing with Carl hurt, but I'd hate to think I've somehow made it worse by what I did with Fraser.'

'What did you do with him?' Kirsten's already warm cheeks seared with flames.

'I took those photos, then I danced with him last night. I saw you leaving after you spotted us. He just seems like a nice guy, I don't feel a reason to dislike him, but I don't want to hurt you.'

'Hmm.' Kirsten rubbed her forehead and steadied her breathing. 'Why not come inside?'

Georgia smiled. 'Thanks, but I should get on. I've got lots of editing to catch up on. I just wanted to say, I'm sorry if you feel that I crossed a line with Fraser.'

'Did you sleep with him?' It was out of Kirsten's mouth before she could stop it.

'No. I didn't.' Georgia's voice cooled. The sheep beyond the fence added their noisy opinion before Georgia added, 'Did you?'

A well of tears rose in Kirsten's throat. She looked away, unable to face Georgia. 'Yes. I did.'

'What?'

Kirsten felt a light touch on her shoulder and turned to see Georgia's hand resting on it. 'What's going on?'

'Yeah, it sounds ridiculous, doesn't it? And it is.' Kirsten shook her head. 'Please don't tell anyone else.'

'I won't, but you're scaring me. Whatever happened doesn't look like something you enjoyed.'

'Oh, I did. I really did. It was like nothing I could have imagined. But that was five years ago.'

Georgia shook her head. 'I don't follow. You knew Fraser five years ago?'

'Yup.' Kirsten bit her lip for a few seconds before relating the story. 'I never heard a thing from him until he turned up here again. And you see him now, strutting around like he owns the place, charming everybody.'

'Oh, my god.' Georgia held her hand to her lips. 'I can hardly believe it. I know he has a grandmother who lives here, but what possessed him to come back and start up tours when he knew you'd be here and that was your job?'

'Yeah, now you see why I was annoyed. I know shouldn't have attached so much meaning to it, he obviously didn't. But at the time, it was like so much more. I felt so alive, and I've literally never felt that good with anyone since, but it just shows how naïve I am, doesn't it?'

'No, Kirsten. You know what a romantic nut I am. I believe if you felt it, it was real. What shocks me is him. How could he lead you on like that?'

'I don't know. I waited on the beach the next day. I even went into the hotel and asked if Fraser was there. The receptionist looked and said a group booked under Fraser's brother's name had checked out that morning. As far as I know, he was always going to check out then. It just makes me feel so stupid and small when I'm around him. He knows how silly I was, and now he can steamroll over me and my business.'

'Wow, I am so shocked. He seemed so nice.'

'Did he try it on with you?' Kirsten's thigh trembled at the memories of him touching her and plying her with kisses. Had he tried the same with Georgia? Of course, Kirsten knew she wouldn't be his only conquest, but the idea of sharing him with a friend was horrible.

'No.' Georgia got to her feet. 'I didn't get the feeling he was looking for anything like that. He was just friendly and easy to talk to. We danced a couple of times, he told me about his tours, he said he lived near his grandmother's croft, and that he'd been in the RAF for fifteen years, but he'd left after a disagreement. That was it. He didn't seem to want to elaborate, and he didn't mention relationships or anything like that.'

'Well, now you know, but you don't know the worst of it.'

'Can you tell me?'

'I still like him. At least in here.' Kirsten knocked her chest. 'But I hate him at the same time, and it's so confusing.'

'Oh, Kirsten.' Georgia sat back down and put her arm around Kirsten's shoulder. 'I can empathise with how you're feeling. Love is the best, but it's also the worst.'

'Just please don't say anything to anyone. Some friends of mine are coming here in a couple of weeks and I'm not looking forward to it. I don't want them to know. They're gossips; they have a way of making me feel backwards and they always tease me about guys. So if you meet them, please don't mention him.'

'I won't, I promise. But, Kirsten, don't let them get the better of you. I understand you regret what happened with Fraser, but they don't need to know that. All they need to know is that you're cool. And if you've had a fling here and there, why not tell them?' Georgia winked and pulled Kirsten in for a tighter hug.

*

A couple of weeks later, Kirsten's eyes sprang open and she realised the visit was upon her. Today! *I'm not ready.* As she showered, she tried to prepare herself. *What will they want to do?*

Turfing Jellicle off the kitchen worktop, she grabbed some toast when she heard a vehicle pull up. Who was it at this time in the morning? She peered out and saw Fraser's SUV parked beyond her window. With a leap in her pulse, she glared. 'What is he doing here?' A shiver ran down her spine. This couldn't be anything good. Jellicle meowed and sprang onto the hall table as Kirsten marched to the door.

She ripped it open and stood with her arms tightly folded. Fraser was on the step, his fist out ready to knock. 'What are you doing? Why are you here?'

'And good morning to you too.'

Jellicle slipped off the table and coiled around Fraser's legs.

'Just explain yourself.'

He smiled at the cat, then squinted about. 'Look, you're not going to like this.'

'Oh, what now?' Kirsten drew in a deep breath and held it, but Fraser's proximity sent a frisson up her spine. Every time he was close, suppressed memories in her body stirred, waking up to possibilities, crying out for more, while her head drummed a furious no, no, no.

'Well, I'm doing a pickup from one of the holiday cottages on the farm.'

'What? This farm?' That was another slap in the face.

'I just wanted to tell you. They booked my tour before they got the cottage. I don't want you thinking they overlooked you.'

'Great. Thanks for letting me know.' Was this a roundabout way of rubbing it in?

'Listen. Don't shut the door. I'd like to think we can still be professional.'

She clamped her teeth into her lip, trying to maintain eye contact.

Voices on the path behind made Fraser spin around, 'Here's my tour but—'

'You better not keep them waiting,' said Kirsten.

'I think they'd tried to book with you first, but you were full.'

'Yeah, ok.'

'Which tells me, there's plenty of room here for both of us.' He quirked a smile that made her knees wobble.

'Your passengers are waiting,' she said

He furrowed his brow, treading forward as if to reach out to her. 'Is everything ok? Can't we be friends?'

'Look, I have to go too.' She stumbled back. 'I have a busy day.' She scraped her hands through her hair.

'Ok.' Fraser glanced back as he strolled down the short path and joined the family at the gate. Jellicle hopped onto the stone wall and purred about with his back arched. Fraser scratched him as he welcomed the family of tourists.

Kirsten rubbed her forehead. Friends? Seriously? Tears pricked. *Just hormones.* Her time of the month always picked a great moment to arrive. Fraser's guests were already admiring his kilt. Back inside, Kirsten put on her boring jacket and headed out for her tour before the main event that evening.

After starting the minibus, she hammered out of the drive a little too fast. Why had he come round? Why did he act like he cared when she knew he didn't? Her hormonal body wanted to sweep away the past five years, pretend he'd never been a jerk and fall into his arms. She'd loved being there. So warm, so safe, so cherished, everything she'd always wanted. When he'd kissed her, she'd let her words slip out. The crazy love she'd felt. Despite her terror that he'd freak, he hadn't given up. He'd said she was beautiful and carried on, taking her nerves and inexperience in his stride. She'd been the most important person in the world because he'd made her feel like that. *Why am I crying? For god's sake.* It didn't change the facts. It made them worse. If he'd been brutal or impersonal, she'd have been happy to see him go. But he'd made her care. *Right, stop!* The next time she saw him, she was going to act like he was not real. He didn't deserve her tears.

Focusing on her tour, Kirsten steered her mind away from Fraser. With a very amiable group of French tourists, she had a relaxing day despite following their request and taking them on the challenging tidal walk to MacKinnon's Cave. She shared in their sense of achievement and was impressed at her bravery when she navigated them past the highland bull in the field. Where was Beth when she needed her?

After dropping them back at their accommodation in Dervaig, Kirsten rushed home to change, trying to ignore her phone vibrating like mad as she entered a Wi-Fi zone. It was a miracle the phone didn't blow up under the weight of messages. Ninety-seven! Seriously? Did they expect her to read them? A detailed account of her friends' journey in gifs and emojis swam before her eyes. They'd arrived but hadn't got to their accommodation. They'd rolled off the ferry and straight into the Craignure Inn.

CHA: See you there ASAP!

Pulling on her most revealing top, Kirsten felt the need to show herself off. She attempted an intimidating line of black eyeliner. A few moments later she rubbed it off, resembling a panda. After watching countless tutorials, she knew the theory, but she couldn't get it right. Her hand shook. Eventually, she settled on smoky eyes. They were easier than trying to get the lines to match. She pressed her pink, sparkly lips together in front of the mirror. *Right, time for business.*

The minibus was like an oven as she drove to Craignure, hoping her sunglasses hadn't made a dent in her makeup, assuming it hadn't melted. Long, balmy evenings were great as long as the midges weren't out. Kirsten had barely got out the bus when a hoard swarmed upon her. She flapped them away before hearing a collective shriek of, 'Kirsten!'

From the beer garden at the side of the Inn, three figures waved from over the fence. Making her way through the bar's cool interior to the entrance, Kirsten waved at Matt as he pulled a pint for some locals. He tipped her a wink. 'Hey. I'll be out shortly.'

A second after emerging in the dazzling sun, it was eclipsed again as she was attacked by several arms and deafening shrieks. After freeing herself from Ann-Marie's grip-hook and her long ebony hair that had twisted around her neck, Kirsten hugged the others and they exchanged the obligatory greetings and compliments.

'Sit,' commanded Rhona, pointing to their table.

'Did you get a drink?' Cha fingered one of her numerous ear piercings. She'd added a nose ring since the last time they'd seen each other. It went quite well with the blue dreadlocks, the grungy vest and the Doc Martins. 'Then you can tell us all the goss.'

Matt swaggered outside, beaming. 'Hey, Kirsten, you're looking especially fabulous again. As are these lovely ladies. What can I get you? One of our special cocktails?'

Kirsten swallowed and blinked, not wanting her friends to think she was still as freaked by guys as she used to be, even though Matt was slightly annoying. She remembered what Georgia had said. Her friends didn't need to know what a pathetic state her love life was in. At work, she'd shed the Roddy restraints. At play, she could do whatever she darn well liked. And tonight, she was determined to have fun. 'I'm driving, unfortunately. Could you whizz me up something non-alcoholic? One of your specialities?'

'You betcha! Matt's your man.' He gave her a wink.

'Thanks, Matt.' She returned his wink and he nipped inside.

'Do you and him have a thing going?' asked Cha. 'That was quite a look he was giving you?'

'Sure. We've been known to... be friendly.'

'Really?' Ann-Marie goggled.

Kirsten enjoyed the banter as they quizzed her, until Matt returned, carrying a tall glass of clear liquid, all bubbles and zing with a fresh green leaf and a parasol, on a small round tray. He placed his other hand behind his back and gave a mock bow. 'Madame.'

Kirsten's friends watched in silence.

'Thanks, Matt, this looks, well, um, as good as you.' Kirsten fiddled with her necklace.

Matt raised an eyebrow, then leaned in, so his perfectly smooth cheek was almost touching hers. 'You're very welcome.' Grinning from ear to ear, he swaggered to the door while Kirsten's friends gawped. Gulping the cool drink, Kirsten glimpsed Matt stepping aside to let someone pass. *Oh no*. It had to be, didn't it? Fraser. *Why here, why now?* Why did they have this uncanny knack of always being in the same place at the same time? Kirsten was quite sure if she wanted to see him, she'd never bump into him. It was obvious he was directing his gaze elsewhere rather than look at her, but he wasn't real. She didn't care what he was doing.

'Isn't that the new tour guide bloke?' Rhona stared quite unashamedly, stroking her blonde hair behind her ear.

Kirsten kept her head down. Ann-Marie coughed, letting her straw drop as Fraser walked to a neighbouring table. 'Oh, wow. That's some competition.'

'Yup,' said Kirsten. 'But without several painful operations and a dramatic change of identity, there isn't much I can do about it.'

'Oh, you're hilarious.'

'He's all alone,' said Cha. 'I wonder what he's doing? Looks lonely just sat there on his phone.'

Kirsten shuffled in her seat.

'Is he single?' Rhona asked.

Kirsten ran her index finger around the rim of her glass. 'I think so.' She contemplated her drink, then glanced at him. He smiled at his phone, seemingly unconcerned at being alone but with a slight frown like he'd sensed her scrutiny.

He raised his eyes and Kirsten found herself staring into them. She blinked, but couldn't draw away her gaze. Fraser lifted his coke bottle, sending a wordless toast in her direction. Heat flooded her neck as she turned quickly back to her friends. *He's not real, he can't affect me.*

'I like the look of him,' Rhona whispered.

'Well, let's call him over,' said Kirsten, a flourish of bravado sweeping through her. 'Let's see if he fancies you too.'

'No,' said Rhona, going pink. Kirsten waggled her eyebrows. After all those years of her friends taking the mickey out of her because of her awkwardness with boys, she finally had the upper hand. A subconscious tug in her chest lured her to peek back at Fraser. Her heart leapt. He was still looking. Had she gone red? It didn't matter. He was not going to get the better of her. She may have been a sweet little innocent five years ago, but not now. With a swift movement, she raised her hand and beckoned him.

'What are you doing?' muttered Rhona.

'Shit,' whispered Cha.

Fraser checked around, his expression asking, 'Do you mean me?' When he'd ascertained she did, he strolled over, stood beside Kirsten, and leaned in. 'What can I do for you?'

'Well, let's see. My friends want to meet you. I think they quite fancy you…' she let the word hang. '…r tours.'

Rhona choked into her drink. Kirsten pulled a sarky smile at Fraser.

He smirked then, taking her by surprise, parked his kilted backside on the seat next to her. Very close. Perhaps deliberately too close. Kirsten chewed her thumbnail and stirred her drink, determined not to notice the citrusy smell of aftershave or the alarming proximity of his thigh. Just a slight movement and their shoulders would brush. Moving away wasn't possible; if she shuffled even an inch, she'd be off the edge.

'Well, hello, ladies, and, Kirsten,' he said. She threw him a disgusted look. 'Just a joke. Sadly, my tours are all booked up this week, though I'm off for a couple of days at the end of the week. If you're really desperate, I could fit you in.'

'Oh no, Fraser.' Kirsten knocked back her drink. Despite its non-acholic properties, it filled her with Dutch courage. 'No one's that desperate.'

'Aren't you the charmer?'

'Well, you would know.' Kirsten ran her finger around the rim of her empty glass.

Fraser drew back and rubbed his neck. 'Indeed. I know all about your charms.'

Kirsten held his gaze before giving him a quick, but pronounced, once over.

'Well,' Ann-Marie coughed, breaking the moment, 'we're doing one of Kirsten's tours, so we probably won't have time to do another one anyway.'

'No worries. I'm actually on a tour just now. I'm hanging about until they finish their drinks. They've got forty-five minutes, then they're getting punted back to their holiday house.'

'The one at our farm.'

'The very same.' Fraser chinked his coke bottle on her glass.

Hyper-aware of her friends watching, Kirsten held her breath. *Must keep calm. He's not real.* An unreal man who happened to look gorgeous, smell heavenly and set her pulse racing? Something somewhere had gone wrong with the plan.

Ann-Marie tapped the side of her glass. 'So, how do you like doing tours? I take it you two get on pretty well together?'

Kirsten knew she was fishing and raised an eyebrow at Fraser. The corners of his lips turned up. What a dazzling smile; one she'd dreamed of so often. He smirked at her. 'We've been known to get along.'

'Haven't we just,' Kirsten said. 'We're quite the explosive combination.'

'Not half.' Fraser sipped his coke.

'Do tell.' Ann-Marie ping-ponged between the two of them, while Rhona and Cha exchanged a glance.

'After you,' said Fraser.

Kirsten smiled at her empty glass. 'I think we'll keep it as our little secret.'

'Very sensible.' He checked his watch and raised his bottle in her friends' direction. 'Cheers, ladies. I should go check my group and see they're ok. Enjoy your night.' Whether he meant to or not, he brushed against Kirsten's shoulder as he stood up. The tremor that passed through her body must have been visible. Fraser cast her a brief glance. 'You look stunning, by the way,' he said before ambling inside.

A tingling sensation swept up her neck and over her face. Her friends' collective stare was rife with intrigued curiosity. Crossed arms, pouts and arched eyebrows; they resembled the comedy version of the Spanish Inquisition.

'Jeezo.' Ann-Marie wafted her top dramatically. 'He is one hot dude, and what the hell is going on? Are you seeing him?'

Kirsten side-eyed the wide-open door. 'No. Whatever gave you that impression?'

Chapter Fourteen

Fraser

A light morning breeze lingered as Fraser led his group towards the Kilmore standing stones. The place resonated with magic. As a boy, he'd played out passages from his favourite novel, *The Lord of the Rings*, here. Even now, he imagined scenes unfolding as he led his group along the path. The view flowed down the valley, towards the village and out to sea.

'Originally,' said Fraser, 'five stones stood here, in a straight line. Only two remain upright, as you can see. Their position is curious. They're alleged to indicate both the southern moon rising and the northern moon setting. Of course, moon worship is intrinsically pagan. But interestingly, the name of these stones is Christian, Kilmore meaning big church. These crossovers are common all over Scotland. When the pilgrims brought Christianity here, they simply adopted places already used by the locals as centres of worship, eventually moving to churches as we recognise them today.'

Fraser remembered so many tales Padre Sloane had told him. He'd always found him fascinating, the way he never shirked from other religions, showed such openness and tolerance despite his own beliefs. His interest in all faiths, beliefs and ideals captured Fraser from the off. Fraser didn't count himself as one thing or another, and the padre didn't mind. The grief of losing him three years ago had been the worst of his life.

'Now, if anyone would like the perfect group shot, don't hesitate to ask. I'm happy to get you all together.' He was handed a phone and leapt onto a tree stump to get the best angle. From his lofty perch, he observed a minibus drawing up and was momentarily distracted as the doors burst open. Kirsten jumped out along with her three friends. *Bugger.* Hastily, he finished the snaps. 'If anyone has any questions, please ask. Otherwise, we'll spend another ten minutes here before we head to Calgary Bay.'

The passengers wandered around without questions. Fraser turned his back on them, checking how close Kirsten and co had got. He wanted to make himself scarce for two reasons. Firstly, he didn't want to get in her way; he knew how touchy she could get. Secondly, he *did* want to get in her way. That really must stop. But whenever she was close, a raw burst of energy drew him to her; old flesh memories returned to niggle him, but he didn't want to encourage that, especially after last night. He knew what she'd been doing, putting on a show for her friends. But he'd felt the buzz – the thrill of flirting with her again. But it was no use. Not this time. If it gave her a bit of fun with her mates then fine, but he wasn't going to get hurt again.

I never learn, do I? Last year, during counselling, he'd met Chevonne. And what a bloody tangled mess that had left him in. Now, Chevonne was back living with her husband. And she had a child. Fraser rubbed his face and sighed. *Ok, don't dwell, there's nothing I can do.* The memory of the day when the message came in sprang to his mind. *I'm pregnant and there's every probability it's yours.* His fingers opened the catch on his sporran, itching with the need to get out his phone and reply to it, but obviously, it was over a year too late, and no matter what reply he sent, it couldn't change the cold hard facts. There was no going back now.

Kirsten's friends approached, smiling and waving. He raised his hand and eyebrows in unison. Kirsten hung back, examining her phone a bit too deliberately, looking unsure. *Not my place to care.* But he did. It tugged his heart to see her like that; a remnant of the awkward girl she'd been five years ago when she'd reeled off stories a little too fast, punctuated everything with nervy laughs and tried not to make eye contact. He could sense the ache in her chest. Meeting up with these friends again brought back her feelings of insignificance. But she was wrong. She was a determined young woman. He might not agree with all her assertions about him, but he couldn't deny her passion for what she did.

'Hi!' One of the friends marched right up to Fraser, interrupting his thoughts. 'This is a coincidence.'

He scratched his forehead. 'Yeah. They happen quite a lot around here.'

'Don't they just,' another friend said. 'I've seen some weird crap going down on this island. I could tell you some real freaky stuff.'

'See, when you turned up at the pub yesterday dressed like that...' The first friend laughed. 'I thought you were the stripper.' She winked and Fraser wanted to stem the flow of heat into his cheeks. 'It's my hen weekend. Do you take bribes?'

'Ha, funny. And no,' he quipped.

'Don't you?'

He hadn't noticed Kirsten joining them. She wore a look of mock shock. 'Well, for you, I might make an exception,' he said. 'Call round later and I'll show you what I've got.' *Seriously. No.* This was exactly the kind of thing he had to avoid. After all his years of shamelessly flirting with anyone, it was hard to stop, especially when his efforts teased out a smile like the one almost permeating onto Kirsten's face. But this was just a laugh. It obviously bought her kudos. What harm could it do?

'If you didn't have a tour, I'd show you a choice hand gesture right now, but I'll save it.'

'Yeah, put that one on ice. I'd like to enjoy it in private.'

'What are you two like?' The blonde friend folded her arms.

'Explosive.' Fraser coughed. 'I better go and round up these folks. We have places to be.' He stalked off to herd his group. On the way back, as he passed Kirsten and her friends, he gave a measured wave.

Putting two fingers in a V shape on her cheek, Kirsten fake scratched it in his direction. *Do not rise.* Not because he was offended, far from it, Kirsten's eyes were almost asking him to come hither, but if he did it would certainly not help anyone. He liked to match like for like, but this time it was safer to walk away.

Calgary Bay was always stunning. Fraser allowed his passengers time to sit, paddle and picnic.

After finishing off the tour, he returned the punters to their hotel. On his way back to Uisken, he stopped at the twenty-four-hour book shed in Bunessan and picked up some neat little finds, including a book on local legends, before returning to his tent.

After a quick chat with his gran, he climbed the hill to a new area. He had to keep shifting, so the tent didn't damage the ground.

Chucking the books through the door onto his sleeping bag, he slung off his sporran and sat outside. The canvas flapped gently in the wind. He closed his eyes. Meditating had become part of his day. Even if only for a few minutes, he needed to shut out the world. It was all part of his therapy. He drew in a deep, filling breath and held it. After slowly releasing it, he repeated. A natural calm flooded his chest. Everything was still. He barely registered the wind on his cheeks. All he saw was a pure, blank canvas. Until a face flashed into view. Keep out! Yes. His eyelids flickered. No.

'For god's sake,' he muttered. 'Will you get out of my head?' He patted his shirt pockets for his phone. Where was it? Crawling into the tent opening, he grabbed his sporran and raided it. Not there. Jogging back to the SUV, he checked around it. Nothing. Agnes gasped with surprise when he appeared at the door again.

'I need to check I didn't leave my phone here.' A cold wave crept over him. Where was it? If he'd dropped it, it could be anywhere. He'd been on tours all day. He called it using Agnes's landline, but there was no answer. Returning to the SUV, he waited as Agnes dutifully called again. Although it was unlikely to get reception, he prayed for the comforting vibration. Nothing. He checked under the seats, in the footwell, the glove box, everywhere he could think of. But there was nothing. Not even the faintest whisper. After thanking his gran and wishing her goodnight, he returned to the tent and sat on his sleeping bag, putting his head in his hands, willing himself to think.

Quite apart from it being brand new, the things that were on it were things he needed every day. He had to find it, even if it meant searching all night.

Chapter Fifteen

Kirsten

There was no let-up for Kirsten. Helping so many people enjoy their holidays made her long for one herself. But the good news was that reviews had picked up. She occasionally had palpitations wondering what Roddy would think, but where was the harm in her changes? If she told legends, she was upfront about their origins and no one had been put off so far; in fact, she was booked out. Robyn had helped her with *wow words* for her website and with Murray taking on the admin, it freed up Kirsten to concentrate on the tours. She almost conceded that maybe Roddy had needed all the time he spent in the office.

It was a pain having to sacrifice a gorgeous day to take her three friends to places they'd already been hundreds of times – but also quite fun. Kirsten wasn't sure whether to be proud or horrified at the blatant flirting with Fraser, but it had come so naturally. And felt annoyingly good. Everywhere they went, they posed for ludicrous 'henny' photos and Ann-Marie uploaded them to Instagram. The ones at Kilmore had possibly been the silliest of all. Ann-Marie had whipped an elf-style cloak out of her jute shopping bag and posed like a wicked elf queen at the standing stones.

With only a couple of days of their visit left, Kirsten felt obliged to meet up with them at every opportunity. But their constant talk of men and boyfriends, weddings and the future grated on Kirsten's nerves. Coupled with the Fraser inquisition, she was on the back foot again. This called for a diversion. Not Fraser. Inviting him to walk with them in the West Mull Woods close to Creagach farm was a step too far. But Georgia would do. She was never one to turn down offers of fun and this was no exception. Her effortless chatter made it easier for Kirsten to avoid the Fraser interrogation. Entertaining as it was, some of her friends' suspicions were getting dangerously close to the mark. If the truth came out, Kirsten wasn't sure she could handle the emotional fallout. Her friends weren't likely to understand just how hurt she'd been. They'd just enjoy the laugh, along with comments like *always the quiet ones you have to watch*. After knowing Kirsten since primary school, they couldn't forget how quiet and awkward she'd once been. It was hard not to lapse back into that mindset in their company, but Fraser's presence had changed that, as Georgia's would today.

'You've done the opposite to us,' said Cha, 'we all left the island as soon as we could. But you purposely came here. What on earth for?'

Georgia smiled; she always did. That smile made people like her, put people at ease, and invited confidence. 'I did an island-hop with some friends, years ago, when I was just out of school. Mull stayed in my mind. I always felt there was something more here for me to discover. So, when I started my photography business, I decided to base myself here. I love it.'

Cha raised an eyebrow. 'But don't you get bored?'

Irritation needled Kirsten. Cha was getting at her through Georgia. This was what her friends did. They just didn't get that she could be happy still living here. And she was happy, but there were always niggles. The what ifs. What if she lived all her days here and never met her soulmate? Would she still think it had been worth it when she reached Agnes or Mary's age? Even if all her dreams with Fraser had played out five years ago, what would she have done? Left the island to be a military wife? Could she ever really have done that?

'I'm not a getting bored kind of person,' said Georgia. 'It depends on what you mean by bored. If you mean do I miss shopping and clubs and things like that, then maybe there are times I do. But living here is anything but boring. This is a living community – it's so rare – I love being part of it.'

'Well, you're braver than me,' said Ann-Marie. 'Growing up here was fun, but these days I'd miss the shops too much. And KFC.'

They all laughed. Kirsten was glad she'd brought Georgia along.

Not far from the boundary between the woods and the farm, they met Murray, who was managing the construction of a new logging road. He approached them, hugging his iPad, and Kirsten was glad Beth wasn't there to witness her friends' unabashed drooling as Murray explained the project in detail.

Georgia caught her eye and winked. 'Everything ok?'

'Good.' Kirsten nodded, not quite meeting her gaze.

'Her tours are fun,' said Ann-Marie. 'We did one yesterday. What a laugh, look at these photos.' She took out her phone and scrolled for Georgia and Murray to see. 'If you're on Instagram, we could all follow each other. I'm Ann_Marie_McIntyre23.'

'Sure,' said Georgia.

'Not me,' said Murray. 'I deleted all that a while ago. Trouble with an ex.'

'Oh dear,' said Ann-Marie, slipping her phone back into the pocket of her jeans. 'That reminds me, did you find out who that phone belonged to? The one we found at the standing stones.'

Kirsten frowned. In the hectic arrangements over the past day, she'd forgotten about it. They'd been taking the photos of Ann-Marie at the stones and seen it face down in the long grass. It looked new, but it was out of battery. It might have lain there for weeks, but possibly one of Fraser's party had dropped it. Kirsten had meant to contact him and ask. 'I forgot. I should hand it in.'

'Charge it and see if anyone has called it,' suggested Ann-Marie.

'Maybe,' said Kirsten, 'but it'll probably have a password on it.'

After what turned out to be a fun afternoon despite her worries, she returned home, took out the phone and shoved a charger into it.

Picking up her own phone, she found Fraser's tour number and called, but it rang out. Hopefully, if it was someone from his tour party who'd dropped it, they hadn't already left the island. She messaged him and explained. The bothy was a tip, mainly because she'd hardly been in it except to dump dirty clothes and the remainders of packed lunches. For once her mum had done as she said and not come in and tidied. *Why did I object?* Now, she had all this to clean too. She buzzed around, shoving clothes into the washing machine and clearing the kitchen area so there was a nice space in place of the dirty dishes and packets. By the time she was done, the phone had thirty percent battery, which was enough to switch it on. She waited for it to go through its opening cycle, then woke it. It needed a passcode, but she could read the notifications. The top one made her brow crease, and she stared at it.

Missed call – Kirsten (Hidden Mull)

Why did the mystery phone have a call from her?

She dismissed it to see *4 Missed Calls – Gran*

Someone's gran was obviously desperate to get in touch with the owner.

She dismissed them, and another one popped up.

1 new message – Kirsten (Hidden Mull)

Underneath, she read the first few words of the message she'd sent to Fraser. She raised her hand to her lips. It was his phone. She didn't know where he was staying. How could she return it? Georgia had said he lived near his grandmother's croft, but where was that? Who was his grandmother? Maybe if she emailed him, he'd see it on a laptop or tablet. People relied so much on their phones these days; he was probably going crazy with worry.

She could ask Georgia. As the washing machine whirred around, she waited. Eventually, a reply pinged.

GEORGIA: Casnock Cottage, Uisken, that's where he said his grandmother lived. He just said he lived nearby. Why? Is everything ok?

KIRSTEN: Fine, just business.

But Uisken, that was the other end of the island. It could take a couple of hours to get there. It was half five and Kirsten had considered meeting her friends for a drink. What to do? Maybe she could pick them up and they could all go. The air was muggy and hot, dark clouds lingered to the west. She reread Georgia's message. *Casnock Cottage.* Hang on. She knew that place. It was where she'd picked up one of the people on her community tour. Riffling through some notes in the drawer in the hall table, she found the list. Agnes Ogilvy. Was she Fraser's gran? Was that why he'd taken her to the Midsummer Party? Kirsten covered her mouth. Could he be the grandson she'd been so pleased about? The one she'd said was coming to camp? Surely, he wasn't camping?

Flooded with intrigue, Kirsten took the phone, jumped into the minibus, and left. Agnes had been a pleasant lady, Kirsten could leave the phone with her. Yes, problem solved.

Calling Ann-Marie on the hands-free, Kirsten made her excuses, insisting she'd discovered the phone's owner and had to deliver it straight away. She didn't let on who the owner was. Her friends might explode with excitement if they discovered where she was going. Pulses of lightning vibrated in her chest. This was the right thing to do, wasn't it?

A taut heaviness strummed in the air. Even with the windows open, the minibus was stuffy. The roads were quiet. Most people were home for their evening meal. Kirsten was used to driving these roads, but Uisken was at the island's southern end down a narrow road and it took an age to get there.

She pulled up outside Agnes's croft. Fraser's SUV was parked on a hardstanding area next to the cute little garden packed with roses in full bloom. A tingle spread across Kirsten's shoulders. Why couldn't it have been someone else's phone she'd found? Dread trickled down her spine. If he opened the door, what would she say? It was after seven. Was that late for Agnes? She didn't want to startle the woman.

Unclipping her seatbelt, Kirsten took a deep breath. She'd come this far. Maybe she could post the phone through the letterbox? As quietly as she could, she closed the minibus door. The mugginess pressed in around her. At the door, she hesitated, then knocked. A few moments passed before there was a shuffling sound and the door opened.

'Hi.' Kirsten smiled as Agnes's lined, paper-like face peered round.

'Hello.' Agnes frowned, seemingly trying to work out who she was talking to.

'I'm Kirsten McGregor, I did your community trip a few weeks ago. You might not remember me.'

'I do, yes. My memory isn't as bad as everyone says. But it's a bit late for a tour, isn't it?'

'I'm not here about a tour. I wonder, your grandson, Fraser, does he live here? I found his phone, and I'd like to give it back to him. I noticed his car outside.'

'Yes, he lives here. Well, not in the house. Silly boy won't live in the house. Wants to give me space, so he says. Lot of nonsense. But maybe it's for the best. Dearie me, when he's in the kitchen he fills the whole room. Very big lad, so he is, and this cottage is only small. He makes me some nice meals, mind.'

'Oh, that's good.' Kirsten rubbed her hands together. 'So, is Fraser…? Well, can you give him the phone?'

'I could,' said Agnes. 'But not until he comes down tomorrow. He's up the top of the hill.' Agnes pointed vaguely behind her head. 'Has his tent there. Always used to do it when he was a lad. Sometimes he forgets what age he is, I reckon. He's been very worried about that phone, been looking all around. Had me calling it, but I can't climb up there to give it to him.'

He actually had a tent? This was getting weirder. Kirsten sucked her lip, uncertain. If she gave the phone to Agnes, he'd get it the next day. But it sounded like he was frantic, and she couldn't shake the mounting desire to investigate. 'I should give it to him.'

'Yes, that would be good. And tell him to come down later if he gets worried.'

'Worried?'

'The storm.' Agnes gesticulated towards the window. 'It's going to be a big one. Those clouds coming over. Fraser probably won't mind. He's a big strong lad, but I worry about him stuck at the top of a hill in a storm with only a tent.'

'Ok, I'll tell him. And thank you.'

'Take care. Don't you be up there too long either. You don't want to be caught out in bad weather.'

Kirsten tramped to the gate and round the edge of the croft, where a small path led past an overgrown field and up the undulating hill. Agnes was a hardened islander and if she said a storm was coming, Kirsten believed it. The clouds hung heavy and the sultry atmosphere agreed with the prediction, though Kirsten hoped not. She wasn't a fan of thunder and lightning. Halfway up the hill, she stopped and admired the sea in the distance. The clouds, some way off yet, were a dark and ominous purply grey. As she got higher, a slight breeze played on her face, the first she'd felt all evening. The closer she got to the top, the louder her pulse drummed in her ears.

On a flat area close to a huddle of gorse bushes, Kirsten spotted the tent, grey with dark green trim. It was a good size for a holiday, but how long had Fraser been in it? Was he crazy? Her feet came to a standstill. There he was, sitting cross-legged at the tent's entrance, which pointed seaward. He wore his kilt, but nothing else. Holy crap. This was her last chance to turn back.

Where was his shirt, his socks? Why did he need to have so much flesh on show? She shivered as she drew closer. His eyes were closed. What was he doing? No matter what she did, she was going to shock him. Should she drop his phone beside him and run? Or just stand still and ogle that body? He was so darned fit. Tanned and honed to muscular perfection. She chewed on her lip. Five years ago, she'd lost her virginity to that body and never found anything comparable since. Because it hadn't just been his body. He'd made love to her with his soul, or so it had seemed. She crept forward. Her foot crunched on a patch of dry grass. Fraser's eyes sprang open, and he jolted around.

'Jesus Christ.' He lifted his hand to his bare chest. 'I nearly died.' With a slight frown, he looked her over. 'What are you doing here?'

'I, er.' She edged forward, swallowing, fiddling with her fingers. Her mouth was dry as a bone. She did a recce of his abs. *Help!* Her gaze shifted to the tent, and she frowned.

'Did you come to inspect my accommodation?' he asked. 'You live in that?'

'Yup.' He gave a one-sided grin, his teeth grazing his lower lip. 'I'm used to living like this.'

'It can't be very comfy.'

'It's not bad.' He stretched and glanced around. A faint low rumble groaned over the sea beyond.

Kirsten squinted towards the approaching wall of black clouds. 'That reminds me.' She wrapped her arms tight around herself. 'Agnes says you're to be careful in the storm.'

'You know Gran's name?'

'Yes, I know her. I did a community tour with her.'

Fraser frowned and shook his head. 'Small world, isn't it? But I love a good storm. I'll go see her later and check she's ok.' He stretched back, leaning on his palms, baring the magnificence of his upper body.

Kirsten swallowed, looking towards the ground. Beside him was a book with a curious cover. She twisted her head to scan the title, *Old Mull Tales and Legends*.

'It's good, you should read it,' said Fraser. Kirsten looked up to find his eyes trained on her. 'Borrow it if you like.'

'Oh, no. It's fine.' A bold flash lit up the sky. 'Holy shit.' Kirsten ducked and put her hands above her head.

Fraser jumped to his feet. So tall. Another grumble of thunder groaned. Kirsten shrank back. 'Hey, are you ok?' Fraser stepped closer.

'Yeah, I just got a shock.'

Fraser stopped directly in front of her and glanced at the sky. 'It's going to be a big one, I think.'

Ears ringing, heart pounding, Kirsten shivered, feeling slightly dazed but weirdly safe. The wind teased her hair as she stood close, feeding from his body heat.

With a slight frown, Fraser focused on her. 'It's ok.' A shudder vibrated up her spine. She couldn't maintain eye contact. Catching his scent on the breeze didn't help the jumbled mess going on inside her head. She'd fallen for him so hard and she could so easily do it again; the feelings had never gone away. Another rumble made her shoulders tense.

'Kirsten.' Fraser's voice was low and mesmerising. 'I never meant to harass you. I admit I started out thinking we'd just have a bit of fun, but you changed me. All those messages were me just trying to make myself understand what had happened. I'm sorry about how it must have sounded.'

'What are you talking about?' Kirsten's mind had stopped working. Blood pounded in her ears. More thunder rumbled. 'What messages?'

'The emails I sent you five years ago. The ones you replied to telling me to stop harassing you. I didn't obey, sorry. I phoned you, you know. Did Roddy tell you? I didn't even think you wanted him to know about us, but he did. I guess you told him, and he warned me off. That was when he said you'd left the island.'

'I didn't tell Roddy about you – ever. And I didn't get any messages.'

'What?'

'If you sent messages, it must have been Roddy who replied.' Kirsten covered her face. 'Oh god, he knew. That's why he kept telling me that rule over and over. He controlled all the emails. I sneaked a look at the main account but didn't realise there was another one in my name until a few months ago, but he must have deleted them by then.' Kirsten felt the need to scream, cry and jump for joy all at once.

'Seriously? Is this for real? Why would the guy do that?'

'Because he was a total control freak.' Kirsten stared at the sky. *Bloody Roddy.* 'My god, Fraser. You didn't run out on me.' She held her forehead. 'I wish I'd seen those messages; if only I'd known about the other account.'

'Well, if I had my damn phone, I'd show you, I saved them all, but I've lost the bloody thing.'

'Oh my god.' Kirsten dug in the back pocket of her cropped jeans, struggling to take in everything he'd just told her. 'I forgot.' A cool breeze ruffled her hair, bringing more drops of rain. With a shaky hand, she pulled out his phone and handed it over. Fraser was still so close, heat radiated from his skin.

He gaped at the phone before taking it. 'Where the hell did you get this? And how did you know it was mine?' The change in his voice was alarming. The sudden harshness.

'I found it at the standing stones. I didn't realise it was yours. Then I forgot about it, I was so busy. I messaged you to see if someone on your tour had lost it, but obviously you didn't get it, as the phone was yours. When I charged it and I saw the message from myself, I worked it out.' Her hands flapped as she explained, and she cringed. He looked furious.

'You had it all that time.' He woke it.

'I told you, I didn't know it was yours.'

'Why didn't you hand it in? I've been back to those stones twice since then. I've retraced my steps all over the island at four in the morning until eleven at night. I've called in at every police station as well as keeping up the tours. When you arrived, that was me bloody praying it would turn up.' He ran his hand down his face.

Another strobe of lightning flashed overhead. Kirsten reeled back. 'Well, your prayer came true then, didn't it? God, of all the people, I thought you'd understand how busy I am. I came here as soon as I realised who it belonged to and when I found out where you were staying.'

Fraser raised his voice as the thunder boomed. 'God, Kirsten, I'm sorry. I didn't mean to sound ungrateful. I was just—'

'Save it. Why should I care?' As she stalked off, another massive flash lit the sky. She let out a shrill scream and ducked in shock. A loud rumble groaned.

'Kirsten!'

Ignoring his shout, she broke into a run. Rain pelted the ground with intense bullets. Within seconds she was saturated. Lightning streaked across the sky. Halfway down the hill, she felt someone grab her shoulder.

'Kirsten, please. Let's not fall out. Not again. Not when we just found out the truth.'

Looking up into his sparkling olive eyes, Kirsten watched a drop of water trickle from a strand of wet hair across his forehead, down the crook of his nose and onto his cheek. 'Ok. But right now, I need to go home. I have an early tour, and this wasn't exactly in my plans.'

'I get that and thank you. Really.'

'You should go to your gran, check she's ok.'

Fraser stared and seemed to sway on the spot. Kirsten felt a stab of terror and desire. Was he going to kiss her? She wanted to close her eyes, lean in and let go, but another boom of thunder brought her to her senses.

'Drive safely,' said Fraser, accompanying her to the minibus. Kirsten started the engine with soaking fingers. As she drove off, she glimpsed Agnes at the window peering out and Fraser at the gate.

He hadn't run out? He'd sent messages. What did that mean? It changed everything. Had he had feelings for her too? Did he still? As another flash lit the sky, Kirsten pushed northwards, wishing to be home, and wondering what in the world could happen now. Did this push open the door of possibilities? Or did it just make things more complicated than ever?

Chapter Sixteen

Fraser

A burst of lightning illuminated the sky. Fraser stood at the gate as the rain hammered his naked flesh. Kirsten had driven off like a bat out of hell. With drips rolling down his face, he checked the phone, now safely returned. Relief was overshadowed by remorse. He cupped his mouth. A lump swelled in his throat. *Why did I get so cross?* She'd accepted his apology, hadn't she? They were good, weren't they? And she'd never got his emails. No wonder she was so angry; she thought he'd behaved like a bastard. *And maybe I am.* He was certainly a mess. Since being medically discharged from the RAF, he'd worked hard to combat the PTSD. Learning new skills at his stage in life was a steep curve. And very little compared to the high of flying a Typhoon.

Knocking on the door, he didn't wait for an answer. 'Gran. It's me.'

Two beady eyes stared at him around the living room door. 'Well, thank heavens you're not sitting up there in this weather, but look at the state of you. Where's your shirt? Put something on. I hope you weren't running about like that when the young lady was there.' Agnes bustled into the kitchen and reappeared with a freshly laundered grey t-shirt.

'Honestly, Gran, this is kind, but you don't need to iron all my clothes.'

'Of course I do. It's not like you're ever going to do it yourself.'

There was no point in arguing. Ironing was a chore he didn't mind skipping. 'Are you worried by the storm? I find them exhilarating, but I'll come sit with you if you like.'

'Och, nonsense. I'm not worried. I've seen hundreds of storms. It's you I'm bothered for. Surely a tent's not safe in this.'

'Probably not.' But sitting out on the hill while the storm roared appealed to him more than sheltering inside Agnes's dim living room. The TV blared and Fraser sighed as he ducked in. Agnes settled in her armchair and turned down the volume with a slightly shaky hand. Her knobbly veins rippled as she fumbled with the remote.

'Did you get your phone from the young lady? I hope she's all right driving home in this.'

'I got it, yeah.' He rubbed his hand over his wet face. He craved her in his arms, cosying close to him in the tent. But what good would that do? Perhaps he could break her heart all over again. What a balls-up he'd made of things. His temper had got the better of him. All the pent-up worry and frustration had blurted out at the worst possible time.

'Good. I hope she drives safely.' Agnes sighed as Fraser lowered himself into the armchair built for someone half his size. Perched on its edge, he cast an eye over the cluttered room. The little side table was packed with photos and to his shock, he saw a little black and white baby scan picture among them. He hadn't spotted it there before. Gran had kept it. Did she show it to people? Tell people?

'Craig called me earlier.' Agnes nibbled on a biscuit from a small tray beside her on a foldout table.

'Did he?'

'Yes, he's had some kind of promotion in the bank, I'm not sure what exactly.'

'That'll please him.' Well, Craig knew how to make money and keep money.

'He's worried you're trying to take my life savings,' Agnes said. 'Though I don't have any. Even if you took everything out of the jar, you wouldn't get far. Everything is so pricey these days.'

'I'm not going to steal anything. The only things I need are the shower facilities and the Wi-Fi, which I pay for.' Fraser suspected Craig didn't realise just how much he'd earned being an RAF pilot. He'd saved and invested for years, owned a penthouse suite in Glasgow and an apartment in Aberdeen, both of which earned quite a lot in rental. 'I'm not sure what Craig is panicking about.' Though he knew fine. Craig loathed the idea of Fraser inheriting the croft. He wanted it for himself so he could sell it and add his share to his already bulging account. Wherever money was concerned he saw it as his right to have it.

Agnes nibbled on her biscuit, peering towards the window at a low grumble overhead. 'Well, Craig's a nice boy, he's intelligent, and he has a lovely wife. The two children send me pretty pictures, even though I've only seen them twice in real life. Ever since you've been here, he's sent me more than ever. I've had letters, pictures, calls. Normally I only get that at Christmas and maybe a postcard from Benidorm in July, if I'm lucky.'

'Well, I don't want you to think I have any higher claim to anything. I've not exactly done much to deserve it and I'd rather have you alive. Craig obsesses over money, but I'd rather things were fair. It stops bad feeling and there's been enough of that in our family.'

'I'm glad you came back. I worried terribly when you were off flying those planes. And I've got all your pictures, I show them to everyone. This is my favourite.' She lifted a silver-framed picture from the shelf. Fraser allowed himself a half-

smile, seeing himself dressed in his number one uniform, affectionately known as his best blue. Being awarded his medal for bravery was something to be proud
of, especially when his actions had initially landed him a court martial. But it was bittersweet even knowing he'd been right in the end. Agnes looked fondly at the picture before replacing it on the shelf close to the baby scan picture. 'Coming here was sensible. I'm not sure about the tent, but I know people need to go to the wilderness sometimes to sort themselves out. Now, I'm very tired. If you want to go back to your tent and dwell some more, that's fine by me. I'm off to bed. If you're worried about the thunder, you're welcome to the spare room.'

'No, Gran. I'm fine with it. Though I might steal a towel.'

Lying in the tent as the thunder rumbled about in the distance, Fraser settled down to his book, but concentrating was impossible. He closed his eyes, listening as mother nature unleashed her fury on the earth. How much better it would be if Kirsten was lying beside him? The dream of making love to her as the storm growled opened a cavern of emptiness in his chest.

By the following morning, a flood of regrets had risen. Now he knew her opinion was based on something beyond his control, he could change it. But things were different. He couldn't pretend the last five years hadn't happened. He'd opened himself to possibilities from a chance encounter. Now a relationship was the last thing he needed or wanted. He had to talk to Kirsten; they could never go back, but having her as a friend was important.

As always, he was up early. After sloshing down the hill, he took a quick shower at Agnes's and set off, hoping to catch Kirsten before her tour. The lack of minibus beside the bothy told him not to bother knocking. He parked roadside for a bit, considering what to do. Her friends were still here.

Maybe she was meeting them. If she was on a tour, she could easily be away all day.

Driving north, he headed to Tobermory without a clear idea of exactly why. It just felt right. After living for so long with the surety of military regimes and discipline or the crushing tension of having to be ready in an instant, it was pleasant to follow whims, go with the mood and be free. Sun poked through the clouds as they raced across the sky. When Fraser got out of the SUV in the car park, a brisk wind brushed his face. The air was so clear after the storm. And he had two days off. After thinking he'd have to use them to go searching for his phone, this was like the get out of jail free card.

Strolling along the promenade, he avoided the side overlooking the water as it was impossible to move for parked cars. Instead, he stuck to the shop side, peering in the gift shop windows. As he passed a small café, he saw hands waving at him. Taking a second to register and focus, he recognised Kirsten's friends at a window table with Georgia. A friend with long black hair and bright red lipstick beckoned him in. Was she Ann-Marie?

Biting the bullet, he opened the door and proceeded to their table, doing a quick scan in case Kirsten was at the till or in the shop area at the back. 'Hey. How's it going?' he said.

'Good,' said Ann-Marie. 'Kirsten's off touring, but we've got Georgia.'

Georgia's smile looked a little forced, but she moved into the seat in front of the window and Fraser took her vacated chair. 'I'm the Kirsten stand-in.'

'Yeah, Kirsten's seeing us off on the five o'clock ferry later. She couldn't get out of her tour today.' Ann-Marie pulled a face to indicate her annoyance. 'She was supposed to meet us for drinks last night, but she pulled out for something.'

'Yeah, that was weird,' said the blue-haired friend.

'Oh. That was my fault.' Fraser fluffed up the hair at his forehead. 'She came to see me. She had my phone.'

'That's why she wanted your address.' Georgia frowned. She didn't look her usual cheery self. 'Why did she have your phone?'

'She found it. She didn't realise it was mine.'

'Oh, was that your phone?' said Ann-Marie. 'We found it at the stones. That's unlucky, you'd just left.'

'Yeah. She returned it when she worked out it was mine.' He cleared his throat. 'I was hoping to see her, I need to talk to her.'

Georgia shook her head, took a sip of her coffee and looked out the window.

'She doesn't seem quite herself,' said Ann-Marie.

Georgia coughed. 'Sorry to butt in, I just remembered something. Fraser, I'm glad you showed up, I've got something in my van for you. Would you mind coming out for it? It'll only take a minute.'

'Sure.' Fraser furrowed his brow as he stood up. *What does she have for me?*

Georgia led the way out the door. She strode for a few hundred metres before turning up a side alley, empty except for a huge gull trying to drag a takeaway box out of a bin.

'What's going on?' said Fraser.

'Listen. I don't know why you want to talk to Kirsten, but will you please be nice to her?'

'What do you mean?'

'Just don't think because she's a quiet island girl you can trample all over her. You may have been a hotshot pilot, but she's a person too, not someone you can just play with and toss aside.'

'Whoa, whoa, whoa.' Fraser threw up his hands. 'I see what's happened here. She told you about us. That's fine. Except you've had the wrong version.'

Georgia folded her arms. 'No, Fraser. Don't tell me you ran off for some "greater good" reason. I've heard these speeches before. I'm a bit more worldly wise than Kirsten, but it doesn't make her feelings any less valid.'

'I know. And that's not what happened. We talked last night. Yes, she thought I'd run out on her, but I didn't. I tried to contact her, but Roddy didn't show her my messages. Then he replied on her behalf with a message telling me she'd left the island. This has all been one big misunderstanding.'

'So what is going on? I know it's none of my business, but she's my friend, and I don't want her to get hurt. Don't try to rekindle something with her if you're going to sail away in a month or two, it's not fair.'

'I know that. I know better than anyone. I don't want to break her heart or mine. I just want to talk to her.'

'Well, she won't be back until late, so you've got a whole day to work out what you're going to say, and make sure it's something good.'

Chapter Seventeen

Kirsten

After saying goodbye to the Mullsketeers, Kirsten raced across the island, taking the shortest road. Still, with tourists everywhere and locals on their way home, it took longer than she'd hoped. Swerving in and out passing places, she finally made it to the bothy.

Pulling out her laptop, she opened it and waited. The following day she had a group of American women booked in and her phone was bursting with messages, emails and missed calls. Every communication was filled with demands, requirements and conditions.

'No, I can't squeeze four more of you into the minibus.' Kirsten glared at the messages. After hashing out replies to them all, she needed air. More notifications pinged in. 'They're going to report me? To who? About what?'

Murray had done a good job with her accounts. Maybe he'd like to take over her communications too. For the first time, Kirsten missed Roddy. At least when he'd been around, she didn't have to worry about crap like this, but it didn't go a fraction of the way towards clearing him. Why the hell had he deleted those emails from Fraser? Messages that could have changed her life.

Not bothering with a jacket, Kirsten left the bothy, ran across the road and into the expanse of valley towards the sea. She stopped at the edge of the bluff, rubbing her arms and looking seaward, her long hair tangled in the wind. *I could scream.*

Her brain couldn't cope with any more, especially when the damned thing just wanted to dwell on Fraser. He hadn't run out. He'd tried to get in touch. What did that mean now? All the old panic returned. Even if she forgave him, it didn't change the facts. If she'd been terrified to discover he'd been a fighter jet pilot, she was even more terrified now that he wasn't. How had he gone from that to here, living in a tent and guiding tours – when he should be living in a camp doing a tour of duty? Something didn't add up.

'Oh, god.' She rubbed her hands vigorously over her cheeks, trying to cajole some sense into her brain. The day's heat had fizzled out with the wind. She wrapped her flimsy cardigan tight and clung to it.

'Kirsten.'

She spun around and stared. Fraser? Again? 'Why are you here?'

'I want to say sorry.' He marched directly to her, and she stiffened. 'I shouldn't have spoken to you like that yesterday.'

Folding her arms, she shrugged. 'I know, you said.'

'I also want to talk to you. Last night, all the stress of the last few days just came out, but there are other things.'

Kirsten arched an eyebrow.

'I can show you those emails now if you don't believe that I sent them. I have them all saved on my phone.'

'I believe you.' Kirsten side-eyed him and let out a sigh. 'I know what Roddy was like. I guess it means I totally overreacted to you being here.'

'Just a bit.' He tilted his head with a little smile. Kirsten tried not to look, but she couldn't help herself peeking. Eventually, she faced him. His smile broadened. 'I'd really like us to be friends.' He moved beside her, just millimetres. 'Or not enemies at the very least.'

Friends? She could almost touch him. Her hold across her body tightened. A deep urge burned within. Her desperate body was about to give her away. Being friends wasn't going to cut the mustard. If he was back, and he was real, her heart desired so much more, even if her head knew it wasn't possible.

'Come on,' he urged. 'I'm only here until the end of the season. It can't hurt, can it?'

Couldn't it? She had to take care and not give in. He wasn't sticking around; this wasn't the time to be rash. Their eyes locked. Desperation tugged her, making her dizzy. She knew what she wanted. They could kid each other all evening that they might be friends, work together, or whatever, but it didn't come close.

'Kirsten, I…'

'I know.' She stared at him, biting her lip. If she could just hug him, that would be enough. A friendly hug, that was all. Smiling, she swung her arm around his neck. He stumbled back, but she held him fast. His resistance melted away and suddenly Kirsten felt a burst of energy. Fraser's lips were on hers. She leaned up and absorbed him. The wind swept her hair back and caution drifted away. *God, yes,* she needed this.

'Kirsten, this isn't sensible,' Fraser whispered.

She gasped, clinging to his neck. 'Since when has that bothered you?'

He kissed her again. And again. She responded hungrily, clinging to every second. Five years of desperate desire poured from her soul.

'Oh god,' she whispered, pulling back, returning her heels to the ground, only just realising she'd been off her feet.

Fraser adjusted his neckline. 'Is that us ok now?'

Kirsten swallowed, not sure if she felt any better or if she'd just opened another can of emotional worms. 'I really don't know.' She adjusted herself, trying to stay casual, though her insides wanted her to jump up and click her heels together. 'Thing is, I need to go. I have a tour arranged tomorrow for a group of American divas. They've sent me about thirty messages with all their special needs. They've also told me they have an extra four people in their party and won't accept I have no space for them on the bus. I'm sick telling them I don't have enough seats. Apparently, they emailed about it ages ago. Well, they didn't email me. I've checked. They've already paid, and they've paid extra for these other four – now they're threatening to pull out, to sue me, and every other horrible thing they can think of. And I have a mountain of paperwork that just won't go away. And what am I doing about it? Standing out here, kissing you and hoping it'll all just go away.'

Fraser took a breath. 'How about I help you?'

'How?' Kirsten clamped her teeth on her lower lip.

'I'm off tomorrow. I could take the extra four and tag along.'

Staring with wide eyes, Kirsten said, 'You'd do that? On your day off?'

Fraser nodded. 'I would for you.'

'Fraser.' Kirsten jiggled her toes and gazed across jagged rocks and green pasture, dotted with sheep. 'I can't—'

'I mean it. I'm not looking for anything in return. Just one guide helping another.'

'But it's an eight o'clock pickup in Tobermory. That's about as far from Uisken as you can get, and you know where they want to go?'

'Don't tell me, back to Uisken?'

'Worse. Iona.'

Fraser laughed. 'So I better get up nice and early.'

Kirsten held her arms even tighter. 'I can't ask you to do that, it's over a hundred-mile round trip.'

'You didn't ask. I offered. And it's fine, really.' Fraser laid his hand on her shoulder.

'Is it?'

Inhaling deeply, he brushed his thumb down her arm and nodded. 'Yes. I've learned how hard this job is at the best of times. And at the worst of times, it's near impossible.'

'Thanks.'

'Any time.' With one step, he closed the gap between them and wrapped his arms around her. She took a shuddery breath that landed beneath the buttons on his shirt. He twitched. The deep heat emanating from within him warmed her cold skin. His masculine fragrance sent a buzz to her brain. He stroked her back; she mirrored him. More nerve ends opened up at his soft touch. 'Time to be friends?'

She gently pulled away, and he released her, but she couldn't stop looking at him. A hundred and one questions sprung up, things she wanted to know about him, but there wasn't time. She had to message the Americans. 'I have to email them and say it's ok before they report me to everyone they can think of.'

Fraser smiled. Kirsten fixated on the way his teeth grazed his lower lip. It was so utterly seductive. 'See you tomorrow then.'

'And no kilt.' Kirsten pointed a warning finger. No way was he stealing the show by wearing that.

'Wow, I didn't realise it was that kind of kinky shit they were after.' He grinned.

'Oh, shut up. I mean, if you're doing my tour, you wear something else.' She flashed him a look before heading for the bothy.

'I know what you mean.' He caught up with her, still smirking.

She swept some errant strands of hair from her lips as the wind teased it. A few steps and she'd be back inside, she could invite him in, but no. She needed to hold on to sensible Kirsten. There was a big day ahead. 'You better get lost, because if you're late tomorrow, I'll be furious.'

'Yes, ma'am.' He doffed her a salute. 'See you tomorrow.'

Chapter Eighteen

Fraser

Fraser had thrown himself into the fire again. Not satisfied with just getting Kirsten back on side, he'd gone ahead and kissed her too. Great. Just bloody great. Having a flirt and a laugh was fun, but hurting her was the last thing he wanted to do. He'd done that already, and although it was a misunderstanding, there was no saying it wouldn't have happened anyway. His days on the island had been numbered five years ago, just as they were now.

As he pulled into the car park of the Western Isles Hotel, his eyes wandered over the car park wall. From the hotel's lofty setting, a stunning view of Tobermory Bay, calm in the morning sun, panned out. It was picture perfect with the bright toytown houses and the little boats in the marina. A current of anticipation buzzed through his veins at the thought of seeing Kirsten again, but he had to keep this professional, for everyone's own good.

His jaw dropped as he glanced at the hotel door. Peering over his sunglasses for a closer look, he gaped as he reversed into a parking place. *What the…?* Had the Kardashians arrived on Mull? The outfits, the jewellery and the hairstyles were all completely unnecessary for the not-so-blinding lights of Iona. Kirsten stood in front of them in navy three-quarter trousers and a plain white top, looking subdued next to their spangles; a pixie in the land of the giants. They were all either tall or wide, and as Fraser got out the car, he realised they had voices to match. Strolling towards them, he ran his fingers through his dark hair. Sighs, chitter-chatter, and squeals issued from the divas. Hell, this was so embarrassing. He tried to smile, adjusting his powder-blue shirt collar. A woman with dark purple lipstick said loudly, 'I'm going in whichever car he's driving.' Then added in a stage whisper with a mock swoon, 'He's gorgeous.' She fanned her neck as two of her friends propped her up, agreeing with her.

Fraser glanced at Kirsten, running his palms down the sides of his cargo shorts. This was going to be a very long day. 'You owe me big time for this,' he said through his teeth, surveying the divas.

'You offered.' Kirsten smirked then added to the group, 'This is the other guide, Fraser.'

With a forced smile, he opened the back door to the SUV and backed off. Purple-Lipstick Girl shoved her way forward. 'Please note, no kilt,' he muttered in Kirsten's ear as they watched the vaguely comical scene of too many large women trying to barge into the SUV.

'Just as well, you'd never had made it out the carpark,' Kirsten whispered. 'You'd have been jumped.'

'Well, depending on who was doing the jumping, I might not have objected.' *Oh, screw me, here I go again.* He wanted to slap himself around the head.

Kirsten flicked him a *you-wish* glance and went to help some passengers onto the minibus. Fraser chatted to a few of the women as they shuffled about trying to get comfy. The usually generous and spacious seating area groaned under their collective size. A few of them budged each other, trying to make elbow room. Every space was filled. Fraser got into the driver's seat and waved to Kirsten, ready to follow on.

'See you at Fionnphort,' she called over.

'Wonderful,' said Fraser.

'Oh, this *is* gonna be wonderful,' said Purple-Lipstick Girl from the backseat. 'I have the best view on the island.' She lolled back, adjusted her giant diamante embellished sunglasses, and pinned her eyes on the rear-view mirror, pouting at Fraser's reflection.

Fraser threw Kirsten a look filled with sarcastic delight. This was horrendous. Though he had a terrifying flashback to a ten-year-younger version of himself who might have enjoyed this kind of flattery, and worse, might have acted on it. He cringed.

By the time they arrived in Fionnphort, his nerves were shattered. He locked the handbrake with a ferocious clunk, wishing he had an ejector seat. Purple-Lipstick Girl leaned through the gap and squeezed his forearm. Fraser patiently removed it and smiled at her, noticing as he looked away that Kirsten was watching.

'Is this it?' asked one of the older women in the party when they'd all mustered. Yes. This was it. A tiny village at the road end. At least the sun was out, making the sea sparkle turquoise. It was alive with glittering beads, like thousands of gems scattered on the surface.

'Yes, this is Fionnphort,' said Kirsten.

'Where's the castle thing?' The woman squinted about.

'It's over there.' Kirsten pointed. 'It's an abbey, on Iona. That's a different island.'

Fraser lurched aside, knocking into Kirsten as Purple-Lipstick Girl sidled up close. Kirsten caught his arm, gripping his hard bicep as he straightened up. She let go quickly.

'So, should we get back in the car then, honeybunch?' Purple-Lipstick Girl invaded Fraser's personal space to talk into his face.

He bit back his response, wondering how she'd feel if the tables were turned. Would she appreciate some bruiser of a guy barging up and shouting at her? 'We can't take the cars over there.' Fraser shuffled back, brushing his hand across the spot where Kirsten had held his arm. 'Only residents can do that.'

'We have to walk?' said the older lady.

'After the ferry crossing, yes,' Kirsten confirmed.

'What? I can't walk too far.'

'You could hire a bike,' suggested Fraser. He'd happily put her on one and send her on her way.

The woman's eyes lingered over him, looking scandalised, then she beamed, displaying what looked like all her teeth. 'My biking days are over, Sunshine.'

'We'll take it slowly,' Kirsten said. 'If you can walk this way.'

'This is joyful,' Fraser muttered in her ear.

'Have you done a tour on Iona before?' she asked.

'No, I haven't actually.'

'I've only done one. I generally steer clear as it's so busy. I'll have to make it up as I go along unless you're a St Columba mastermind.'

'Of course I am.' He beamed.

'Seriously?'

'No!' He gave her a nudge. 'But I had a wonderful padre in the RAF, he taught me a few tricks.'

'I'm not sure we need any of your tricks.'

'No? I guess not. These days I can't do anything that exciting, even though I used to do a mean tailslide in the Typhoon.'

'I don't even know what that means.'

'Probably just as well.'

Kirsten threw him a tiny smile. 'How about we do this tour together? As in properly, like we share the talking and guiding.'

'Good plan.'

The crossing was glorious. The oohs and aahs from the divas were a welcome change to the lewd comments on the drive there. 'I'm glad something appeals,' Kirsten muttered to Fraser as they leaned side by side on the railing, looking out to sea.

'Oh, you have no idea. I can tell you what appeals to my four, though it certainly doesn't appeal to me.'

'Got yourself a date, have you?' Kirsten pulled a windswept strand of hair from her lips.

'More like an orgy.'

Kirsten smirked. Her wrist brushed against Fraser's forearm, and he felt the warmth from her seeping into him.

After making sure they got safely off the ferry, it took a lot of effort and much puffing and panting to get all sixteen Americans up the short but steep path through the village to the abbey.

'This place is so cute.' The matriarch held her phone high, snapping pictures of the sea, the ruined nunnery, and the chocolate box houses on the shore.

'I'll see to the admin,' said Kirsten. 'I need to tell the manager I have four more people than planned. If you could give the divas some chat about the island.'

'Sure.' Fraser pushed open the door to the admission's cabin, leading the group straight out the other side as Kirsten went to the desk to give the updates. He jogged to a grassy area in front of a huge Celtic cross in the grounds and hopped onto a mound to start his speech. When Kirsten came out, he welcomed her to join him. He caught the look of trepidation on her face. This wasn't her style, and he knew it, but if she played along, it would be fun. 'I've just been telling the ladies about the island. Now, how about the abbey?'

'Well.' Kirsten rubbed her neck. Fraser nodded his encouragement. 'Iona Abbey was first built in the sixth century for St Columba.' She gestured at the stone building behind. A winding path led through green banks and low walls. A light gust ruffled the grass.

'And who's he? I hear you ask.' Fraser grinned and flicked her a wink. 'Columba is a very interesting character.'

Purple-Lipstick Girl tilted her head, fluttering her eyelashes. 'I adore his Scotch accent, it's gorgeous.'

'Scots,' Kirsten muttered into her hand. Fraser winked at her. *Yup, I'm not a whisky. Though I might need one shortly.*

Fraser gave a little cough and continued. 'St Columba was a fascinating character, and I like to think of him as a survivor as well as a saint. And there's no reason why he couldn't be both, is there?'

'No,' said Kirsten, flicking Fraser a half-annoyed, half-amused glance, but playing along. 'I guess we have a warped image of saints these days. That's mostly down to the way they were portrayed by romantic painters.'

'Exactly, but Columba came to Scotland from Ireland in a coracle. A distance of around a hundred miles. It may not seem far today, but when we go inside, there's a reconstruction of a coracle and you'll see for yourself.'

'And when you're looking,' said Kirsten, 'think about not only the distance but the depth of the Irish sea and the weather. Today we're lucky to have sunshine and a gentle breeze, but things change in a flash in the Hebrides. Try and imagine the journey for yourself.'

'Huge waves, high winds.' Fraser lifted his hands and gesticulated. 'And nowhere to stop off and rest. No possibility of rescue if you capsized. It paints a picture to me not only of a holy man but a man with strength and survival instincts, perhaps even a spirit of adventure. A saint and an adrenaline junkie too.' His gaze found Kirsten's and for a moment he was transfixed. Such a lovely face. Sparkling eyes shining bright; the gatekeepers to her soul. Something tugged inside him. The word soulmate had never meant much to him, but suddenly it clicked.

Kirsten cleared her throat. 'If you'll walk this way.'

'He's an absolute babe,' said Purple-Lipstick Girl.

'Well, she's not at all embarrassing,' Fraser muttered, giving Purple-Lipstick Girl a wide berth as they headed towards the main chapel.

'I thought you'd like it, having all the ladies eating out your hand.'

'She's not exactly my type.' He glanced at Kirsten. 'But you… Well, what kind of an awesome team are we?'

Kirsten smirked, her twinkling brown eyes never leaving his face. 'Yeah, that was—'

'Seamless?'

'Yeah. Oh, your fans await.'

Purple-Lipstick Girl beckoned Fraser forward. Pulling on his cheesiest grin, Fraser joined her. 'So, I'm about to open the door.' He rested his fingertips on the handle. 'But before I do, Kirsten will tell you a bit about it.'

'This is not the original abbey.' As Kirsten spoke, Fraser swept up his arm, drawing an arc in the air to indicate the building. 'A new abbey was built here several centuries after that. It's this later one you see today. It too fell into ruin, and only in the last few years has it finally been restored to former glories. It's a working church, a place of peace and holiness. Please respect that as you walk around.'

'And take time,' said Fraser, 'to reflect on your own life or beliefs, whatever they may be. There's a prayer corner if you're religious or if you feel this is the right time to appeal for help or forgiveness, for yourself or others. Please take your time to enjoy this moment in these beautiful surroundings. We'll meet back here in—'

'An hour,' said Kirsten. 'That'll give you time to look around fully, visit the shop and get a coffee.'

'Perfect.' Fraser pulled open the door, allowing the masses to pass through.

Kirsten shivered visibly as she stepped inside the cool stone chamber under the high vaulted ceiling. A few people sat around in quiet reflection. Purple-Lipstick Girl reflected a bit louder than everyone else.

'I don't suppose this is really the way you wanted to spend your day off,' Kirsten said.

'Not my first choice, no. Though it's not all bad.' Fraser's focus roved over her. Spending time with a friend was never a bad thing, and she could be a friend. Just that.

Shaking her head, Kirsten edged into a pew near the back. 'Let's see if you're still saying that after the drive, if you're still alive. They might maul you on the way.'

Fraser laughed a little too loudly. It echoed in the cavernous interior. His hand jumped to his mouth. 'Oops. Better mind my Ps and Qs, I'll get excommunicated.'

'Or lynched. Uh oh, here comes your friend.'

As Purple-Lipstick Girl approached with three others from the party, her grin was huge, and she giggled. Such a randomly squeaky noise from someone so large. 'Can we get some photos with *you*?' She batted her eyelids as though making the request embarrassed her, though she looked ready to eat him for breakfast. Or murder him if he said no.

Giving a little cough, Fraser adjusted his collar and stood. 'I guess so. Wouldn't you rather I took one of you all together?'

'Oh, do that too, but we need one with our guide.'

Fraser glanced back at Kirsten. She turned away and poked her tongue into her cheek indicating for him to go right ahead.

'Actually, Kirsten's the guide, I'm just assisting.'

'Really?' Purple-Lipstick Girl said. 'Why are you doing the speeches then?'

'I er. I'm training.'

Kirsten's eyes flicked around and she stared, looking like she was on the verge of a laughing fit.

'Wow.' Purple-Lipstick Girl raised her hand to her chest. 'You're really good.'

'Thanks. Hopefully, I pass the test. But I'll need lots of instruction to be as good as my boss.' His eyebrow twitched.

'Isn't he doing great?' Purple-Lipstick Girl pouted at Kirsten.

'Not bad.' Kirsten gave him the once over and he looked away.

'Hey, d'you mind if I steal him for a bit? Only, he'll look great in our photos.'

'Why not? Keep him as long as you like. It's good practice for him.' Kirsten gave him a little wave as he was dragged off between them. He tried sending her a parting glance containing a plea for help, but she didn't budge, just grinned forward. As he left, he saw her lean back and close her eyes. Lucky her, getting to shut out the world as he was hauled away like a lamb to the slaughter.

Chapter Nineteen

Kirsten

In the cool interior of Iona Abbey, Kirsten kept her eyes shut. Dreams and desires she'd tried to repress for years snapped back. Fraser hadn't abandoned her, and now he was here, helping her. But how could things be different? No matter how much her heart ached for him, he wasn't sticking around. That part had never changed. Enjoying the thrill of his company was one thing, stressing about the outcome was another. If he asked, she'd have him in a minute. The raw well of desire suppressed all the complications; fiddlesticks to tents and reasons for leaving the RAF. What did it matter if she could have him? She knew her brain would provide all the answers if she let it, but for some reason, her heart was blocking the replies.

A tap on her shoulder roused her. Her eyes flickered open and her neck cricked as she straightened up. *Was I asleep? For how long?*

'They've gathered outside,' said Fraser. 'We await your command.'

'What?'

'Have you been sleeping on the job? Naughty, naughty, boss.'

'Shut up. Jesus, is that the time?'

'Language, remember where we are.'

'Bloody hell.' She jumped to her feet.

'That's not a great improvement on the expletives front.'

'I said, shut up. And let me out. What will this look like? I bet I get slated on Trip Advisor again.'

'Relax. They're taking pictures of St Martin's Cross, I told them it was considered good luck if they touched it and said a prayer.'

'You did? Oh my god.'

Fraser grinned and coughed. 'Blasphemy.'

'My tours are meant to be realistic,' she muttered through gritted teeth. 'I've added some new stuff, but I can't let you just tell them any old rubbish.'

'It's not as if they're going to remember. Most of them probably think if they touch it, they'll get sucked back to 1745 and be whisked off by a naked Robert the Bruce wielding a claymore and riding a lion rampant.'

Kirsten's mouth fell open, and she glared at him. 'I can't even begin to tell you what's wrong with that statement.'

'I already know. I'm joking. They don't care. All they want is the romance, none of them will remember the history five minutes after they get back in the bus.'

'Spoken like the mainlander you are.'

'Hey, I have island blood.'

'It still doesn't give you the right to make up blatant lies and nonsense on the spot.'

'That's not what happened, well, ok, it is a bit. I was just giving them some fun. But, Kirsten, I'm not trying to preach or to tell you how to do your job. It was you who inspired me to come back and do this. I know from your itinerary that you climb Ben More, you walk to the Carsaig Arches, you go to McKinnon's Cave. These places aren't easy to get to, and when you've got a group of people you're responsible for, it's even worse. I think what you do is awesome.'

'Do you?'

'Yes.'

'Right, well, thanks.' She swallowed the bubble of pride building inside. 'But right now, I really need to go out.'

Fraser reversed from between pews and stood aside to let her pass. Hurrying outside, Kirsten gathered the group together. As she explained the possibilities to them, a split emerged. Some were keen to walk to the other side of the island where there was a magnificent pebble beach, others wanted to stay in the village and check out the various craft shops, island galleries and the Heritage Centre.

'I'm going wherever he's going.' Purple-Lipstick Girl ogled Fraser as he hung on the periphery, looking serenely casual.

'Fraser will lead the tour to the beach,' said Kirsten. *He can have her all afternoon and the further away the better.* 'I'll take the rest of you around the village.'

'Is it a long walk?' the matriarch asked.

'No,' said Kirsten. 'But first, we're heading to the St Columba Hotel for our lunch. It's nice enough to sit outside today.'

Kirsten marched ahead of the party along the winding road through the village. She clenched her jaw as she heard Purple-Lipstick Girl talking to Fraser. Their tone of voice was enough to tell her they were laughing. Even with someone Fraser was clearly not attracted to, he had a knack of sounding at ease, being friendly, even flirty. *Don't I know it.* Perhaps that was another reason his tours were so popular. Being more sociable with clients didn't come easy to Kirsten, but she was trying. She might not be best chums with her guests, but it didn't mean they couldn't be friendly acquaintances. *I've been so blinded.* Following Roddy's rules had made her cold and detached. The terror of getting too close had plagued her ever since Fraser. But recently, she'd lightened up. It felt good.

After Kirsten had sorted out the guests with their lunch seating arrangements, she joined Fraser at a table near the fence, far enough away from the main party to allow them privacy. 'I hope lunch is provided.' He lifted the menu and eyed her over it.

'Within reason.'

'Ha. We've passed reason. After what I've put up with today, I think I'll order two of, let's see, sirloin steaks, salmon. Oh, venison.' He checked up and winked.

'Let's stick to sandwiches, shall we?'

'If you insist, boss. Just remember I've got to get to the other side of the island with my fangirl.'

'She'll probably give up halfway,' said Kirsten.

'As long as I don't end up carrying her.'

'I'd pay to see that.' Kirsten smirked as the server came over.

After they'd ordered, Fraser examined her with a keen glance and said, 'This has been a tough shift.'

She raised an eyebrow. 'Surely it's not a patch on flying jets into a warzone.'

'Ha, don't you believe it.'

'You miss it, don't you?'

Fraser steepled his fingers in front of his lips. 'Yes, and no. There's nothing in the world like piloting a jet and leading the squadron; the rush of adrenaline, the speed, the responsibility. It's a crazy, mind-blowing experience. You're on hyper-alert all the time, and even when you're relaxing, you never really are. It's like a high you can't replicate, and sometimes, yeah, I miss that. But it takes its toll. I signed up young, straight out of school. My mum didn't want me to. She hated even the idea of the military, which made me want to do it even more.'

'Why?'

'Because it showed me she cared.'

'What do you mean?' Kirsten frowned.

'I was her least favourite son. Seeing her upset I was leaving made me feel more wanted than I'd ever been. I know it sounds twisted, but I was only seventeen.'

'I don't know how you did it. I've never been on a plane. Even the idea terrifies me.'

'We lived near Lossiemouth – I saw the jets every day. It made me want to do it. I dreamed one day I'd be stationed there, and it happened.'

'Didn't you go to Afghanistan?'

'I did. I went to lots of places.'

'So why did you leave?' Kirsten's cheeks grew warm. Something in Fraser's expression suggested he didn't want to discuss it. 'Sorry, if you don't mind me asking.'

'No, I don't mind.' He sighed and ran his fingers through his hair. 'It started when I made a decision that went against my Wing Commander. I'm glad I did because it saved a lot of lives, but disobeying a superior is an instant court martial. I got grounded, and that doesn't mean I got shut in my room for twenty-four hours.'

Kirsten smirked. 'I guessed that. But what happened?'

'We'd been on a recce mission of a site suspected of holding missiles. There were several things not right about it, but my commander was insistent that I'd got it wrong. I decided to go out on a limb and find out. I was right, but, as you can imagine, he wasn't impressed. I was a desk pilot for months while they investigated. And it didn't suit me. I wanted to be out in the field again, but I just had to sit tight and wait. It got me thinking, wondering if it was what I wanted to do. I started considering other options like becoming a commercial pilot or instructing. Then one day, out of the blue, I discovered the Squadron Leader who'd taken my place had been killed on a mission.' Fraser looked to the sky and pressed his lips together.

Kirsten held her breath, waiting.

'It wasn't my fault, just a god-awful coincidence, but it set off a chain reaction in me. I was awarded a medal for bravery and given the chance to go back, but I couldn't. By then I was in a different place.'

'I don't follow. What different place?'

'I was diagnosed with PTSD.' He took a deep sigh. 'No one wants to be the one it hits, and, in some ways, I was lucky. I know people who've had it a lot worse, but I was stricken with grief, guilt, and anger. I felt it was all my fault that this officer had died when it should have been me.'

'Oh, no.' Covering her mouth, Kirsten watched him, her heart racing. She lowered her hands and held one out to him. 'I'm sorry.'

He linked his fingers through hers. 'Thank you. I was medically discharged, but I got help. I know how to control things better now. I'm sorry the other night when I let rip at you… It's not an excuse, but if I get stressed, sometimes I just can't stop. That's the only time it's happened since I've been here, and for me, that's a big deal.'

'Is that why you came to Mull?'

'Yes. The pace of life and quiet is good for me. I meditate, I have cognitive behavioural therapy, and look around, just being here is food for the soul. But I'm not someone who can just sit about, chilling. Much as it sounds nice, it's not me. I decided to do this to keep me busy. I deliberately started small and made sure I had plenty of time off, but I needed something. I had no idea the business would take off like it has.'

'You've done well.'

'You inspired me to do it.' He removed his hand from hers as their lunch arrived. Kirsten's mind reeled at all the new information. Knowing he'd opened up to her filled her chest with warmth. Their eyes locked and energy vibrated between them. 'I don't make it common knowledge,' said Fraser. 'I'm not ashamed of it, I just think people's mindsets change when they find out. They instantly think I must be unhinged, or untrustworthy.'

'I won't tell anyone.'

'Cheers.'

'And, for what it's worth, I don't think you're unhinged… or untrustworthy. Not any more. In fact, well…' She took a long, deep breath. 'I really do like you, Fraser.'

He blinked and his mouth twitched before he toasted her with his glass of coke. 'Well, let's see how much therapy I need after my afternoon with you-know-who.' He winked and took a sip.

*

Three hours later, Kirsten waited at the harbour for Fraser and his group to return. Her half of the group, well and truly spent, had gone into the Martyr's Bay seafront café for drinks and snacks. As the little ferry dotted back and forward, Kirsten stood on a small beach close to the jetty. A familiar laugh alerted her attention. She turned to see Fraser and co on their way. Smile still intact, only his eyes gave him away. He didn't need to roll them for Kirsten to see he was thoroughly pissed off.

After showing the group into the café, he hopped down onto the shore. 'Oh god.' He held his hand to his forehead as if checking for a fever. 'That was some afternoon.'

'Well, we're almost at the end. Just the drive home.'

'Just as well. And if my purple-lipped shadow gets in my car, you can drive it back. I don't think I can stand another second with her.'

'Yeah, sadly you're not insured to drive the minibus.'

'Are you kidding me? I've driven worse, I'll risk it,' he muttered, hurling a stone across the waves.

It had been one of the longest days on record. Kirsten was so exhausted when they got back to Tobermory, she'd happily have crashed overnight in the bus. After making sure the divas were all safely back inside, Kirsten turned to Fraser. He looked back. Moments passed without words. Kirsten's heart rate picked up until she couldn't hear anything else. She didn't want to let him go, ever.

Chapter Twenty

Fraser

Confessing to Kirsten had lessened a weight on Fraser's mind. No matter how much his counsellor had told him not to be ashamed, he couldn't wholly disassociate himself with the idea that somehow he was a failure. Despite having considered a change of career before his discharge, leaving in that manner left a black cloud over what had been a beloved career for a long time.

He smiled at Kirsten, blinking slowly. Neither of them had moved from their position in the Western Isles Hotel car park. Hitting the memory rewind button, he remembered doing this before, in a different carpark and what felt like a different life. Then he'd asked her to come for a drink with him. And where had that led? Giving his hair a rake, he tried to unscramble the mess in his brain. He was desperate to ask her again, but he couldn't. Kirsten's eyes betrayed her. The connection Fraser felt with her let him into her thoughts. Now she'd discovered the truth, she thought they could pick up and carry on, maybe start a new life together. For her, it might work. *But not for me.* Fraser couldn't encourage her because it would break her heart. He'd already let slip with his silly flirting and lapses into his old ways, but no more.

'Well,' said Kirsten. 'Should we... Well, are you ok?'

'Yeah, I was thinking, that's all.'

'You can still think after today?' She scraped back her

hair and pinned it to the top of her head. 'They were so gruelling. I'll sort out the payment later in the week, I guess I owe you.'

'No, really. I don't need anything for it.'

'Nothing?'

He nodded and considered her before running his hand down his face. No. He didn't need anything from her.

'Are you ok? All the things you told me earlier... I'm sorry, it must be so hard. I could help you.'

'No, I don't want you to feel sorry for me. I've done a lot to sort it, and I'm pleased with what I've achieved. I'd say I'm almost back to normal. When I snapped at you, that was my first lapse for a long time. This place helps me. It's quiet, but at the same time, it's not easy. This job and lifestyle are enough to challenge me. But I'm not staying here, Kirsten.'

Kirsten frowned and mouthed something. 'I, well, um, ok.'

'It's not because of you. It's because of myself.'

Kirsten stretched out and took his hands, glancing up at the hotel windows, her cheeks reddening slightly.

In silence, they looked at each other. Rain started to drip. Leaning over, Fraser removed one hand from her grip and stroked his palm down her cheek. 'Kirsten, if I give in now, it'll only be a temporary fix. I'm leaving when the season ends. I want to fly again; it won't be with the RAF, but there are still opportunities.'

'Please.' Kirsten leaned up and brushed her lips against his. She dropped his hand and looped her arm around his neck. Everything else washed away; sound vanished. He could kiss her like this all night, but it was just making things worse in the long run. The rain was getting heavier and there were voices on the golf course path behind the car park. 'Oh, god.' Kirsten pulled away and edged back. 'If one of the divas sees us, I'll be slated on Trip Advisor. Why don't we take this somewhere else?'

'No,' Fraser mumbled, feeling punch drunk. 'Not this time. I can't...' He swallowed, trying to keep himself together. 'I should go, I have an early tour tomorrow. You do too. We're friends, Kirsten. I like you, I care about you, but that's it. Nothing else. We can't go back, too much has happened in between. I know there are unresolved feelings but doing something rash will just make it worse in the long run, and I don't want to hurt you again.'

'But...' Her expression fell.

Jumping into the SUV, Fraser's heart pounded a tattoo. He'd done the right thing, hadn't he? He waited at the hotel gates as a group of totally drenched young golfers went by, pulling carts. One of them looked directly into Fraser's window, narrowed his eyes and flicked some wet hair from his face with a contemptuous stroke. Fraser sighed and looked away. Matt, that irritating barman from the Craignure Inn. Resisting the urge to pull the finger up at him, Fraser waited until the group had safely passed before turning out. A nauseous wave threatened to overpower him. If Kirsten ended up with that bloody barman. *Well, if you don't want her, you better get used to the idea that other people might.*

Chapter Twenty-One

Kirsten

Kirsten's hand shook as she wrestled with the gearstick. What was going on now? Why couldn't things work for them? Even though she'd always known Fraser would leave, she couldn't help wishing for a different outcome. Maybe she could go with him. What if that was the answer? Could she sacrifice her life here, go to the mainland and make a new life? The minibus stalled. She'd never get over the regrets if she didn't at least try. Clamping back a swell of emotion, she grabbed her phone and started typing a message.

I'm sorry if this comes across as desperate, maybe I am. You said you hadn't stopped harassing me even after you thought I'd told you to. Well, for what it's worth, I'm not done harassing you yet. Just this one message. Please don't disappear on me again. I couldn't stand it if you did. Friends isn't what I want, but I'd rather be that than nothing. If you're leaving, why don't I come with you? I don't know what I'll do or how to live away from the island, but I could try.

She paused, desperately wanting to add *I love you.* She'd said it before, but she wasn't sure she dared. The first time it had burst out through raw emotion. Maybe this was the same, but she felt it deep in her heart. No one else had ever stoked up feelings like this in her. Could she let him walk away and lose him all over again without even attempting to say how she felt? In and out went the words. She wrote, deleted, wrote again. A knock on the minibus window made her jump. Her thumb knocked the send button as she looked up.

A bedraggled figure with a golf cart waved to her. Matt played golf? She zapped down the window.

'Hey,' he said.

'What are you doing?'

'I chose the wrong day to try golf.'

'Oh? It was lovely on Iona.'

'Well, it's chucked it down nearly all day up here. I'm bloody soaked, but I need to return these clubs, I borrowed them from a guy in the village.'

'Do you want a lift?'

'Na, it's just along there. Just thought I'd say hi. Do you want to go for a drink?'

'No thanks, I'm exhausted, I've had a very long day. But get in. Even if it's just a few metres, you look ridiculously soaked.'

Matt smirked and made his way around to the passenger side. With a lot of clattering, he heaved the clubs in and sat diagonally behind Kirsten. 'Thanks. It's on Breadalbane Terrace.' He tapped the back of her seat. 'Drive on, Parker.'

'Funny.'

'Listen, can I tell you something?'

'I suppose.' Kirsten didn't look in the mirror. After all the silly flirting, she hoped he wouldn't get any ideas now.

'I don't want to pry or anything, but I saw you just now with that other guide. The bloke who wears the kilt and loves himself.'

'Fraser.'

'The very one. So, it's none of my business really, but are you and him, you know, seeing each other?'

Kirsten tugged a strand of hair around her shoulder, waiting to get out of the drive. 'It's really not your business, Matt.'

'I know. But I like you and I'd have been happy for us to have some little get-togethers. But I also know you're a sensible girl who wants a lot more than a fling. Which let's face it, I can't do much more than that seeing as how I'm leaving next month. But I wouldn't like you to be hurt.'

Kirsten pulled out. 'And you think Fraser's going to hurt me?'

'Possibly. It sounds cheap, and maybe I'm just biased because I don't like him much. All that showing off with the kilt just bugs me.'

'Look, Matt. Can you just say what it is you have to say?'

'Actually, it just sounds like I'm trying to score a cheap point.'

Kirsten tilted her head and eyed him in the mirror. 'You can't say that and then not tell me.'

Matt sighed. 'Well, it's total hearsay, so it could be crap. My landlady was talking about him the other day. She has all these folks going on his tours. Her friend knows his grandmother, and this friend told her that Fraser... has a baby.'

Kirsten's mouth opened, and she gaped.

'Yeah, she says the grandmother keeps a picture of the scan. But before the baby was born, he dumped the mum and never sees either of them. That's why he came here, to hide from the responsibility. And apparently, he lives in a tent, so he can move around and claim he's homeless, so he doesn't have to pay maintenance.' Matt screwed up his face. 'Though it sounds a bit farfetched to me and my landlady is the world's worst gossip.'

Kirsten's hand jumped to her mouth. 'What?' The realisation hit her with a sharp force. 'He has a baby?'

'So the story goes. Stop here, this is the house, please.'

'Wow.' Kirsten slammed on the brakes. She had to get Matt out. The tent part of the story was true, so was there reason to doubt the rest? Was this why Fraser was hiding? Hot bile bubbled in her chest. She might be sick.

'Look, I better get this golf stuff back to the guy. Thanks for the lift and take care. And you know, I don't want to blacken the guy's name. Maybe I shouldn't have said anything.'

Kirsten's brain turned numb. She grabbed her phone. Oh, shit. She'd sent the *I love you* message and there was no getting it back. Terror gripped her insides. What if he changed his mind and wanted to get together? How could she now? What kind of man abandoned a baby then hid in a tent?

Was it even true?

The desperation to find out was outweighed by the fear of detonating something in him. What if mentioning it was a trigger that sent him spiralling back into a place he'd worked so hard to get out of? She didn't want to do that. But at the same time, the idea that somewhere in the world a baby was missing its father because of him made her sick to the core.

Chapter Twenty-Two

Fraser

Fraser sat in his tent, staring at his phone. Was this message for real? Kirsten was already guilty of saying *I love you* at unexpected times, but she'd written it in a text and sent it. That had to mean something. It did. A lot. That wasn't a phrase people just bandied about. *Not to me anyway.* She was now the first and second person in his life to have said it.

He lay back and stared at the canvas, listening to the raindrops pattering. How to respond? As if he was shaking his life in a sieve, Fraser tried to sift out everything that wasn't important. What did he really want? Right here in this message, a woman he cared about was begging him to stay and telling him she loved him, even offering to give up her beloved home for him. Why throw it away? He'd never meant this to be long term. It was an exercise to get his head back in gear. If he passed his mental health assessment, he could get a job as a pilot for a private company or be an instructor. But if he did that, he wouldn't have Kirsten. Or would he? Was she serious? She'd leave the island for him? How could he do that to her? If she left, she'd never be the same. Her heart belonged here.

There was no mobile reception now he was back atop the hill at Uisken, which for once was a blessing. He had time to think about his reply.

Being maxed out on tours kept him busy, but the message played on his mind all week. It was Gala Week, and there were events all over the island. As he wasn't constrained to hidden places like Kirsten, he lapped it up and took his guests to everything and anything as part of the island experience.

The culmination of events was the Gala Week Fair on Sunday. Now his name was known, Fraser had been roped into helping. He didn't mind, these things could be fun, but Kirsten would be there too. Stopping in a layby, that Saturday evening, Fraser checked he had reception, then with a deep breath began typing a response.

Thank you for your message. I appreciate your words. My future is uncertain. I don't want to leave you, but I don't see how I can stay. My life is complicated at the best of times. I'm going to the fair tomorrow. Maybe we could talk.

He read it over. How to sign it? *Love, Fraser?* Did Fraser Bell love anyone? He looked out the window and frowned. Yes, he did. That was what had made everything so hard. Because he did love her. The realisation floored him like a force nine gale. He sent the text signed only with a kiss. He loved Kirsten, but he didn't want to say it in a text. No, he was going to tell her to her face; he owed her that much.

*

The following day, Fraser jostled through a crowd on the small grassy area beside the Dervaig Village Hall. Gazebos loaded with bunting covered tables packed with goodies. The end of Gala Week Fair was in full flow, but Kirsten was nowhere to be seen. Fraser had abandoned the games stall to have a wander, leaving Donald Laird in charge of *Feeding Nessie* and *Hook-the-Duck*.

Across the field, he spied the most bedecked gazebo on the field. Georgia's art and photography stand was set up to Instagram-perfect standards. Fraser sidled up beside her, looking over the shabby chic explosion that was showcasing her paintings, photographs and driftwood crafts. Even her bright blue tea-dress looked handmade. She reminded him of someone on a 1940s re-enactment stall, apart from the pink streak she'd added to her hair.

'Hey,' he said, 'this all looks interesting.'

'Thank you, all made by me.'

'I rather guessed that. You have quite the talent, don't you?'

'We all have our own special talents, Fraser. Like you can fly a plane and look good in a kilt. Maybe next year, you should do both at the same time.'

'Yeah, thanks. I'll think on that one.' He scanned around. 'Have you seen Kirsten? I really need to talk to her.'

'Why?'

'Nosey.' He raised his eyebrows. 'I just... There's something really important I need to tell her.'

Georgia frowned and pursed her shiny lips. 'I think she's on her way. That's her mum on the baking stall. If you mind this stall for a minute, I'll go and ask if Kirsten's coming.'

Fraser paced with his hands in his pockets until Georgia returned five minutes later.

'Yes, she's coming as soon as she can, but she has a tour.'

'Ok, I better get back to the games.'

Feeling like he was back in the rapid response team, Fraser was on high alert as he helped some kids chuck beanbags into the giant cut-out Nessie. Where was Kirsten? It was almost three-thirty, and the fair ended at four.

Eventually, he saw the minibus pull up. It took all his restraint not to run to her there and then. Patience. Only twenty more minutes stuffing Nessie's face, and then he could tell her.

Chapter Twenty-Three

Kirsten

Georgia waved brightly at Kirsten, her broad smile filling her face. Kirsten returned it, but her chest burned with mounting panic. She had Fraser's message, and her heart was doing somersaults. Not the pleasant kind. What did he want to tell her? About the baby? *Oh, god.*

'I'm so late.' Kirsten approached Georgia. 'There's no point in me helping anyone now.'

'Don't worry. Listen, Fraser was over here a while ago. He said he wants to talk to you. He looked really serious. Is everything ok with the two of you?'

'Oh god. I don't know.'

A screech over the tannoy stopped their conversation. With a fair amount of crackling, Carl's voice rang over the field. 'We're approaching the end of this year's fair. We have a few results to announce before you all head home, so if you would like to make your way to the main marquee.'

Georgia grabbed Kirsten, and they walked arm in arm. 'I hope I've won best-decorated gazebo.'

'If you haven't, the judges need their eyes tested,' said Kirsten. The marquee sides flapped in the breeze, several strings of bunting had dislodged and were trailing down the sides. The grass underfoot had been worn to dust with all the comings and goings. Georgia beamed around, waving to lots of people. For someone who'd only come to the island the year before, Kirsten wasn't sure how she'd got to know so many people so quickly.

Carl began announcing the winners of everything, including the best scarecrow from the round island competition. 'I hope it's not that freakish one that looked like a drunken granny pole-dancing,' muttered Georgia. A few minutes later she was skipping up to the front to collect a rosette for her best-decorated gazebo. She kissed Carl on the cheek before returning to Kirsten with a full beam.

'Now, we also have some wider community awards,' said Carl.

Kirsten stifled a yawn. Carl had a pleasant voice, but these Roddy-like speeches didn't make for entertaining listening no matter who did them. What she wanted was to find Fraser. How could he talk his way out of this one? She clapped robotically as some outstanding community members were praised. Through the crowd, she spotted Fraser, leaning in and talking to someone. She needed to get to him. Before she looked away, he turned, and his gaze landed on her. He started towards them.

'Let's go,' said Georgia. 'We can start getting the gazebos down.'

'You go, I need to talk to Fraser.'

'Oh, right.' Georgia spotted him and, giving Kirsten a pat on the arm, left her to him. Kirsten waited, not sure where to look.

'Hey,' said Fraser. 'Can we talk?'

Kirsten glanced sideways and saw Beth looking over her shoulder. Fraser held out his hand, indicating they should step outside. 'Um, yes.'

'Listen, I need to tell you something, Kirsten. It's very important,' he said as they moved into the wind.

Kirsten shook her hair off her face. 'I already know.'

'You do?' He shook his head. 'I don't think so.'

Why was he smiling? This was hardly something to joke about. A fiery heat burned in Kirsten's cheeks. 'Yes, Fraser. Nothing stays a secret for long on this island.'

'Ok, now I'm confused.' He pressed his hands together in front of his lips and stared.

'Your baby, Fraser.' Her words crackled through the air. The sound from the marquee seemed to drop simultaneously. Its sides shuddered in a strong gust.

'What? How do you know about that?' The colour rushed from him.

'People talk,' she muttered, holding her hand to her mouth.

'What? Did my gran say something?'

'Is it true? You don't even deny it?'

'It depends on what you want me to deny.'

'That you abandoned some woman with a baby.'

He put up his hands and drew back. 'Ok, keep your voice down. Please.' He stood up tall and took in a very obvious breath. 'I don't want to discuss this with the entire field.' His fists balled. People were coming out of the marquee. Beth and Murray were there, and Georgia. They looked over.

'Why aren't you with your child? How could you abandon a baby? Is this what you're really escaping from? Do you pay for the child's upkeep?' The words tumbled out in desperation.

'No, I don't.' His voice snapped like a gunshot.

Kirsten shook her head. 'Oh my god, no more.' Tears welled in her eyes and she ran towards the minibus, leaving Fraser standing stock-still and alone.

*

Slamming the bothy door, Kirsten flung the minibus keys onto the hook in the hall, almost knocking it off the wall. Nothing could excuse Fraser now. The growing feelings of the past few weeks would never atone for what he'd done. A baby was missing a father because of him, and he didn't even care. How could she risk that he might do the same to her?

A knock on the door. Kirsten hadn't even made it out of the hall. Beth's head poked around before Kirsten could open it.

'What's up?' Kirsten tried and failed to look aloof with a lopsided shrug.

Beth folded her arms and raised an eyebrow. 'Nothing's up with me. What's up with you?'

'Nothing. What do you mean?'

'Come on, Kirsten. I wasn't born yesterday. What was going on at the fair? Georgia said you and Fraser didn't always get on, but what were you talking about? It sounded like some serious stuff. I think you should tell me what's happening. If he's bothering you.' Beth rubbed a fist over her palm.

'He's not. Look, it's nothing like that. It's so ridiculously complicated, there's no point in me even explaining.'

'Try me.' Beth ducked inside the door and strolled to the living room.

With a deep sigh, Kirsten followed. Beth took a seat, waiting with her long legs stretched out, crossed at the ankles. 'Is he the same guy you went to the Argyll Hotel with a few years ago?'

'How the hell do you know about that?' Kirsten dropped into her seat, frowning. 'Did Georgia tell you?'

'She knows, does she? My goodness, I'm out of the loop. No, it wasn't her. Will Laird saw you.'

Kirsten half-closed her eyes. Seriously? She remembered seeing him there, talking to someone. Bloody nosey island gossips. 'And what exactly did he see?'

'You and some guy Will described as "not a bad-looking tosser". Apparently, you were snogging this guy on the beach, then, later on, he saw you driving off and the same guy was standing topless looking out an upstairs window. When you came back and seemed fine, I let it go. Will's worse than the girls when it comes to gossip, I take everything he says with a pinch of salt. I thought he was just making up shit.'

Kirsten covered her face. 'Well, this time he was right.'

'Fraser didn't hurt you or anything?'

'No. But he disappeared, and I thought he'd vanished without a word until he turned up here this summer.'

'Awkward.' Beth lolled back and tented her hands.

'But then he told me it had been a mistake. He insisted he'd sent me emails and spoken to Roddy, but I don't know. I'm not sure what to believe now. Did Roddy delete those emails?'

'Let's find out.'

'What do you mean?'

'I spoke to Fraser after you left. He didn't say much, but he did say you'd got him all wrong. Maybe you have, but we can find out about those messages.' Beth jumped to her feet and went into the hall. 'What's Roddy's number?' She returned to the room, holding the landline phone.

'You're going to ask him?'

'I bloody am.'

Kirsten read out the number, quite sure this could get very ugly, very quickly. Beth maybe thought Kirsten's ears were too sensitive to hear the full conversation as she wandered back into the hall. But the interior walls of the bothy were thin. It was impossible not to admire Beth's guts. She wouldn't let go. Kirsten stood up and looked into the hall as Beth paced, saying, 'Did you have any right to do that? How was it protecting her? Bloody nonsense. And no, I will not watch my language. I'm extremely annoyed with your interference.' Red in the face, Beth slammed down the phone. 'Never liked him.'

'What did he say?'

'Yes, he got the emails, replied on your behalf and deleted them. Then he told Fraser you'd left the island to stop him harassing you. Apparently, he knew Fraser's parents and his father did something like that to his mother, so he assumed Fraser was just as bad. Bloody stupid man.'

The new information appeased Kirsten for a few minutes, but it didn't last. How could it? It didn't alter the fact that Fraser had a baby and had abandoned it. *At least it wasn't me.* The idea made Kirsten sick. But Fraser had been so well-prepared five years ago, it seemed hard to imagine him making a mistake. Well, thank heavens he'd been ready for her, or she could be sitting in this bothy with a child of her own.

The season had almost finished. Fraser would soon be gone. Nothing could keep him now. There were only two weeks left until the end of August. A stabbing pain caught Kirsten in the heart every time she thought about those moments of near perfection they'd shared. The feelings it had taken years to dissipate flowed back. Now she needed to go through it all over again. A flood of unbearable anguish spread through her veins.

After nearly three months of running into Fraser all over the island, he must be lying low because she hadn't seen him since their argument at the fair. Everywhere she went, a tense trepidation buzzed around her. What would she say if he turned up? Just ignore him? Look away. Act as if she hadn't noticed him; didn't know him. *Because that's what it feels like. Like I never knew you.*

Returning from a tour that had been quiet and distinctly end-of-seasonish, Kirsten flung off her jacket, leaving it on the floor and stamping her foot. Five years ago, she'd been equally wretched. It had started all over again. 'I am sick of men!' she yelled at her kitchen. 'Sick of them.' Why couldn't

Fraser just be the man she wanted him to be? He'd come so close so many times, but there was always something. *We weren't meant to be. He was always a big hotshot and I'm just an island girl.* Opening the fridge, Kirsten barely took a glance before slamming it shut. Nothing. Well, nothing of the medicinal alcohol variety she wanted. Wine, gin, whatever, right now she'd take a neat whisky. Mum might have something. She pulled on her shoes, ready to run up to the farmhouse when there was a knock at the door.

'Hello.' A beaming Georgia stood on the doorstep, waggling a bottle of Prosecco. In her candy pink dress, she looked like a good fairy. 'I thought you might need this.'

'I do. How did you know?'

'Sixth sense.'

Kirsten fetched two glasses from the kitchen as Georgia pulled out a bottle of sparkling elderflower and screwed up her nose. 'I guess I better be good.'

'Island life.' Kirsten poured herself some Prosecco. God, she needed it. All too often she was the one on the soft stuff as there wasn't a pub in walking distance and she was rarely on anyone's route home.

Georgia smiled. 'I don't mind. I'm happy with this stuff, it reminds me of flavoured gin. I'm good at using my imagination.'

'That's what I need to do.'

'How do you mean?'

'To imagine that day five years ago never happened.'

'No, don't do that. Even mistakes are important. They teach us things. I've made a shed load of them, but that just means I still have lots to learn, and learning is fun.'

'You sound like a nursery teacher.'

'I'd probably make more money doing that. But listen, let's get to it. What is happening with Fraser? Matt told me a story about him.'

'The baby?'

'Yup, but Matt's a twat. I thought he was ok; now he just gets on my nerves.'

'I think the story's true. Fraser admitted it.'

Georgia's eyes widened, and she put her glass on the table. 'I saw him in the Co-op last week. He looked so sad.'

'Did you talk to him?' Kirsten finished her second glass.

Georgia leaned back into the soft armchair. 'I just said hi and asked if he was ok. He said he'd been worse, and that he was winding down for the season.'

'He's leaving after he finishes in a couple of weeks.' Kirsten grabbed the Prosecco bottle. 'He wants to fly again.'

'Yeah, he mentioned that. I think he misses it. Maybe he'll go back to the child and try and make things up with the mum. I hope he does, for the child's sake. Something just feels odd. I always got a good vibe off him.' Georgia poured herself another drink.

'Yeah, well.' Kirsten glugged more Prosecco. Fraser was on a roller coaster, he'd admitted it. PTSD didn't just go away. Maybe he wasn't as far on in his recovery as he thought.

'What if there's another story?' said Georgia.

'Such as?'

'No idea. Maybe he was emotionally scarred in the RAF, it's quite common. What if he came here, hoping to find peace and all he's found is himself at the centre of a web of intrigue? He just looked like a lonely soul who needed a hug. I don't feel I'm the right person for that job, but you might be.'

'I want to. I really do. I know he's been scarred, but what could explain away a child?'

'I'm not sure, but every story has two sides. Maybe we should give him a chance.'

Kirsten flopped into her seat with a jitter. Was it wrong to hope this was true? Was there any possible way to redeem Fraser? Ridiculously, she'd loved him for five years. First as an adoring angel, then as a desperate hopeful, now with her heart and soul. But she wasn't sure if she could forgive something as huge as someone abandoning his own flesh and blood.

Chapter Twenty-Four

Fraser

Fraser sat on a bench inside the eagle hide as his group leaned forward, binoculars primed. His heart was black and blue from the many poundings he'd taken in his life, but Kirsten's words had hit him hard. Somehow, she'd heard that bloody story. The one his gran made worse with her denial and her wish that somehow there had been a mistake. He got that she wanted him to be normal, settle down to a wife and kids, but she couldn't accept his version of events, not when they so wholly contradicted the story he'd originally told her. And he'd only done that because he'd been so misled himself.

If he hadn't talked himself around to the idea of becoming a father, he could have forgotten all about Chevonne. She could have been tossed on the pile of pointless flings that had littered his life. But the baby he'd set his hopes on had been snatched from his grasp. Now he didn't know what he wanted, or where to find it.

He closed his eyes, drawing a breath and holding it. A solitary tear rolled down his cheek and caught at the side of his lips. He turned to the panelled wall, making sure no one could see him brush the tear away. Tilting his head upwards, he stared into the cobwebbed rafters. *I wish you were here, Padre. I need help. I've made such a mess of my life and I don't know how to put things right.*

With tours booked for another fortnight, he had to honour them, but the struggle was real. Where he'd grown to see magic, he saw a barren landscape. Grim and unforgiving, bleak and harsh in the fading summer. Trying to see past the mundane became a daily battle.

Donning the kilt gave him the confidence to act his way through the days, but the passion had died. He said the words on rote; he had no feelings left. During his RAF days, he'd learned how to shut down emotions. Now he didn't have to try, he was just a body.

One blessing was the sight of his gran's smiling face. She appreciated him being there, even if she didn't say so. Maybe that was something positive to take on his next adventure, whatever it was. On the flipside, he hated to imagine how she would cope with him gone.

Staying wasn't a viable option, but he hardly dared say a word to her about it. He hated the pain in her eyes. The worry. The knowledge she'd have to rely on others to help her with shopping and lifts. The loneliness. Even though Fraser had stayed all summer in the tent, he'd dropped in and out every day. Soon she'd have no one.

'Can't you and Kirsten sort something out?' Agnes said as they ate breakfast together.

'Pardon?' As they'd been talking about tours the moment before this took him totally by surprise.

'She does tours as well, you know. She took us on a lovely community tour. Why don't you and her work together? Instead of leaving. It can't be easy for two of you competing.'

'It's not that. My tours have done well, but I never planned to keep them going.'

'She's a very nice girl, you know,' said Agnes. 'I think she quite likes you.'

'She did, but I'm not sure she does anymore.'

Agnes nibbled on her toast. 'Oh, Fraser. What have you done?'

'Nothing.' He stood up and washed his plate. 'Her opinion of me is warped. She wants me to be something I can't ever be.'

'And what's that?'

'A normal guy without any kind of baggage.'

'What are you talking about? You are normal, aren't you?'

'Not the kind of normal she wants. She wants a neatly packaged guy with no history and no faults. Well, I've failed spectacularly on every level. Someone told her I had a baby which, I'd like to remind you, I don't. That baby isn't mine. Please, will you get rid of the picture?'

'But what if there was a mistake?'

'There wasn't.' Not in the test. *Only in my judgement.* 'Please. It's bad enough Kirsten knows or thinks she does.'

'Then why not tell her it's a mistake if you're so sure?'

'Because it doesn't change anything. I still can't stay here. I belong in the sky. I need to get back to flying.'

'Oh, Fraser. Please don't choose a career over a person.'

'I'm not. The man Kirsten wants isn't real. I'm a fantasy that changes with the wind. It's ironic, for a girl who loves her facts so much, when it comes to people, she can't stomach the truth.'

'Oh, Fraser. I hate to see you throwing away a chance.'

'A chance of what?'

'Of having a home with someone who loves you.'

Fraser stared at his gran, then out the window. Drizzly rain blew past. Could this be home? This beautiful wilderness? 'No, Gran. I can't.' Drying his plate, he sighed. 'I have to go to Iona today. Looks like it's going to be a wet one.'

He dreaded a return to the abbey, retracing the steps he'd taken not so long ago with Kirsten. The party were seasoned travellers happy to be shown the best spots while enjoying Fraser's endless Columba lore.

'I think you were Columba in a past life,' said a woman. 'You talk about him like you were there.'

'I'm not a saint.' Fraser laughed, though he appreciated the difficulty of surviving in wild lands. What he didn't comprehend was how to put down roots and maintain meaningful relationships. And that was what life was all about. So far, the only life he knew was in the RAF. He was safe there. The irony. Could he go back? Even if it meant being an instructor for the rest of his days, he would at least have the security.

The party dispersed for their investigations. Fraser leaned his forearms on the stonewall extending around the abbey grounds, watching the ferry being rocked by gusts, forging its way across the little channel back to Fionnphort. It reminded him vividly of the story he'd imparted to the tourists about St Columba traversing the wild seas in his coracle. A man willing to sacrifice his life for the love of god. Fraser had lived many years willing to sacrifice his life. Every time he'd sat in a cockpit was a risk; anything could happen. Maybe if he was going to make a new life, a different kind of sacrifice was required. At last, out here in the wild, surrounded by the aura of saints, wind blasting his hair and flapping his kilt, he began to realise what he had to do.

He clumped towards the main chapel and pulled open the wooden gothic door. As it thudded shut, the blasts ceased. Still air cooled his windburned cheeks. The eerie quiet from the high vaulted ceiling drew him deep into the chamber. He edged into an empty pew and sat quietly, staring towards the altar. He didn't speak but let the peace wash over him.

Don't give up, son. Have a good cry, then swallow the tears, stand up and look the world in the eye. You're a strong man. But strength isn't just in the body. It goes deeper than that. So does courage. You're

*brave enough to fly at four thousand miles an hour into a war zone, but
following orders is just one kind of courage. Doing what's right can be
the hardest thing of all.*

Padre Sloane's words played inside his head. Fraser
remembered them so well. He'd said them the day Fraser had
disobeyed orders to save his unit. What was the right move
now? He couldn't just go; abandon Kirsten again and not
even try to explain himself. His heart compressed inside his
ribcage. If he'd not been such an arse, what chance might he
have had there? Maybe his gran was right. Kirsten was good,
kind and stable; exactly what he needed, but he'd messed up.
He'd got mad when she'd recounted that story. The
humiliation of her finding out about his messy life was
unbearable, but maybe he hadn't given enough credit to the
strength of her feelings. She'd begged him not to leave, but
if he stayed, he'd have to sacrifice flying. Mull wasn't exactly
an aviation hotspot.

Standing up, he padded to the far end of the great
chamber. Tucked away in a darkened cloister was a quiet area
filled with twinkling tealights. Messages of hope and
remembrance on little slips of paper sat alongside each one.
Fraser rummaged in his sporran, pulled out some coins and
threw them into the wooden collecting plate. His hand shook
slightly as he lit one of the candles. Placing it on the row, he
picked up a card and wrote: *Padre, I miss your words of wisdom.
What I wouldn't give to talk to you right now. Fraser.*

He clutched the card for several minutes before laying it
beside his candle. Time was pressing. He gave a last look at
his note, and his eye strayed to the one beside. His brow
furrowed as he read *P.S. Never give up on love, follow your heart
and you'll find the key to flying high.*

Fraser stared at it. Ok, it was a stretch. But PS? Padre Sloane? He grinned. Coincidence or some stroke of Iona magic? It didn't matter. He had an answer. Or a lifeline. Maybe the tiniest flicker of hope.

He'd never have closure if he didn't tell Kirsten the truth about the baby. Everything else aside, he owed himself that much, and her. She'd confessed her love for him on two occasions now. Armed with that knowledge, he had to find her, though it would mean a confrontation and, whichever way he squared it, he felt more nervous and sick than he'd done facing the court martial. How could one pint-size woman terrorise him more than the Commodore? Because he couldn't stand the idea that she didn't care about him any more. He needed her. He had done for a long time, but he'd let lesser stuff get in the way.

At the end of the week, he dropped a tour party in Tobermory. Bracing himself, he took the road towards Calgary and Creagach farm. Now or never. As he approached the bothy, he had the distinct impression this wasn't meant to be. Kirsten's minibus wasn't there. But he was psyched and ready. Should he wait? Drawing onto the verge, he stopped. Time ticked on. White clouds raced across the blue sky, accompanied by perfunctory gusts that rattled the car.

Where was she? It was almost seven o'clock. She could have had a late tour and a drop off miles away. Then again it was Friday, maybe she'd gone for a drink or a meal with friends. With a two-hour drive to Uisken, Fraser didn't want to hang about too long. He pulled off and travelled south on the coast road towards Ulva Ferry and Gruline. Gorgeous sea views twinkled to his right. Foam spritzed as it hit the black rocked coastline.

Some miles down, he approached Eas Fors. There were no signs, not even a proper car park. It really was a hidden place known only to locals and people who went on Kirsten's tours. A blue flash glinted in the distance, close to the verge where he'd parked the SUV for the only tour he'd taken there before Kirsten had banned him. He drew closer and his heartbeat raced. That was her minibus. Something told him this wasn't a tour. This was a chance. His belt was off and he was out of the SUV almost before he'd pulled on the handbrake. Scrambling down the winding path at a dangerous speed, he peered into the clearing. No voices, no people. Stop. Make that one person. One solitary figure stood before the Eas Fors. *You can do this.* Fraser braced himself. *Take one step forward. One step. Then speak.*

Chapter Twenty-Five

Kirsten

Kirsten stooped and trailed her finger in the pool. Sighing a sad smile, she remembered her granny's stories about the place. The breeze played a whispery tune in the hanging branches. This was a beautiful place to think and breathe whether or not people believed in its magic. She traced the heart shape onto her forehead.

'Kirsten.'

Almost breaking her neck, she turned to stare. *No way. This is not possible. My imagination.* Never had she doubted herself this much. So much so, she nipped the skin on the back of her hand. *Ok, I just checked to see if I was alive, or awake, or whatever.* But whatever it was, Fraser was still standing there, clad in his kilt, his olive eyes bright, his expression wary. Why had her knees turned to jelly? Fire burned low, desperate for his hold. Every unsuitable feeling churned up, threatening to collapse her insides. Speech was impossible. He treaded closer, running his fingers through his hair.

'I saw the minibus,' he said. 'And I need to talk to you.'

She stared at him, her brow furrowed. In him, she saw so much she admired. But her desperate heart had invented an image that didn't match the reality. He was the only man she'd felt so strongly about, that was all. It had warped her perspective. He'd since shown himself to be a man who cared only for himself. 'What about?' She folded her arms.

'I can't change my past but at least let me tell you about the baby.' He sat on a large flat boulder by the pool and patted it, glancing up with a flicker of hope and desperation. Kirsten chewed her lip, then inhaling slowly, she dropped down beside him, conscious of his heat and his scent. The deep-rooted desire to wrap her arms around him and bask in his warmth almost overpowered her. Why was she such a hopeless case? If he could just be an average guy ready and willing to make his life here things would be super simple. She nearly let out a laugh. Somehow she knew she wouldn't fancy him half as much as she did if that was the case. And she could have the Carl Hansen situation all over again.

'Two years ago,' he began, 'when I came out the RAF, I attended counselling. Through that, I met Chevonne, a trainee counsellor.' He shook his head and closed his eyes, as though something was replaying in his mind. 'I know it was part of her job to dig deep and to seem concerned. I latched onto her. It felt good to believe someone cared about me, and I think she felt sorry for me. I should have kept it professional, but one day things developed.'

'I get the picture.'

He nodded and looked down. 'A few weeks later, she messaged me saying she was pregnant, and the baby was most likely mine. Well, this came as a huge shock to me, I'm always careful. Still, I didn't have any reason not to believe her. These things happen. And it made me reassess my life. This was like a chance. So, I embraced it, decided the time had come to grow up and become a dad. Chevonne and I weren't in love. We weren't even a couple as such, but I was ready to give it a go. But she got strange and distant.' Fraser scraped his hands over his face and took a deep cleansing breath. 'That's when I found out she was already married. Initially, she'd wanted to use me and the baby as a chance to leave her husband, but when it came to the crunch, she valued her steady life better than a pie in the sky chance.'

'What?'

'Yup. Then she started trying to cover up at work. She changed her tune completely and said the baby wasn't mine after all. I was so confused and stressed. I'd looked up to her and here she was making everything worse. I wanted her to get a paternity test. By law, I had no right to demand one without taking her to court, but I threatened to tell her employers. She was livid, but also devastated. Her relationship was on the rocks and this had been her feeble attempt at ending it. By that time, I was past caring about what she did. I just wanted to know for sure if the baby was mine, although I already suspected.'

'So, the result was…' Kirsten swallowed, not sure she wanted to hear. After despising him for having the child at all, she now felt a cold dread creeping up her spine.

'Not a match.' Fraser's voice was hoarse. 'Chevonne said she was sorry she'd dragged me into it, but I'd already told my family. Chevonne had sent me the baby scan photo. I guess at that point she really was planning to leave her husband. For someone training to be a counsellor, she was one of the most twisted and messed up people I've ever met. I'd already forwarded a copy of the photo to Gran and my mum. Then it all went pear-shaped and left me looking like an idiot again. All I wanted was something to be proud of.'

'But, Fraser, they are proud of you, I'm sure. Look at the career you've had.'

'Maybe. But whatever I do is never enough for them. I imagined being a dad, maybe flying with a local airline, and showing my family I could be normal.'

Kirsten looked away and sighed. 'You are normal. You're just a lot braver than most of us.'

'You think? I'm not a stable guy. You know that. You've seen me get mad. You know I can't settle at anything. I don't have a home. I can't even see a day ahead. I just live right here and now.'

'Fraser, five years ago, I saw something in you that I liked. And those feelings never stopped. I was silly thinking you could ever return them. I see that now. I know you're not here to stay and I understand how important flying is to you.' Chewing on her bottom lip, Kirsten looked skyward. 'But I...'

'No.' Fraser placed his finger on her mouth. 'You haven't been silly. You've been honest. If I'd recognised your true feelings from the start, I could have spared us a lot of pain.'

Kirsten swallowed and frowned. 'How?'

'When I came looking for you at the fair, I didn't want to tell you the story about Chevonne. I wanted to tell you something else.' He closed his eyes and breathed. 'Something incredibly important to me right now.'

Tears clouded Kirsten's vision, and she covered her mouth. 'You're going back to the RAF?'

Fraser's eyes glistened. He shook his head. 'No. I'm not. I wanted to tell you...' He lifted his finger and trailed it down her cheek. 'That I love you too.'

Still holding her lips, tears streaked her face. 'Really?'

'Yes, really. You disarmed me five years ago saying that to me and it's bothered me ever since.'

'Oh, god. You remember.' Kirsten threw her face into her hands, the embarrassment searing through her.

'Of course I do. It was a pivotal moment in my life.'

'I just blurted it out. I was overwhelmed, but so safe and happy. I was completely out of my depth.'

'No, you weren't. I was the one out of my depth. I knew what to do physically, but emotionally, I didn't have a clue.

You said what you felt, and I realised I felt the same. That moment changed me for the better. You changed me. I'm not denying I made mistakes, but they were mistakes of the heart. Before you, I didn't have a heart, or at least I didn't know how to work it properly.'

Kirsten stared at him for a moment, then swung her arms around him. 'I was stupid to say it, but I meant it.'

'I know you did.' He stroked her back. 'I could feel it. I still can. That's how I know I'm home, where I'm meant to be, with the person who loves me most in the world.'

'Yes.' A shiver trembled down her spine as he pulled back and brushed the tears from the corner of her eyes. 'I do, and I'll go anywhere with you.'

'We're not going anywhere. I'm staying right here with you.'

Kirsten smiled and Fraser returned it, looking more beautiful than ever. Her gaze fell on the Eas Fors as they played their cyclical rhythm behind them. 'Maybe they're magic after all.'

'I think they must be, or you are. I suddenly feel, I don't know…' He rolled his shoulders. 'Free. Like I can do anything.'

'But what about the planes?'

'Don't worry about that, I have a cunning plan. I'll tell you later. Right now, I just want you.' He leaned forward, cupped her chin in his hand and pulled her towards him. The softness of his lips was flawless. Edging closer, Kirsten melted into his arms, holding the kiss. Lifting one hand to his hair, she spread her fingers through it. He clutched her back, feathering her lips with soft kisses. The Eas Fors rushed. The birds sang, and the crickets danced. Five years had passed since they'd started this, but they had all the time in the world to finish it. *And my god am I going to enjoy it!* Kirsten smiled as she drew Fraser in even closer.

Epilogue

Kirsten

Kirsten pulled her jacket tight around herself as she huddled amongst the group of friends and family assembled close to the pier at the Glen Lodge Hotel. The weather had forgotten the summer as September had rolled in and the tourist season calmed. Kirsten should have felt the familiar pang and worry about how to make ends meet over the winter. But as the wind bit her ears and she stared out over the sea, all she felt was a buzz of excitement.

'What are we waiting for?' asked Agnes Ogilvy, wrapped up in a headscarf and a brown tweed coat.

'You'll see,' said Kirsten, winking at her mum. Gillian held up her palms, indicating she was none the wiser either as Agnes looked over at her.

'Well, shall we assume it's something to do with Fraser?' asked Georgia with a pouty grin.

'Well, yes.'

'I should certainly hope so,' said Agnes. 'But where is he?'

'He'll be here soon.' Kirsten checked her watch, then twisted it, searching around.

'He tells me the two of you are dating now.'

Kirsten nodded and caught Georgia sharing a grin with Beth.

'About time too. Silly man couldn't see what was in front of his nose.'

'Men usually can't,' said Gillian.

Kirsten tried not to roll her eyes and avoided looking at either Carl or Murray, neither of whom she was sure would dare contradict Gillian.

'Well, before Fraser gets here, I have something to tell you,' said Agnes.

'Oh?' Kirsten moved closer to Agnes, blocking the others. She wasn't sure why, but she had a feeling this wasn't going to be something she wanted everyone to hear.

'I suspect we're waiting here because Fraser has done something crazy again. Maybe it suits you, you're a young woman and I know my grandson has a way of turning the heads of the ladies with all his daredevil stuff. I told you the first time I met you, you'd like him.'

'So you did.' Kirsten couldn't help smiling.

'But he's always been rash and impulsive. What he needs is someone like you, someone with their head firmly screwed on.'

'Thank you.'

'And what's more, he needs a house. He can't stay in that ridiculous tent forever and I know he could stay with you, but underneath the tough guy, he has a kind heart. He thinks if he goes, I'll be lost without him. He forgets I've survived here for a long time, but he has a point. I've got used to him being about, and I won't lie, I like it. I wouldn't let that get in the way of his life though. But there might be another solution.'

'Is there?' Kirsten bit her lip. Was this going to be something useful? In the rush of the past month, she'd not cared where Fraser was as long as it was in her arms. He'd promised to look for sensible accommodation, right after he'd indulged one remaining fantasy. Despite thinking he'd lost his mind, Kirsten went along with it and had got carried away in planning this day as much as him, but it didn't solve anything in the long term.

'I've never told anyone, even Fraser's mother. I knew she'd tell Craig, and if Craig knew, he'd be up to visit with a shotgun.'

'What do you mean?'

'Fraser's grandpa, god rest his soul, and I owned our croft for many years. After our daughter, Marion, left with Craig's father, we were always worried something would happen and she'd end up on her own again with the two boys. Thankfully, she didn't. Now, I wonder, did you happen to notice the large field behind our croft?'

'The overgrown one?'

'The very one. Well, it belongs to me. Fraser's grandpa and I bought it so if his mum needed a home, we could build one on it. It was dirt cheap in those days, but now, it's worth a mint. People want to put holiday houses on it.'

'Wow.'

'And, Kirsten, I'd be happy to give it to you.'

'What?'

'Yes. A wedding present for the two of you.'

Kirsten's cheeks burned hot. 'No one said anything about getting married.' She and Fraser had only just started letting the excitement of being a couple sink in.

'I know.' Agnes smiled. 'I'm happy for you to have the land now. You can build a house on it, shove a caravan on it, even put up that silly tent. It's yours, and one day, when you're married, you can tell everyone it was your wedding present.'

Kirsten couldn't quite believe her ears, even if she was trying to ignore Agnes's assumptions regarding a future she could hardly begin to comprehend in her wildest imaginings. 'Thank you. I don't know what to say.'

Agnes stretched out her frail hand, and Kirsten held it. 'Just take care of each other.'

The buzz of an engine sounded from beyond. Kirsten raised her eyes and caught Carl smiling. He was in on the surprise. He'd already used his talents to ensure the Glen Lodge Pier was suitable for Fraser's dream. Kirsten flicked him a wink.

'Has Fraser bought a boat?' asked Beth. 'Is he going to be doing boat tours next year?'

With a broadening smile, Kirsten trained her gaze seaward as the engine sound increased. Fraser loved boats, she'd have been happy to talk him into having one of them, but that wasn't what he really wanted.

'Oh, my god,' said Beth, saying aloud what everyone was thinking.

A dazzling white seaplane glided into view, and Kirsten felt a surge of emotion. Fraser was in that. He had the skill, the talent and the nerve to fly it. Hand covering her mouth, she stared as the plane drifted perfectly from sky to water. It took her breath away and she shook her head, slowly. *Wow.*

'That's not Fraser, is it?' Agnes's mouth fell open. 'I knew he could fly planes, but my goodness, that's just, well, unbelievable.'

'I know.' *And he's mine, all mine.*

*

Fraser

Fraser manoeuvred the plane alongside the modified jetty, skimming his fingers over the control panel. Ok, it would never rival the rush of flying a Typhoon, but getting back in the air was like Christmas come early. He removed his headset and looked out at the throng approaching, Kirsten leading the way. Time for her biggest surprise.

He lifted the cockpit door and climbed out, alighting on the jetty in time to whisk her off her feet.

'Oh my god,' she squealed. 'Don't drop me in the sea.'

'As if I would. I'm going to do something even more fun.' He kissed her on the cheek. 'I'm taking you up.'

Her face fell, and the colour drained from her cheeks. 'No way. I've never been on a plane.'

'Come on. You can't date a pilot and expect to keep your feet on the ground. And besides,' he whispered in her ear, 'you and I have been through some first times before with somewhat spectacular results.'

'Oh, shut up.' She flicked him on the shoulder.

Fraser put her back on her feet. 'Hi, folks. Nice to see you all here. So, this is my new plane. Next year, I'm going to do air trips, even though I mostly got her for fun. I'm happy to give you all a whirl, but maybe the first time I could take Kirsten.'

'Oh, Fraser,' said Agnes. 'Take whoever you like, but it won't be me. I'm quite happy to watch from the window, with a strong tea.'

'Just take care of my daughter,' said Gillian, eyeing the seaplane suspiciously. 'I'm happy the two of you have found each other, but I don't want to lose you so soon afterwards.'

'I'll be very careful.' Fraser doffed her a salute. Stretching his hand out to Kirsten, he led her up the ladder, feeling her wrist shaking.

'I can't believe I'm doing this,' she said.

Fraser handed her a headset, strapped himself in, looked over and winked at her. 'You'll love it. You've walked the cliff path to the Carsaig Arches. Believe me, this is nothing like as risky.' Making the final checks, he flicked the switches and overhead controls, pushed the lever and the plane eased forward. 'She's an absolute beauty… Just like you.'

'Isn't this like driving a moped for you? I mean it can't be as exciting as a Typhoon… Shit.' Kirsten's voice burst from the headset and she clung to her seat as they drifted forward, gaining speed.

Keeping his eyes forward, Fraser grinned. 'I don't know, I could try looping the loop?'

'Oh my god, no. Are we up? Hell, we are. Oh god, they're all waving, look how small they are.'

Fraser laughed and manoeuvred them into the air. 'Let's fly over Uisken, we can look for the tent.'

With white knuckles on the seat, Kirsten craned her neck to look out. 'I can't believe I'm in the air, and what a view. Look at everything, it's like Google maps, only real.'

'Amazing, isn't it?'

'Totally.' She released her grip on the chair and let out a deep breath. 'Agnes owns a plot of land behind the croft, you know. She's giving it to us.'

'What? She never told me that.'

'She wants it to be a wedding present.' Kirsten's cheeks reddened. Fraser pretended to concentrate, but he only had eyes for her.

'Is that a proposal? In the air. Wow.'

'Well, um, no.'

'Pity. I thought flying a seaplane had got as exciting as the Typhoon for a second there.' He cast her a glance.

'But eh… Well, do you even want to live together?'

'Don't you? I thought that was the general direction we were heading in.'

'It is, but… are you ready?'

'Yes, Kirsten. You and I have always been meant to be. I was just too stupid to see it. Now I can see past the end of the day and I see you there. I see a future and I like how it's looking.'

'Me too.' She slid her hand onto his leg and gripped his thigh.

'Careful now, I made a promise to get you back in one piece, don't go distracting me.'

'Why not land this thing in the middle of the ocean and let me distract you a bit more? Just think of the stir you'll cause next year when we have kilted pilot tours.'

Fraser chuckled. 'Yeah, nice one. Ok. I'll bring her down somewhere quiet.'

After a smooth landing, Fraser pulled off his headset, leaned over and planted a kiss on Kirsten's rosy pink lips. 'I love you, you're the most special thing that's ever happened to me.'

'And I love you too,' said Kirsten. 'And if you want that proposal to be real, I could try again.'

Fraser's grin split his face. 'Be my guest.'

Clouds raced across the blue sky, and breakers fizzed against the floats. Together Kirsten and Fraser held fast, drifting on the edge of the future, ready and waiting for the magic to start.

The End

Share the Love!

If you enjoyed reading this book, then please
share your reviews online.
Leaving reviews is a perfect way to support authors
and helps books reach more readers.
So please review and share!
Let me know what you think.

Margaret

About the author

I'm a writer, mummy, wife and chocolate eater (in any order you care to choose). I live in highland Perthshire in a little house close to the woods where I often see red squirrels, deer and other such tremendously Scottish wildlife... Though not normally haggises or even men in kilts!

It's my absolute pleasure to be able to bring the Scottish Island Escapes series to you and I hope you love reading the stories as much as I enjoy writing them. Writing is an escapist joy for me and I adore disappearing into my imagination and returning with a new story to tell.

If you want to keep up with what's coming next or learn more about any of the books or the series, then be sure to visit my website. I look forward to seeing you there.

www.margaretamatt.com

Acknowledgements

Thanks goes to my adorable husband for supporting my dreams and putting up with my writing talk 24/7. Also to my son, whose interest in my writing always makes me smile. It's precious to know I've passed the bug to him – he's currently writing his own fantasy novel and instruction books on how to build Lego!

Throughout the writing process, I have gleaned help from many sources and met some fabulous people. I'd like to give a special mention to Stéphanie Ronckier, my beta reader extraordinaire. Stéphanie's continued support with my writing is invaluable and I love the fact that I need someone French to correct my grammar! Stéphanie, you rock. To my fellow authors, Evie Alexander and Lyndsey Gallagher – you girls are the best! I love it that you always have my back and are there to help when I need you.

Also, a huge thanks to my editor, Aimee Walker, at Aimee Walker Editorial Services for her excellent work on my novels and for answering all my mad questions. Thank you so much, Aimee!

Margaret Amatt's Honorary Dispatches

Forde, Helen

SACW Forde Airwoman

Receives a mention for her distinguished answering of all my RAF related questions and her swift and detailed replies. These notes were used to forge ahead in the battle of this book and helped win through in the end. Thank you, Helen! It was invaluable!

More Books by Margaret Amatt

Scottish Island Escapes

Season 1
A Winter Haven
A Spring Retreat
A Summer Sanctuary
An Autumn Hideaway
A Christmas Bluff
Season 2
A Flight of Fancy
A Hidden Gem
A Striking Result
A Perfect Discovery
A Festive Surprise

Free Hugs &

Old-Fashioned Kisses

Do you ever get one of those days when you just fancy snuggling up? Then this captivating short story is for you!

And what's more, it's free when you sign up to my newsletter.

Meet Livvi, a girl who just needs a hug. And Jakob, a guy who doesn't go about hugging random strangers. But what if he makes an exception, just this once?

Make yourself a hot chocolate, sign up to my newsletter and enjoy!

A short story only available to newsletter subscribers.

Sign up at
www.margaretamatt.com

A Winter Haven

She was the one that got away. Now she's back.

Career-driven Robyn Sherratt returns to her childhood home on the Scottish Isle of Mull, hoping to build bridges with her estranged family. She discovers her mother struggling to run the family hotel. When an old flame turns up, memories come back to bite, nibbling into Robyn's fragile heart.

Carl Hansen, known as The Fixer, abandoned city life for peace and tranquillity. Swapping his office for a log cabin, he mends people's broken treasures. He can fix anything, except himself. When forced to work on hotel renovations with Robyn, the girl he lost twelve years ago, his quiet life is sent spinning.

Carl would like nothing more than to piece together the shattered shards of Robyn's heart. But can she trust him? What can a broken man like him offer a successful woman like her?

A Spring Retreat

She's gritty, he's determined. Who will back down first?

When spirited islander Beth McGregor learns of plans to build a road through the family farm, she sets out to stop it. But she's thrown off course by the charming and handsome project manager. Sparks fly, sending Beth into a spiral of confusion. Guys are fine as friends. Nothing else.

Murray Henderson has finally found a place to retreat from the past with what seems like a straightforward job. But he hasn't reckoned on the stubbornness of the locals, especially the hot-headed and attractive Beth.

As they battle together over the proposed road, attraction blooms. Murray strives to discover the real Beth; what secrets lie behind the tough façade? Can a regular farm girl like her measure up to Murray's impeccable standards, and perhaps find something she didn't know she was looking for?

A Summer Sanctuary

She's about to discover the one place he wants to keep

secret

Five years ago, Island girl Kirsten McGregor broke the company rules. Now, she has the keys to the Hidden Mull tour bus and is ready to take on the task of running the business. But another tour has arrived. The competition is bad enough but when she recognises the rival tour operator, her plans are upended.

Former jet pilot Fraser Bell has made his share of mistakes. What better place to hide and regroup than the place he grew to love as a boy? With great enthusiasm, he launches into his new tour business, until old-flame Kirsten shows up and sends his world plummeting.

Kirsten may know all the island's secrets, but what she can't work out is Fraser. With tension simmering, Kirsten and Fraser's attraction increases. What if they both made a mistake before? Is one of them about to make an even bigger one now?

An Autumn Hideaway

She went looking for someone, but it wasn't him.

After a string of disappointments for chirpy city girl Autumn, discovering her notoriously unstable mother has run off again is the last straw. When Autumn learns her mother's last known whereabouts was a remote Scottish Island, she makes the rash decision to go searching for her.

Taciturn islander Richard has his reasons for choosing the remote Isle of Mull as home. He's on a deadline and doesn't need any complications or company. But everything changes after a chance encounter with Autumn.

Autumn chips away at Richard's reserve until his carefully constructed walls start to crumble. But Autumn's just a passing visitor and Richard has no plans to leave. Will they realise, before it's too late, that what they've been searching for isn't necessarily what's missing?

A Christmas Bluff

She's about to trespass all over his Christmas.

Artist and photographer Georgia Rose has spent two carefree years on the Isle of Mull and is looking forward to a quiet Christmas... Until she discovers her family is about to descend upon her, along with her past.

Aloof aristocrat Archie Crichton-Leith has let out his island mansion to a large party from the mainland. They're expecting a castle for Christmas, not an outdated old pile, and he's in trouble.

When Georgia turns up with an irresistible smile and an offer he can't refuse, he's wary, but he needs her help.

As Georgia weaves her festive charms around the house, they start to work on Archie too. And the spell extends both ways. But falling in love was never part of the deal. Can the magic outlast Christmas when he's been conned before and she has a secret that could ruin everything?

A Flight of Fancy

She's masquerading as her twin, pretending to be his girlfriend, while really just being herself.

After years of being cooped up by her movie star family, Taylor Rousse is desperate to escape. Having a Hollywood actress as a twin is about all Taylor can say for herself, but when she's let down by her sister for the umpteenth time, she decides now is the time for action.

Pilot Magnus Hansen is heading back to his family home on the Isle of Mull for his brother's wedding and he's not looking forward to showing up single. The eldest of three brothers shouldn't be the last married – no matter how often he tells himself he's not the marrying type.

On his way, Magnus crashes into a former fling. She's a Hollywood star looking for an escape and they strike a deal: he's her ticket to a week of peace; she's his new date. Except Taylor isn't who he thinks she is. When she and Magnus start to fall for each other, their double deception threatens to blow up in their faces and shatter everything that might have been.

A Hidden Gem

She has a secret past. He has an uncertain future.

Together, can they unlock them both?

After being framed for embezzlement by her ex, career-driven Rebekah needs a break to nurse her broken heart and wounded soul. When her grandmother dies, leaving her a precious necklace and a mysterious note, she sets out to unravel a family secret that's been hidden for over sixty years.

Blair's lived all his life on the Isle of Mull. He's everybody's friend – with or without the benefits – but at night he goes home alone. When Rebekah arrives, he's instantly attracted to her, but she's way out of his league. He needs to keep a stopper on his feelings or risk losing her friendship.

As Rebekah's quest continues, she's rocked by unexpected feelings for her new friend. Can she trust her heart as much as she trusts Blair? And can he be more than just a friend? Perhaps the truth isn't the only thing waiting to be found.

A Striking Result

She's about to tackle everything he's trying to hide.

When unlucky-in-love Carys McTeague is offered the job of caring for an injured footballer, she goes for it even though it's far removed from the world she's used to.

Scottish football hero Troy Copeland is at the centre of a media storm after a serious accident left him with career-threatening injuries and his fiancée dumped him for a teammate. With a little persuasion from Carys, he flees to the remote Isle of Mull to escape and recuperate.

On Mull, Carys reconnects with someone unexpected from her past and starts to fall in love with the island – and Troy. But nothing lasts forever. Carys has been abandoned more than once and as soon as Troy's recovered, he'll leave like everyone else.

Troy's smitten by Carys but has a career to preserve. Will he realise he's been chasing the wrong goal before he loses the love of his life?

A Perfect Discovery

To find love, they need to dig deep.

Kind-hearted archaeologist Rhona Lamond returns home to the Isle of Mull after her precious research is stolen, feeling lost and frustrated. When an island project comes up, it tugs at Rhona's soul and she's desperate to take it on. But there's a major problem.

Property developer Calum Matheson has a longstanding feud with the Lamond family. After a plot of land he owns is discovered to be a site of historical importance, his plans are thrown into disarray and building work put on hold.

Calum doesn't think things can get any worse, until archaeologist Rhona turns up. Not only is she a Lamond, but she's all grown up, and even stubbornly unromantic Calum can't fail to notice her – or the effect she has on him.

Their attraction ignites but how can they overcome years of hate between their families? Both must decide what's more important, family or love.

A Festive Surprise

She can't abide Christmas. He's not sure what it's all about. Together they're in for a festive surprise.

Ambitious software developer Holly may have a festive name but the connection ends there. She despises the holiday season and decides to flee to the remote island of Mull in a bid to escape from it.

Syrian refugee Farid has made a new home in Scotland but he's lonely. Understanding Nessie and Irn Bru is one thing, but when glittery reindeer and tinsel hit the shelves, he's completely bemused. Determined to understand a new culture, he asks his new neighbour to educate him on all things Christmas.

When Holly reluctantly agrees, he realises there's more to her hatred of mince pies and mulled wine than meets the eye. Farid makes it his mission to inject some joy into Hollys' life but falling for her is an unexpected gift that was never on his list.

As their attraction sparkles, can Christmas work its magic on Holly and Farid, or will their spark fizzle out with the end of December?

Printed in Great Britain
by Amazon